EDA BLESSED

A KI KHANGA STORY COLLECTION

....

MILTON J. DAVIS

MVmedia, LLC
Fayetteville, GA

Milton J. Davis/MVmedia, LLC
PO Box 1465
Fayetteville, GA 30214
www.mvmediaatl.com

Book Layout ©2017 BookDesignTemplates.com
Cover Art by Stanley Weaver, Jr.
Cover Design by Uraeus
Interior art by Stanley Weaver, Jr, Hasani Claxton, and Bryan Syme

Ordering Information:
Quantity sales. Special discounts are available on quantity purchases by corporations, associations, and others. For details, contact the "Special Sales Department" at the address above.

Eda Blessed/Milton J. Davis. -- 1st ed.
ISBN 978-0-9992789-7-0

Contents

To the Ki Khangans. May Eda Bless you.

KEPT

Omari Ket rifled through the dead merchant's pouch with his left hand as he held a bloody knife in his right. The men who killed the unfortunate man glared at Omari but kept their distance. The man was their prize, but Omari was in his right as *mtu wa kwanza* to take what was due to him. The alley where they ambushed the man was his domain, and all who 'collected' there were required to share a portion with him. The rouge who attempted to defy Omari held his wounded forearm, blood running through his fingers. It was his blood that stained Omari's knife. The others scowled but made no effort to stop him. Each had faced him before and received a sound beating for their efforts. Omari frowned when he looked at the meager cowries in his palm.

"This was a waste of time," he said.

"Then give it to us," Kunju, the leader of the rouges, replied.

Omari stuffed the cowries in his pocket. "Not today. Consider it payment for soiling my alleyway."

"What's going on here?!?"

Two nyanas, Sati-Baa law enforcers, entered the alley brandishing their infamous throwing clubs. Omari bolted; the others cried out as the clubs smashed against their bodies. Omari ducked instinctively and a club cracked the stone wall beside him at head level. A flash of fear swept through him; they were trying to kill him. He turned the corner to the narrow street just as a second club struck his thigh, knocking his legs together and sending him sprawling into the crowd. Pedestrians cursed as they avoided him; he was just another street rat about to get what he deserved. Omari rolled back onto his feet then limped through the throng, the nyanas blowing their cursed nut whistles to clear the way for their pursuit. Eda smiled on him; the market was packed, slowing down his pursuers. He dipped in and out of three different alleyways before finally losing them.

Omari leaned against a wall, rubbing his thigh where the club struck him as he caught his breath. He would have to find a job soon. The nyanas were more diligent than ever due to high merchant season and everyone worth robbing had bodyguards. He limped down the street as he considered his options. Goods flowed into Sati-Baa from every direction but despite this, work and vice were scarce near the docks. He would have to travel to the northern district and see if there was work in the fields. He reached into his pocket then pulled out the cowries. There was enough for a piece of bread and maybe bush meat. Omari melded into the crowd, continuing to massage his bruised leg. He found a small market then persuaded the vendor to sell him meat, bread and a gourd of goat milk for half the price. Omari was well aware of his talents, most of all those gifted to him by Eda. In short, Omari was a beautiful man. He was tall but not overly so, with a well-proportioned body that spoke of vigorous activity. His umber skin highlighted his perfect teeth when he smiled and he was much stronger than his physique conveyed. Any *mvulataani* knew well how to take advantage of every strength to survive the streets and Omari was no different.

As he strolled down the thoroughfare enjoying his meal, he heard clopping hooves then stepped aside. A pair of well-groomed horses trotted by, pulling a large wagon common to the wealthier inhabitants of the city. The wagon slowed, keeping pace with his steps.

"*Vulaana*," a woman called out.

Omari continued walking, ignoring the woman's insult.

A whip cracked by his head; Omari glared at the gaudy coachman.

"Didn't you hear my *bibi* speak to you?"

"I heard your bibi speak to a boy, which I am not."

The coachman drew back his whip. Omari took a stance, ready to take the blow on his forearm then yank the man from the wagon.

"Stop, Tanbasi," the woman said.

Omari finally looked into the wagon. What saw almost made him drop his meal. The woman was gorgeous, her ebony face enveloped in a cloud of black hair laced with golden strands. She smiled and Omari briefly forgot his hunger.

"What is your name, bwa?" she teased. Omari could never claim being a bwa, nor would he ever be.

"Omari, bibi," he said.

"Well, Omari. My name is Mariama. I own a farm north of the city. It's harvest and I could use someone like you."

Omari remained silent and Mariama smiled.

"I pay two sheks a day and three meals. I also supply lodging until the end of the season."

"And after the season?"

Mariama grinned. "We'll see."

"I accept your offer," Omari said. He didn't have a choice.

"Good," Mariama replied. "Follow us. We are not far."

The coachman cracked his whip and the wagon sped off. Omari took a bite of his stale bread then took a long drink from his gourd before following the wagon. The coachman was trying to make it hard for Omari to keep up but Omari matched the pace. The city clutter gradually dissipated, giving way to the grasslands that dominated the landscape north of Sati-Baa. The Cleave Mountains loomed in the distance, their colossal size making them seem closer than they were. It would take a good two weeks travel on a good horse to reach the foot-hills, a journey no one in their right mind wished to make.

The air cooled and Omari wished he had a cloak, or at least a thick blanket. The sight and smells of the farm gradually reached him. He grinned as it came into full view; it seemed the bibi understated her property. Her 'farm' sprawled for miles before him. Omari imme-diately began to suspect how she had accumulated the wealth to purchase such a large plantation.

A thick wall the height of two tall men encircled the farm, another sign of the woman's wealth. Two armed guards flanked the gate; they opened it as the wagon approached then scowled at Omari as he trotted through. He smiled and waved; there was no reason to be nice to the help, but he didn't want to make any premature enemies either. This farm would be like any other situation he'd encountered. There would be a hierarchy among the workers and it would do him well to figure out as soon as possible where he fit. Whatever the position, it would be temporary. Omari had a plan. He always did.

It took ten minutes to traverse the road through the fields of grain, vegetables and fruit. The wagon halted when they reached the road separating the fields from the estate. The coach master climbed down, taking a small stool from behind his seat them placing it under the coach door. He opened the door and the bibi stepped out. Omari's grin widened; her body was as beautiful as her face. The bibi noticed his attention then grinned.

"You're ambitious," she said. "It may serve you well eventually, but not now."

She signaled the coachman.

"Send for Chuk. Tell him I have a new laborer for him."

"As you wish, bibi."

The coachman smirked as he shuffled off to the fields.

"So what is it you wish me to do, bibi?" Omari asked. He was anxious to see what lay beneath the silk dress.

"I expect you to work," she replied. "Chuk is my foreman. He's been with me longer than any of my husbands. Put in a good day's work and he will pay you well. Do otherwise and he'll send you away. "

Omari's mouth dropped open. "But I thought . . ."

"I know what you thought," she replied. "Do your tasks and maybe I won't tell the nyanas know where you're hiding."

She smiled sweetly as Omari glared at her. Before he could hurl an insult, her bodyguards appeared, three massive men armed with swords and orinkas. They stared at Omari impassively.

"Boy!" someone shouted.

Omari turned to see a stocky man with ebony skin waddling toward him.

"What are you standing there for?" he said. "There's work to do!"

Omari took one last look at the woman then stalked toward the overseer. The man looked him over then nodded.

"You're in better shape than most," he said. "We'll put you with the wood-gatherers. It's hard work but it pays better than being a field hand."

"Thank you," Omari said.

"Don't thank me yet," Chuk replied. "Come on, I'll take you to your hut."

Omari followed Chuk across the fallow fields to an encampment of conical huts arranged in a circle around a spent bonfire.

"You're lucky," Chuk said. "You won't have to share a hut. The bibi usually brings two of you rats back."

"This is how she gets her workers?" Omari asked.

Chuk laughed. "Works every time. You street rats are so stupid. Did you actually think she would take you to her bed?"

Chuk's laugh was like a knife in Omari's ribs. He thought about punching the man as hard as he could, but there was a lot of property between him and the gate and there was a slim chance he could get by the guards. And then there was the bibi's threat to notify the nyanas.

"You are a good-looking one though," Chuk said. "Still, best focus on the work ahead."

Omari stuck his head into the hut. It was filthy, but he'd spent the night in worse places.

"Come with me," Chuk said. "We'll go to the tailor and get you fitted."

Omari followed Chuk across the camp to the tailor's hut. The rhythmic rattle of a working loom reached them before they entered. Inside, a lanky gray-haired man sat before the loom, singing to himself to keep pace. His voice was terrible.

"Hanisi! I have a new one for you!"

Hanisi looked up from his loom, squinting his eyes to study Omari.

"You're a big one," he said. "I think Saka's garments will fit you."

The man climbed to his feet then shuffled to a pile of clothes pressed against the opposite wall.

"What happened to Saka?" Omari asked.

"A tree fell on him," Chuk replied.

Hanisi stepped between Omari and Chuk with a ball of cloth.

"Try this on," he said.

Omari disrobed then put on Saka's used clothes. The shirt fit tight across his chest and the pants were too long. Despite the ill fit the fabric felt good against the skin. He pinched the cloth between his fingers and nodded.

"This is a fine weave," he said.

Hanisi beamed. "Thank you! I take pride in my work. It's nice for someone other than the bibi to notice."

Hanisi glared and Chuk and the foreman glared back.

"I could care less how the damn thing feels, as long as I'm not naked."

"We're all thankful for that," Hanisi said.

Hanisi took a notched stick then placed it against Omari's shoulders, legs, and back, mumbling as he did so.

"Come back at the end of the week," he said. "I'll have two uniforms for you."

"Thank you," Omari said.

"Don't thank me yet," Hanisi replied.

Chuk and Omari walked to the edge of the woods. Chuck took a pipe from his shirt then packed the bowl with a shredded material.

"What's that?" Omari asked.

Chuk grinned. "It's heaven in a pipe."

"Water root?" Omari said with a frown. He'd smoked the root before and found it a waste of time. All it gave him was a horrible smell and a bad headache.

Chuk spit. "Cleave no. I wouldn't touch water root if you paid me ten stacks. This is the divine leaf, dagga."

Omari's licked his lips. He'd heard of dagga. It was a rich man's indulgence, something far above his status. It should have been above Chuk's wages as well.

"How did somebody like you get your hands on dagga?"

"We grow it," Chuk said. "With the bibi's permission of course. She likes to smoke a bit herself and she makes a hefty profit from it."

"May I?" Omari asked.

"No," Chuk replied. "You got work to do. Besides, dagga is earned, not given. Do the work and the bibi will allow you a ration."

Omari frowned. So far, this new job was a mix of perks and problems. His brooding was interrupted by the sound of rattling wagons. Two oxen-drawn carts emerged from the bush, both piled with freshly chopped wood. A group of men walked beside them, two of them guiding the oxen with words and whips. One of the woodcutters, a big bare-chested brute with massive arms and a thick moustache sauntered ahead of the wagons toward Chuk and Omari. The man stopped before them, sizing up Omari with a discriminating stare.

"This is the new one?" he asked.

"Yes," Chuk answered.

The man sucked his teeth.

"I'll give him two weeks before the bibi has him pulling weeds in the sorghum fields."

"You'll lose that bet," Omari replied.

"Ain't nobody talking to you," the man said.

"I'm talking to you," Omari retorted.

The man was fast, but Omari was faster. He ducked the looping punch meant for his jaw and the backhand meant for his cheek. Omari retaliated instinctively, hitting the man with a jab and a solid right cross in the mouth, splitting the man's lip. The man didn't flinch. He licked the blood from his lips then grinned, showing his blood-stained teeth. Omari realized he was in trouble. He braced himself for the eventual beating. Instead the man laughed.

"Not bad pup," he said. "Not bad at all."

He looked at Chuk. "He works with me."

"I don't know if I want to," Omari said. "I don't fancy being killed in my sleep."

The big brute laughed.

"He's funny, too. Put him on my team, Chuk."

"He's yours," Chuk replied.

Omari was dumbfounded. Chuk grinned then extended the pipe to Omari.

"This is Gituku," Chuk said. "You couldn't have a better boss to work for."

Gituku grinned, blood still running from his lip.

"We're the best paid woodcutters on the farm," he said. "We always exceed our quota and we always come in on time. You're a skinny one, but we'll get you in shape quick."

"I'm stronger than I look," Omari said.

"We'll find out. Help us unload the wagons."

Omari was about to take a pull from Chuk's pipe when Gituku snatched it from his hand.

"No time for that now," he said. "We got work to do. I'll be damned to the Cleave if you'll drop a log on my head."

Gituku sauntered away. Omari looked at Chuk pleadingly and the foreman shook his head.

"You heard the boss. Come see me later. I might have a few leaves left."

Omari sulked as he followed his new boss to the wagons. He fell in step with his workmates. Their stares were not pleasant.

"Not another new one," one of the ox drivers said. He was a thick man, though not as tall as Gituku.

"We take what the bibi gives us," Gituku said. "This one has spunk. He busted my lip."

The ox driver laughed. "You're going to pay for that tonight in the ring."

Omari's eyebrows rose with his worry.

"The ring? What is the ring?"

"It's a little thing we do every night. Looks like you and Gituku will be tonight's entertainment."

Omari looked at Gituku and the big man grinned.

"Don't worry," he said. "I'll be gentle."

The other men laughed.

"Shit!" Omari muttered.

Gituku pointed at the ox driver.

"This is Bupe. And this—he pointed at the other man—is Kibwe. We're the bibi's best woodsmen. Now that we all know each other, let's get some work done."

The wagons pulled beside the woodpile and they set to work. Omari was no stranger to hard labor so he fell in with the others as they unloaded the wood.

"Don't bend your back," Gituku advised. "You'll be too stiff to work tomorrow and it will ruin you over time. Just drop it."

Omari and the woodmen worked until sundown, Gituku and the others sharing their wisdom and stories along the way. It was hard to imagine that the same man helping him would try to kill him later that day.

The unloading was complete sooner than Omari would have liked. Gituku placed his hands on his waist, scanning the pile like a proud parent.

"Now that that's done, it's time to play," he said.

Omari dropped his head and cursed.

Follow me," Gituku said.

The men walked single file to the opposite side of the farm. A stream flowed nearby, a natural divider between the forest and the fields. The water originated in the distant Cleave mountains, weaving through rocks and woods before reaching the farmland. The men stripped down to their loincloths then jumped into the cold water, exclaiming various expletives as the cold water chilled their skin. Omari stood on the bank, frowning at them.

"What's wrong?" Gituku called out. "Jump in!"

"He's a street rat," Bupe said. "He's not used to being clean!"

"Right!" Kabwe added. "I hear those street rats don't bathe because the only thing they own is their funk!"

The woodsmen laughed raucously. Omari stuck his toe in the water and his teeth chattered.

"It's all or nothing, rat," Gituku said.

Omari ran then jumped into the stream.

"Shiiiiiiiiit!"

Numbness spread through his limbs and he thought he was going drown.

"Keep moving!" Gituku shouted. "You'll get used to it after a while."

Omari's teeth chattered. "Who in the Cleave could get used to this?"

He swam to the shore then jumped out of the stream. Omari paced back and forth as the warm air dried his skin while the others continued to frolic in the waters. He was becoming agitated by it all, more than ready to get his beating over with so he could go to sleep. After what seemed like forever the trio waded out of the stream then sauntered to a round space of dirt.

"Come on street rat," Gituku said. "Let's see what you got."

"It's about time," Omari replied. He stomped to the ring, ready for his thrashing.

Omari stood on one side of the circle, Gituku on the other. He studied the hulking man and concluded there was no way he could defeat him, at least in a match of strength. There was only one way out.

"Begin!" Kabwe shouted.

Omari ran up to Gituku then locked arms with the brute. As soon as Gituku grabbed him, fear took over Omari's eyes and he back pedaled. Gituku chased him, his face twisted with a frown.

"Get back here, street rat!"

Omari continued to run backwards, Gituku gaining ground. Omari took a quick glance backwards then slowed. Gituku finally caught up with him.

"I got you now!" Gituku said.

"Yes, you do," Omari replied.

Omari grabbed Gituku around the shoulders then rolled onto his back. He jammed both of his feet into the man's gut, knocking the wind out of him then continued to push out with his legs as he rolled. He let go of Gituku and the man flew briefly before landing on the ground and rolling away.

Omari rolled onto the balls of his feet then spun around, facing the direction where he tossed Gituku. The big man scrambled to his feet, his dirty face shaking with anger.

"I'm going to break you in half!" he yelled.

"No you're not," Bupe said. "Fight's over."

Gituku jerked his head toward Bupe. "What do you mean the fight's over?"

Bupe pointed at Gituku's feet. The massive man was standing on the wrong side of the ring.

"AAAAAAAAAAA!"

Bupe and Kabwe laughed. Omari joined in as well, laughing more from relief than humor. Gituku's snarl slowly gave way to a grin. He sauntered up to Omari and extended his hand. Omari grabbed it and was pulled into a crushing hug.

"You're a crafty one, street rat!" he bellowed. "I'll break you in half the next time!"

Omari couldn't answer. Gituku was squeezing him so tight he could barely breathe.

Just before he was about to pass out, he heard clapping behind him. Gituku released him as the laughing ceased. Omari gasped for breath as he turned about. Standing at the ring's edge was the bibi. Mariama grinned at him as she continued to clap. Gituku backed away as she approached.

"That was clever," she said.

"I've been known to be from time to time," Omari replied.

"I've never seen Gituku thrown from the ring."

"There's a first time for everything."

"Yes, it is."

Mariama's expression suggested all types of possibilities.

"Gituku, is our new worker any good?" she called out.

"He's got stamina, but he hasn't swung an ax yet. He's a smart ass too."

"Should I keep him?" she asked.

"I'd say yes, at least for a few more days."

"You heard the man," Mariama said. "You'll stay for a few more days. We'll see if you're going to be permanent later."

"Thank you, bibi," Omari said, sharing a look that made his intentions clear.

"Still over-reaching," she said.

"You haven't said no," Omari replied.

Mariama turned and strolled away. Gituku walked up beside him.

"Be careful, rat," he said. "You were very close to disrespecting the bibi."

"I don't think so," Omari replied. "Besides, the bibi is a woman of power and privilege. I believe she can handle herself. She doesn't need a woodcutter looking out for her."

Gituku struck him on the back, almost knocking him over.

"I don't know whether to like you or kill you," he said.

"Please make up your mind soon," Omari said. "The suspense is killing me."

The servers arrived after the fight and set up a meal table for the woodcutters. Omari grabbed a loaf of bread and a chunk of goat meat then retired to his hut. He was sore everywhere it was possible. He sat on his cot and was about to finish his rations when the door swung open. Chuk entered with a bottle and a bag.

"Courtesy of the bibi," he said with a wink. "Don't indulge too much."

Chuk sat the items on the table then left. Omari opened the bottle and grinned. It was filled with palm wine. He opened the bag and shouted.

"Eda be praised!"

He took the short pipe and flint from the bag, then removes a smaller bag. He opened the bag then inhaled the fragrant aroma.

"Dagga," he whispered.

He fumbled as he packed the pipe bowl with the herb then lit it with the flint. Omari settled into relaxation, sipping on the palm wine while nibbling his meal and taking a puff on the pipe. All things considered, he'd been in worse situations. He decided he would stay around until things cooled off with the nyanas, or at least until the dagga ran out. If the bibi allowed him to.

The wine, the dagga and fatigue took its toll. Sleep hit him like a thrown stone, knocking him out onto his bed while the wine cup and dagga pipe fell from his hands.

* * *

"Wake up, street rat!"

Omari bolted upright then collapsed in pain. His head throbbed, whether from the palm wine or the dagga he didn't know. He gripped his head then moaned.

"I told you to take it easy," Chuk's said through the painful haze.

Chuk grabbed his arm then pulled him from the bed. Omari tried to stand but his head began spinning as he pitched forward. He yelled as he hit the dirt floor. Chuk grabbed his limp arms then dragged him from the hut.

"Damn you to the Cleave!" Omari shouted. "What are you doing?"

"Taking you to work," Chuk replied. "There's wood to be cut."

Someone lifted him off the ground then dropped him into a wagon.

"Good morning, rat!" Gituku shouted. "We got real work to do today."

Gituku dropped the ax on his chest, knocking the wind out of him.

"The Cleave take you!" Omari wheezed.

"Such a foul mouth," Gituku said. "Save your curses. You'll need them for the trees. Not that they will care."

Omari spent the majority of the ride to the forest attempting to sit up. By the time they reached the forest he was somewhat sober. He picked up his ax, fell out of the back of the wagon then stumbled after the others. Everyone set about chopping trees except Gituku. He waved his hand before Omari's face to get his attention.

"You're with me today," he said. "Need to make sure you know what you're doing and don't kill the rest of us before we let you on your own."

He guided Omari to a fairly tall tree.

"These are the trees we cut first," he said. "You want to hit the tree an angle first then cut straight. The purpose is to cut the tree the way you want it to fall."

"And where do I want it to fall?" Omari asked, his head still aching.

"Away from us," Gituku answered. "Watch."

Gituku hit the tree before them with two blows then it fell to the ground. He took Omari to the next tree.

"Your turn, rat," he said.

"Don't call me that," Omari replied. He raised his ax then chopped at the tree. His ax didn't penetrate nearly as deep as Gituku.

"What is this?" Omari said. "Is this ax dull?"

"No, you are," Gituku said. "Takes time to learn how to swing an ax, street rat."

"I said don't call me that."

"So earn another name," Gituku said.

It took Omari ten chops to fell the tree. He was winded by the effort and they had the rest of the day to work. He did the best he could, felling trees until Chuk arrived with food, a thick porridge that tasted better than it looked. After a brief rest they were chopping again. Gituku called a halt a few hours before dusk and they switched to chopping the trees into manageable logs. At the day's end they loaded the logs onto the wagon and began their walk back to the farm.

"So how did I do?" Omari asked.

"Not bad for the first time out," Gituku said. "The real test is tomorrow."

"What's so different about tomorrow?" he asked.

"You'll see. I just have one word of advice."

"What's that?"

Gituku grinned. "Work through it."

When they returned to the farm, they stacked the wood in the shed. Omari went to the river to wash before the evening meal. He stripped naked then waded into the frigid water, more concerned about getting clean than freezing. He was splashing about when he heard a familiar voice.

"I heard you did well today," Mariama said.

Omari grinned as he turned to face the woman. He waded to the shore, his body rising from the water until everything was exposed except his privates.

"You seemed to be keeping a close eye on me," he said.

"You're an investment," she replied. "I'm trying to determine if you're worth it."

"I'm just a woodcutter."

"For now," Mariama said. "You have potential."

Omari stepped out of the water, fully exposing himself.

"Maybe if you told me what I was working for I would be more . . . motivated."

"A man shouldn't need incentive if success is truly in his heart," she replied. "Such a man would find his possibilities endless."

"I'm not that kind of man," Omari said. "I need to see what I'm working for."

"You have," Mariama replied.

Omari stepped toward Mariama and she raised her hand.

"The distance between us is wide . . . for now," she said. "Don't bathe too long. You'll miss your meal."

Omari watched Mariama walk away before wading back into the water. He smiled as he floated. The bibi was playing a game with him. He wasn't sure if she planned to tease him to distraction or actually allow him in her bed. He'd slept with women of lineage before; there were plenty in Sati-Baa whose wealthy husbands only satisfied their financial needs. A young handsome man like him was always in demand, although it was not his preferred way to earn his cowries. But a street rat was not in a position to argue about the source of his or her income. He decided he'd stay a few more weeks to see how this would work out.

The end of the week brought the much-awaited day of rest. Omari and the others dressed in their best clean clothes while Gituku waited in his wagon to take them into Sati-Baa. Omari was taking a chance going into town so soon after his run-in with the nyanas, but he was tired of fields, trees and Mariama constant teasing. A smile came to his face as he thought of Aisha. It had been a while since he'd seen her and he found himself thinking about her smooth dark skin and twinkling brown eyes. They were a match for each other in every way, yet Sati-Baa would not allow them to be lovers in the true sense of the word. They both needed to survive on the streets, and they had learned that they could not do so together. Still, he looked forward to finding her and hopefully spending some special time with her.

Omari followed his cohorts to the wagon. As he began to climb into the back of the wagon Gituku raised his hand.

"Not you, street rat," he said. "The bibi has chores for you."

"What do you mean chores?" Omari said. "It's our free day."

"Not yours," Gituku replied. "When there is additional work to be done the low man stays behind to do it. You are the low man."

"Damn to the Cleave!" Omari said.

"No need for profanity," Gituku said. "It won't change the situation. The bibi requests that you meet her at the main house."

Omari sulked as he trudged to the bibi's abode. After thinking of Aisha, he was in no mood for the bibi's games. Whatever it was she wanted him to do he would finish it fast then walk to town. He wouldn't have much time, but just a few moments with Aisha would be worth the effort.

Two guards flanked the entrance to the house. Apparently, they were expecting Omari for they stepped aside as he approached. The door opened and the bibi's house master, Haddas, took its place. She was a voluptuous woman who would have a pleasant face if she didn't frown constantly. She wore a bright blue khanga that exposed her right shoulder. A golden turban covered her towering hair. Haddas eyed him as if inspecting a mbogo for slaughter.

Omari stopped at the door and executed an elaborate bow.

"I have answered the bibi's summons," he said. "How may I serve her?"

"Smart ass," Haddas replied. "Follow me."

Omari stepped into the bibi's house. Any doubts he harbored of her wealth were dispelled as he strode through her atrium. He was no stranger to such displays, but the bibi's collection was the most elaborate he'd ever seen. Huge elaborate masks carved by the wood masters of Kongo hung from the walls, separated by lengths of the famous kenteke cloth from Asanteman. Bronze statutes from Oyo rested on soapstone pedestals under the masks, their exaggerated expressions capturing his attention. As they reached the end of the atrium, Haddas spun to face him. To Omari's surprise the woman attacked. He found himself in her iron grip as she flipped him onto his back then dropped her knee in his chest. Her hand flashed under her dress, snatching out a slim dagger. Haddas pressed the tip to his neck.

"Just because the guards remain outside does not mean the bibi is unprotected," she said. A crooked grin came to her face. Omari grinned back.

"You're point has been made," he said as he glanced down at the dagger. "And it seems that you can smile."

"Get off of him, Haddas," the bibi said.

Haddas obeyed, pressing her knee into Omari's chest for good measure. Omari stood and quickly forgot the attack as he gazed upon the bibi. She wore a simple low-cut white tunic that ended midway on her thighs. Thin golden chains circled her hair. Emerald earrings dangled from her ears, complementing the necklace that rested against her chest.

"You can go now," she said to Haddas.

Haddas bowed then walked away. Mariama smiled then gestured for Omari to follow her.

"Come, I have something that needs your attention."

Omari followed the bibi's swaying hips into her chamber. The atrium was small in comparison. A large pool occupied the center of the room, the bibi's enormous bed beyond it. Omari's attention shifted back and forth from the pool to the bibi.

"Get in," she said.

Omari stripped off his clothes then grinned at Mariama as he waited for her to disrobe. Instead she shook her head.

"You need to bathe first," she said.

"I did," Omari replied.

"Not in that filthy river," she retorted. "I can still smell that swill on you. Take a bath then come to my bed. I'll be waiting."

Omari jumped into the warm water, creating a tremendous splash. He grabbed the nearby towel and black soap then scrubbed every inch of his body as if he was preparing for a healing. Once done he toweled dry then jogged to Mariama's bed. The dress lay on the floor nearby. Mariama lay on the bed, her eyes roaming his body.

"I approve," she said.

Omari scrambled into the bed, but Mariama held him at arm's length.

"Slow down," she whispered into his ear. "We have all day."

She wrapped her arms around his neck then pulled him on top of her.

* * *

It was almost dark when they finally relented from their lovemaking. Omari lay on his back in sweet exhaustion, Mariama pressed against his side. He was famished; despite not wanting to leave he had to eat something. He tried to stand but Mariama pulled him down.

"Where are you going?" she asked.

"Back to my room," Omari said. "I'm hungry."

"I'll have Haddas bring us food," Mariama said. "As for your room, you won't be going back there."

Omari's joy dissipated.

"So are you done with me now?" he asked.

"No, Omari," she replied. "We're just beginning. I have a new role for you."

"And what is that?"

"You're to be my escort," she said. "You will accompany me when I leave the compound and on all of my travel excursions. You will provide companionship and protection when needed. For your services you will be paid three times what you are receiving now. You will also take a room in the servant wing of my home."

"I can stay here," Omari said with a smile.

"Of course not," Mariama replied. "Unless our relations demand it."

"And what if I refuse this position?" Omari asked.

Mariama's mouth went wide.

"Refuse? Refuse?"

Omari fought hard to keep from laughing. People like Mariama never expect their offers to be rebuffed, especially by a street rat. They either become enraged or they express their true intentions. Omari picked Mariama to be the latter.

"I don't want to complicate my life," Omari said. "It would be simpler for me to work out the season then be on my way."

"And what awaits you, Omari?" Mariama asked. "A life in the streets stealing and fighting? You won't live long. I'm offering you steady work and stability."

"And you?" he asked.

"I am not yours to have," Mariama replied. "But I will share my time with you. Much of it."

"Then I accept your offer," Omari said.

"Excellent!"

Mariama shared a smile Omari knew was genuine. She'd gotten her way, or at least she thought she did. Time would tell different.

"Your instruction will begin tomorrow," she said.

"Instruction?" Omari was puzzled.

"You are now the escort of one of the most powerful people in Sati-Baa," Mariama said. "You will be exposed to people and places far beyond your current status. You must represent me in all these situations with the appropriate skill and decorum."

"What kind of instruction are you talking about?"

"Can you read and write?" Mariama asked.

"Well enough," Omari said.

"Well enough is not acceptable. I will arrange for you tutelage. And your fighting skills need improvement."

"I think I can hold my own," Omari said, somewhat offended by her remark.

"Holding your own is not enough," Mariama replied. "My house maid took you down."

"She caught me by surprise," Omari said.

"That should never happen. You will not be only protecting yourself; you'll be protecting me."

"I see," Omari replied.

Mariama grinned then sat on his lap as she kissed him.

"Did I hurt your feelings?"

"A little," Omari said. "But you're doing a great job making up for it."

"And this is the last time I'll do it," Mariama said. "Remember that everything I do for you I do to make you a better person."

"I'll try to remember that," Omari said as he gripped her butt with both hands.

"Who will my fighting instructor be?"

"Balogun Ojetade," Mariama said.

Omari let go of Mariama's ass then pushed her away.

"Balogun Ojetade? How can you afford him?"

"Balo and I are old friends," she said. "For me he's not so expensive."

"Oh."

"What's wrong?" she asked.

"Nothing. I'm looking forward to his guidance."

Omari let Mariama pull him into her arms as he tried to keep a fearful look from coming to his face. Many years ago, he was foolish enough to try to rob the master fighter and was beaten to an inch of his life. Ever since that day he made it a point to keep far away from the man, and now he was going to be instructed by him. Unless he remembered who he was. Then he was going to be killed by him. Before he could fall into complete panic Mariama began pressing her hips against his and he let himself be coaxed into more amorous thoughts. His death imaginings would have to wait until much later.

He woke the next morning before Mariama then dressed. When he opened the door to the bedroom Haddas greeted him with a snarl.

"Good morning," he said with a smile.

Haddas pushed by him without speaking.

"I can do that," he said.

"No, you can't," Haddas replied. "What you can do is go out back and bring more firewood. You are no longer needed here."

"I don't take orders from you," Omari said.

Mariama sat up in the bed. She rubbed her eyes then smile at Omari.

"Yes, you do," she said.

"Do what?" Omari asked.

"Take orders from Haddas. She is over my household. So, if she needs your help, you will help her."

Haddas gave him a victorious smile. "What are you waiting for?"

"I'm waiting to see if the bibi wishes me to join her for breakfast."

"No," Mariama said. "I always eat breakfast alone. Now fetch the wood."

Omari stomped out of the room. He hated being dismissed, no matter who it was. He immediately had second thoughts about taking Mariama's offer, but his survival instincts won out. He couldn't think of a better situation for him at the moment, and when he tired of it, he would simply leave.

Omari stepped out the back door as the wood wagon pulled up. Chuk was driving the wagon, with Gituku standing in the back. Both looked shocked when they saw him but their emotions quickly changed. Chuk took on a sad look then shook his head. Gituku spat in his direction then glared.

"So, you're the bibi's lap dog now?" Gituku said.

"Escort," Omari corrected. "And it's better than being your punching bag."

"How about we do more punching?" Gituku jumped from the wagon.

"Get back in," Chuk said.

"This street rat thinks he can . . ."

"Get back in the damn wagon, Gituku!"

Gituku hesitated then climbed back into the wagon. He grabbed the wood in his arms then threw it toward the house. Chuk jumped out then stood before Omari, his arms folded across his chest.

"You've done it now," he said.

"Omari grinned. "Yes, I have. A few times, actually."

Chuk didn't seem to think his joke was funny.

"You're in the spider's web now," he said. "Eda bless you."

"What are you talking about?" Omari said. "I consider this a step up."

"You don't know these kinds of people," Chuk said. "To them, we're nothing. You're a toy to be used then disposed of when it suits them."

"You seemed to have survived."

"I worked for the bibi's parents," he replied. "I was here before she was born. Don't think she keeps me around because of some emotion. I'm like the house and the trees. She keeps me because she's used to me. Best you take off now before it gets bad."

"This suits me fine," Omari said.

"Then as I said before, Eda bless you."

Chuk climbed back into the wagon.

"Be careful, street rat, and be wary."

Chuk cut his eye at Gituku. The big man still glared at Omari as Chuk turned the wagon about and they rode away. Omari shrugged then stacked the wood before bringing a load in for the kitchen. Haddas was waiting, tapping her foot impatiently.

"After you prepare the fireplaces, I need you to go into town and pick up a few things at the market," she said.

"Yes, bibi," Omari replied.

"Don't mock me," she warned. "Remember yesterday. Besides, I would never let someone as scrawny as you into my bed."

"That's comforting to hear," Omari quipped. "And don't let yesterday go to your head. You caught me off guard."

Haddas charged him, but this time he was ready. He sidestepped her blow as he grabbed her arm then twisted it behind her back. She attempted to back kick him in the gonads but Omari had anticipated her attack. He swept her feet then eased her fall to the floor. He sat on her back then put her into a chokehold.

"You're from the streets, just like me," Omari whispered into her ear. "Your tricks will protect you from some stupid merchant, but I know them all. So, let's try to be nice to each other, even if we don't want to."

Omari held her a bit longer to emphasis his point. When he let her go, she gasped for air.

"Now where's that shopping list?" he asked.

Haddas pointed to the butcher block. He picked up the list then headed for the door.

"What about money?" he asked.

"The bibi's credit is good," she croaked. "The list has her seal."

Omari frowned. He hoped to tuck a few cowries in his pocket. He shrugged then headed to the stables. The stable hand gave him a good horse and Omari was on his way. It was his first time back to the city since taking the job with the bibi and if felt good to be in familiar surroundings. With the horse he would make good time, so he decided to take a detour before visiting the market. First, he had to get rid of the horse. He rode the horse to a stable near the market then called on the stable master, a short dark man with a noticeable limp. Omari recognized him as Kenjan, most likely the slave of the true owner.

"How can I help you?" the man said in heavily accented Ki Khangan.

"I need to leave my horse," Omari said.

"Ten cowries,' the man said.

Omari reached into his pocket then took out the bibi's symbol. The man nodded as he took the horse's reins.

Omari sauntered into the chaos of the northern market, but he had no intentions of filling Haddas's list, at least not yet. He had someone to visit, someone he had planned to see before he was so pleasantly interrupted by Mariama. His stroll took him to the Mamba's Mouth, a section of Sati-Baa few ventured, a piece of the city where people like the bibi had never seen. It was Omari's home, if he could claim any part of the city as home these days. He ambled through the jaded inhabitants, knowing just how to carry himself to keep anyone thinking of robbing him at bay. His walk took him to a row of weathered tenements. Although the exteriors spoke of tenants with few prospects, Omari knew different. A person living in the Mouth never displayed their wealth.

He finally reached his destination. Omari knocked on the door then braced himself. He heard the peephole cover slip open, followed by a gasp. The door jerked open and he stared into the beautifully surprised face of Aisha.

"Come in here, you!" she exclaimed. She grabbed fistfuls of his shirt them pulled him into a tight embrace, kissing him all over his face. They didn't make it to the bedroom; Omari kicked the door close just before they made love furiously on the floor. When they were done they lay half-naked, Aisha on top of Omari.

"I see you missed me," she said.

"Not as much as you missed me," Omari replied.

"Where have you been?" she asked.

"Working."

"That's a lie."

"No, really. I have."

Omari took out the bibi's seal and showed it to Aisha. Her eyes brightened.

"Let's go to market!" she said.

She clambered off Omari and dressed.

"Slow down," he said. "We can't blow her money."

Aisha turned to face him, hands on her hips.

"Why?"

"Because I'm going back," he said.

Omari saw disappointment in Aisha's eyes. The two of them had a committed relationship, at least as committed as a relationship could be with people of their circumstances. Both of them knew they might have to make certain decisions to survive, and they both understood that would mean taking on other relationships. Still, it didn't lessen the pain.

Aisha's emotional face withered away, replace by her practical mask.

"So what's the deal?"

"She hired me as a woodcutter, but I've been promoted to personal escort."

"How much is she paying you?"

Omari shrugged. "Sixty cowries a week. But she's hiring me a tutor and a fight instructor. I'm also living in the main house."

Aisha smirked. "I guess you didn't miss me as much as I thought."

"No one can replace you," Omari said. "You know that."

Aisha rolled her eyes. "This sounds long term."

"It might be," Omar confessed. "But you know I'll always come back to you."

"Really?" Aisha said in a sarcastic tone.

"Of course. You are my heart."

Aisha grabbed his hand.

"And you are my soul. Now put on your clothes and let's spend a little of the bibi's money."

Omari and Aisha browsed the market, careful to haggle for deals so the spending would not exceed the allotted cowries. After escorting Aisha back to her home, Omari picked up his horse then returned to the farm. Haddas waited for him as he entered.

"What took you so long?" she said.

"I'm not used to paying for items in the market," Omari replied. "I usually steal them."

"Next time be quick about it," Haddas said. She snatched the basket from his hands.

"The bibi is waiting for you in the public room."

Omari strolled to the room, happy he was not meeting Marianna in her bedroom. He didn't have the energy or desire for a tryst. Aisha had drained him physically and emotionally. The bibi sat in one of her cushioned chairs, flanked by two middle-aged men sitting on stools. Their conversation ended upon his entering the room. One was familiar to him, the other a stranger. Both men scrutinized him, one with a disapproving expression.

"Ah, you have returned," Marianna said. "Honored ones, meet your pupil, Omari Ket."

Omari bowed to the men. The man to the bibi's right stood, his robe hanging loosely from his wiry frame. His head was shaven as was most that practiced his profession.

"Omari, can you read and write? the man asked.

"Yes," Omari replied. "My parents taught me the Seven Tales and Eda's Songs."

The man smiled.

"Impressive. Where are your parents?"

Omari's mood fell as the memory of his parents' demise appeared in his mind.

"Dead. They died during the bacillus plague," he replied.

A flash of terror crossed the man's face.

"Eda's mercy," he said. "I am so sorry."

Omari shrugged. "It was a long time ago."

"I am Akin Bobala," the man said. "I will be you tutor of the sciences and the arts. I will also instruct you in proper manners."

Omari's eyes shifted to Mariama.

"I thought I was to be your bodyguard," he said.

Mariama nodded. "You are."

"Then I would assume that the last thing you would want be to do is observe the proper manners when protecting you."

"There will be situations where your service must not be so obvious," the bibi said. "In such situations you must be able to carry yourself in a manner that reflects my status."

"I see," Omari replied. So he was to be a dancing mbogo as well.

"We will begin your lessons tomorrow," Akin said. He returned to his stool.

Omari tensed as Balogun Ojetade stood then sauntered toward him. The fight master was tall with light brown skin and a bald head covered by a light blue cap. He wore the traditional warrior garb of Oyo, light blue shirt and pants with symbolic patterns. He stopped, his arms folded across his chest as he looked Omari up and down. Omari was no fool; the master assumed a fighting stance, preparing to attack. Omari did the same.

"The street rat has found a home," Balogun Ojetade said.

"I have," Omari replied, ignoring the Bodua's insult. He stood before one of the deadliest men in Sati-Baa. Ojetade's martial skills were legendary. He trained the Sati-Baa nyanas, and was the only man never defeated in the Ibuthodili, the annual worldwide wrestling tournament that took place during the Baa Festival.

"I remember what you attempted to do," he said.

"I am sorry, bodua," Omari said.

"A warrior does not apologize for his actions," Balogun said. "Whatever he does he does with intent. I will teach you better."

Ojetade turned to walk away. Omari's relief was cut short by a kick to the gut that sent him flying across the room. He crashed on the floor then curled into a ball as he gasped for breath.

"Was that necessary?" Mariama asked.

"Yes," Ojetade replied. "No one tries to steal from me without consequences. Besides, he's a street rat. He's suffered worse."

Omari finally regained his breath. He stood then approached Ojetade.

"I deserved that, bodua," he said. "I promise you that I will be an attentive and diligent student."

Ojetade grinned. "If only for the chance to pay me back."

Omari grinned. "Of course."

"Good," Ojetade said. "It will push us both to our best."

"You will spend you mornings with Akin after your chores," Mariama said. "Your afternoons will be spent with the bodua. Your schedule is subject to change based on my needs."

Omari held back a smirk when Mariama mentioned her needs.

"Yes, bibi," he said.

"You may leave," she said.

Omari bowed to the three then went to his room. He immediately collapsed onto his bed and fell asleep, exhausted by the day's activity. His sleep was interrupted by a naked body pressed against his and perfume wafting into his nose.

"Are you well rested?" Mariama asked.

Omari opened his eyes and grinned.

"Well enough," he replied.

Mariama pressed her lips against his as she wrapped her legs around him.

* * *

Omari's routine took shape over the weeks. His days began with the market, where he would slip in time with Aisha when she was available. Back at the compound he would perform a few mundane tasks until it was time for his teaching. The sparring sessions with Bodua Ojetade were brutal but instructive. Afterwards there was a long bath to soothe his wounds. Most of the time he bathed alone, but sometimes Mariama joined him when she couldn't wait for their nightly encounters. As his household schedule became more comfortable, his relationship with the compound workers degraded. While Chuk was himself, the others grew more distant. Their friendly insults disappeared, replaced by glares and curses. Worst of the lot was Gituku. He said nothing when Omari appeared, responding with a glower and a spit. Omari knew the look from years in the streets. Sooner or later there would be another confrontation between them, and when it happened it would be far from friendly.

Omari was struggling with a complex math problem when the bibi entered the room.

"I have an engagement tonight at the Grand Merchant's compound," she said. "You will accompany me."

Omari smirked. "Those merchants can be a dangerous lot, I suspect."

Mariama did not smile. "You'll be surprised. There is a uniform waiting for you in your room. Be ready by sunset."

No sooner did Mariama leave the room did Akin clap his hands.

"At last!" he exclaimed.

"Why are you excited?" Omari asked. "She asked me, not you."

"She is finally introducing you to her better friends," Akin replied. "You'll have a chance to use everything I've taught you."

"So?"

"If all goes well the bibi will increase my pay!" Akin said.

"I'll do my best to make you proud," Omari lied.

He completed his lessons, happy to skip practice with Ojetade and avoid the usual afternoon beating. He entered his room and frowned when he saw the uniform laying on his bed. It was a Sati-Baa nyana outfit, a red kanga instead of nyana blue. Beside the bed were a short sword and sheath, a wrist dagger and two throwing clubs. He winced as he looked at the clubs; he'd been the recipient of those foul weapons more than once. At least the ones that struck him were toothless; he'd seen the damage a toothed throwing club could do. He undressed then put on the uniform. It was a perfect fit. When he returned to the foyer Mariama was waiting. She was breathtaking. The gown she chose to wear was tastefully revealing. The look on her face told him it would be in his hands before the end of the night.

"You look respectful," she said. "Let's go. We're late as it is."

Chuk waited for them with the carriage. He was dressed formally as well, a blue turban held together by a sapphire broach sitting on his head. He shifted uncomfortably as they approached. Omari took Mariama's hand and helped her into the carriage. He took a seat beside Chuk.

"I don't know why I have to wear these clothes!" Chuk said. "I'm not going inside."

"You work for me," the bibi called out. "Your appearance affects my reputation."

"Your baba never forced me to wear this thing," Chuk retorted.

"I am not my baba, nor my nana. If you value your position, I will hear no more of this ever again."

Chuk reined the horses and the carriage jerked to a start.

"You look ridiculous," Chuk said to Omari.

"True, but it's only temporary. Tonight, I'll be naked."

"About that," Chuk said.

"Spare me the lecture," Omari replied.

"This is not a lecture, it's a warning. Try not to flaunt your status so much. There are many who hoped to be in your place and they are not pleased that you were the one selected."

"That's their problem," Omari replied.

"No, it's your problem. None of us are obligated to work the bibi's farm. We could pack our things and walk away during the night. If that happens, you'll find yourself doing much more than warming the bibi's bed."

"You would leave the bibi?" Omari asked.

"Of course not," Chuk said. "I told you how I feel. But the others have no qualms, especially Gituku."

"He's a problem," Omari said.

Chuk nodded. "A problem you'll have to deal with sooner or later."

"Let's make it sooner," Omari said.

They continued the ride in silence. Omari's musing was interrupted as they entered the Sati-Baa merchant district. It was one of the few city districts he wasn't familiar with and he was awestruck with the amazing architecture. The district was a shrine to the wealth of those who controlled it, each family compound vying with its neighbor for opulence. The streets were so clean you could drop your food on them and retrieve it to eat with no compunction. The wide avenues glowed from large fish oil lanterns spaced like soldiers along the sidewalks. There were few pedestrians at such a late hour, most retired to their homes with the exception of nyanas and groups of people that seemed to be headed to the same destination as the bibi. All were well dressed and walked with an air of privilege and confidence.

Chuk guided the carriage to the largest structure in the district, the compound of the Grand Merchant. Once again Omari was captured by opulence; there were enough jewels embedded in the door alone to support him for the rest of his life. He was tempted to remove a stone or two on his way inside but fought down the urge. He was a hired man now, not a street rat.

The wagon halted and Omari jumped from the buckboard. He opened the carriage door and assisted Mariama from the wagon.

"You've been paying attention," she whispered.

"I'm a fast learner," Omari replied.

"Yes you are," she said. Her comment referred to other skills he's acquired since he began servicing the bibi.

"How do you know I wasn't holding back?" he said.

Mariama's eyes widened as she grinned mischievously.

"I look forward to your future revelations."

Mariama took his arm and he led her to the entrance. The entry guards opened the doors without hesitation and Omari entered the world of the high merchants.

The foyer of the Grand Merchant's home was three times as large as the largest drinking house in Sati-Baa. Music flowed through the massive room with ease, projected by a system of Darmacen amplifiers, large funnel-like objects placed near the ceiling. Omari didn't understand how they worked; apparently there was nyama involved. Such nyama didn't come free; it was another example of the Grand Merchant's wealth. The main floor writhed with dancers, some professionals, others guests doing their best to match the hired dancers' skill. Merchants and their companions wore a myriad of outfits, some signifying their origins and city districts, others in fashions unique to Sati-Baa. Omari stared at them all wide-eyed.

Mariama tugged at his arm.

"Stop looking like you chew grass," Mariama said. "Kansoleh is waiting for me."

"Kansoleh Dembele? The Grand Merchant?"

Mariama grinned. "We are old friends. She won't begin her meal without me. The guests are probably starving."

Mariama led Omari through the crowd to a large round table at the opposite end. Merchants in gaudy costumes sat at the table while servers swirled about with trays of food. Kansoleh Dembele, the Grand Merchant, looked down on the spectacle, her seat raised to signify her elevated status. The seat beside her was empty. As Mariama and Omari approached, everyone came to their feet and bowed.

"You had no idea," Mariama whispered to Omari, reading his thoughts.

"No, I didn't," he whispered back.

"This is why your behavior is very important, so forget about embarrassing me."

"Forgotten," Omari replied.

Mariama greeted the celebrants with generous platitudes as she neared her seat. Kansoleh stood, her arms outstretched. Mariama walked into her embrace and they hugged, pressing their cheeks together.

"You're late dada," Kansoleh said.

"I always am," Mariama replied.

Kansoleh opened her eyes, looking at Omari.

"Is he the reason?" she asked.

"Not this time," Mariama replied.

Mariama walked to her seat. Omari took position behind it as the bibi sat. Kansoleh's eyes stayed focused on Omari.

"He's beautiful," Kansoleh commented. "Young, too."

"Not as young as he appears," Mariama said.

"I sense the street about him."

"You're perceptive," Mariama said.

"Be careful," Kansoleh said. "The feral ones are the most dangerous."

"How would you know?"

Kansoleh answered Mariama with a mischievous grin.

"You are so full of secrets!" Mariama said.

"Enough of this," Kansoleh replied. "Your food is getting cold. I had your favorites prepared."

Mariama's eyes widened as she scanned her plate.

"I see. Thank you!"

Mariama looked at Omari.

"I don't need you for now," she said. "You can join the others in the small room."

Omari bowed then strode away having no idea where the small room was located. He looked about until he saw other persons similarly dressed walking toward an entryway near the entrance. He entered the room and frowned; it was cramped, filled with guards standing around small tables. A few looked up at him then continued their meals. Omari found an unoccupied table; moments later a servant appeared.

"How may I serve you," the boy said.

"What do you have?"

"We have spinfin stew, jackgoat chops and thin beer," the boy replied.

"I'll take all three," he said.

"As you wish," the boy replied. "May I ask who your patron is?"

"Bibi Mariama," Omari said.

The boy stiffened then fell to his knees at the mention of Mariama's name.

"Please pardon my insult!" he said.

He jumped to his feet then grabbed Omari's arm.

"Please come with me," he said.

Omari let the boy lead him, taking full notice of the others has they gawked. The boy led him to another room which was much larger and smartly decorated. There was a table like that of the grand merchant's but significantly smaller. Sitting around the table were other guards, most dressed similar to him. They looked up in unison, greeting him with warm smiles. Omari smiled back as he sat.

"So, what is this? The high table of servants?"

The men laughed.

"It's special, isn't it?" one of the guards said. He was a big man with thick arms and a thick neck. The man extended his hand and Omari took it. His grip was so strong Omari suppressed a yelp.

"Kofi Ansah, the man said. "Personal guard of Bibi Dambele."

Kofi let go of his hand and Omari flexed his fingers to make sure nothing was broken.

"Omari Ket. Bibi Mariama's guard."

The other guards responded with whistles and winks.

"You're a lucky one," Kofi said.

"How so?" Omari asked.

"First, you're here with us. The food is almost as good as the merchants."

As if on cue the boy arrived with his food. It was everything he ordered but prepared with much better care. Omari tasted the spinfin soup and his eyes rolled back in pleasure.

"This is Eda touched," he said.

Kofi grinned, exposing his perfect teeth. "Second, Bibi Mariama is known to be most generous."

Omari sipped his soup, suppressing a comment.

"Many a merchant in Sati-Baa owes their start to her. Serve her well and she will return the favor. Cross her and you'll disappear."

The last part of Kofi's statement caused Omari to pause. He never considered what would happen if Mariama became dissatisfied with him.

"It's my job to make her comfortable."

"Good answer," Kofi said.

"What about you?" Omari asked. "What has the Grand Merchant done for you?"

"Working for her is reward enough" Kofi said. The other guards burst into laughter.

"Bibi Kansoleh keeps him busy," one of the other guards said.

"As I'm sure Bibi Mariama does you?" Kofi said.

Omari smirked. "So basically we're whores."

Kofi laughed. "Pretty much."

Omari smiled as more hot food was placed before him.

"I'm good with that," he said before he stuffed his mouth.

A loud crash followed by hysterical screams cut his meal short. In an instant Omari and the guards were on their feet with weapons drawn, running through their chambers and into the main hall. They plunged into chaos. They were under attack, and whoever was attacking the gala dressed similar to the guests making it difficult to determine who to fight.

"To the main table!" Kofi shouted. "Kill anyone with a weapon that is not a guard!"

Omari had already determined as much. He pushed his way through the crowd toward the table. A number of the attackers scattered among the others as a distraction, but the main group worked their way to the main table. If not for the people fleeing before them, they would have reached it. Omari ran around them, reaching the table first. He glimpsed Mariama hugging Kansoleh, their faces twisted with terror. He turned to the armed horde. This was not him. With odds like this he would have run away. Life was more valuable than a fight he was bound to lose. He glanced at Mariama, their eyes meeting. It was at that moment Omari realized he actually cared for the woman.

"Shit," he whispered.

He stabbed the first assassin in the throat then cut his blade free with the slash of his dagger as he tripped another interloper who tried to run past him. The man's chin slammed into the table as he fell; Omari spun and severed his spine. As he turned about a fist struck him in the face, knocking him against the table. He kicked out instinctively, landing his foot in the man's gut. Another attacker attempted to get by him and he threw his dagger, the blade sinking into the man's head.

A roar rose from behind the attackers; Kofi and the others had arrived. Omari fought on, his actions a blur as he attempted to keep the onslaught at bay. He was about to hack down with his sword when someone gripped his wrist then spun him around.

"That's enough, killer," Kofi said. Blood trickled from a wound on the man's forehead as he smiled. "We got 'em."

Omari was met by Mariama as he turned about. "Get a healer immediately!" she shouted.

Omari was confused. "What?"

Weakness washed over him as he fell face forward to the floor.

* * *

The sound of trickling water let Omari know he was still alive. Something warm and soothing pressed against his abdomen and he moaned in response. A smooth hand touched his forehead; moments later a pair of familiar lips pressed against his. His lips parted in reflex and a mint-scented tongue teased his teeth.

"Mariama," he whispered.

"You've come back," she said.

Omari opened his eyes. The bibi stood over him, a smile on her face as she ran her hand from his stomach to his crotch. Her smile widened.

"I feel you've recovered completely," she said.

"Apparently," Omari replied.

He attempted to sit up but she pushed him down. "You need more rest. I shouldn't be here."

"How long have I been here?" he asked.

"Two days. You almost died."

Omari shook. "Really? But I didn't feel anything."

"You were stabbed with a sliver sword," Mariama said.

Omari closed his eyes. Sliver swords were an assassin's tool, a thin piece of pitted steel designed to deliver poison without leaving a mark. It was meant for one of the people at the table, most likely the Grand Merchant.

"Who planned the attack?" Omari asked.

"We don't know," Mariama replied. "Those that were not killed by you and the other guards killed themselves when the Nyana arrived."

"Where did they come from?"

"No one knows. They wore local clothing. They bore no markings that would identify their people."

Mariama looked pensive.

"What?" Omari asked.

"Some suspect they may have come from the Cleave."

Omari burst out laughing, which almost made him pass out with pain.

"It's not that funny," Mariama said.

"It is, because it's impossible," Omari replied. "Nothing lives in the Cleave."

"How do you know?"

"Good question," Omari replied. "I'm speculating that any place struck by Daarila's Axe would be barren of life."

Mariama shrugged.

"That's a discussion best left to priests and prophets," she said. "You should rest and heal."

She kissed him then left him alone.

Omari watched Mariama leave before laying back onto the mattress. Kofi was right. He was blessed. He couldn't imagined a better situation. But he was practical enough to know it wouldn't last. He was young and interesting. One day Mariama would tire of him and send him back to the forest to chop wood or send him away altogether. He would make sure he was long gone before that day arrived.

After two weeks of rest and healing herbs Omari was almost himself again. No sooner did he show signs of strength did Mariama invade his bed, vigorously making up for lost time. She seemed more caring than before, spending time to linger and talk about mundane and insignificant things. Omari, usually annoyed by such chatter, found himself enjoying the moments. They were growing closer and he wasn't sure how he felt about it.

The morning came when he was ready to assume his duties. He dressed in his uniform, and then met Haddas in the kitchen for the market list. Although his relationship with the bibi had progressed, things between him and the house maid remained the same. At least she knew better than to threaten him again.

"Here," she said as she shoved the list against his chest. "And don't take so long!"

Omari took the list then headed for the stables. He met Chuk along the way.

"Good to see you up and about," Chuk said.

"Good to be seen," Omari replied.

"Going on your market run?"

Omari nodded.

"You had a visitor while you were healing," Chuk said.

Omari stopped. "Really?"

"Yes. A pretty woman from the city. She said she was selling breads, but he asked about you."

Aisha, Omari thought.

"I told her you were fine," Chuk said.

"Thank you," Omari replied.

He was about to mount his horse when Chuk grabbed his arm.

"Omari, be careful."

"I always am."

Chuk tugged his shoulder. "I'm serious. The bibi has always favored you, but now she cares for you."

"And that is a bad thing?" Omari replied.

"Very bad. She and her kind don't know what true feeling is. Everything in their world has a price. It would be the same even if you were her equal, and you're not."

Omari was irritated by this conversation. He spent his entire life in the streets being treated less than Ki Khangan.

"Are you done?" he asked.

"No. All I'm saying is that you are a possession to her, and she's selfish about what she owns. If she were to find out about you and this other woman . . ."

"She would what?" Omari asked. "If I feel threatened, I'll walk away and disappear into the streets. I'm good at that."

Chuk sighed. "I did my duty. I wipe my hands of it."

He let go of Omari's arm then walked back to his wagon. Omari went to mount his horse.

"Street rat!"

Omari dropped his head then looked up to see Gituku striding toward him, a thick wooden staff in his grip. Omari looked into his former boss's rheumy eyes and could tell he'd been drinking. This was not going to end well.

"What do you want, Gituku?"

"You don't deserve her!" Gituku shouted. "I've worked hard for the bibi."

"It was her choice," Omari said.

Gituku stopped before him. "If you had not come, I would be wearing your fancy clothes and sharing her bed."

"Careful, Gituku," Chuk said. The old man had come from his wagon, his eyes shifting between Omari and Gituku. Omari began circling Gituku.

"You told me I would have to deal with him one day," Omari said to Chuk.

"That was then," Chuk replied. "Walk away, Gituku. You're no match for him now."

Gituku didn't answer. He ran at Omari, the staff held high. Omari stood still, waiting until Gituku swung down. At the last moment he sidestepped, maneuvering behind Gituku. Before the wood master could turn Omari had him in a chokehold. Gituku fell to his knees with Omari on his back, clutching at Omari's arms. Omari leaned close to Gituku's right ear.

"I could choke you to death," he said. "Balogun Ojetade taught me well. But that would mean trouble for me. When I release you, I want you to walk away and never speak to me again or come near the bibi. If you do, I'll kill you."

Omari let Gituku go then shoved him face first into the dirt. Gituku rolled onto his back, gasping. Omari strode to his horse, cutting his eyes at Chuk. Chuk shook his head and trudged back to the wagon.

"Fools," he whispered.

Omari mounted his horse then rode into town in good spirits after handling Gituku. He stabled his horse then headed to Aisha's dwelling. He'd barely knocked when the door flew open. Aisha grabbed his shirt then dragged him inside.

"You bastard!" she shouted. "What the Cleave did you think you were doing? You could have died!"

Before he could answer she kissed him hard and long. When she released him, he grinned.

"But I didn't," he said.

"We have a rule," she fussed. "Never risk our lives unnecessarily, remember?"

Omari pushed by her, walking to the nearest chair and sitting down.

"I know. I got caught up in the moment," he said.

"You never get caught up in the moment," Aisha replied. She walked to the table and sat opposite him.

"Tell me the truth. Do you care for her?"

"No," Omari said.

Aisha slapped him.

"Liar."

Omari dropped his head.

"I don't care for her as much as I care for you."

Silence fell over them like a damp, cold fog from the Cleave Mountains.

"Go," she said. "Leave before I slap you like I mean it."

Omari stood.

"Aisha, I..."

"Remember our promise? Never let them get close. Never care. Never."

"It's not that simple."

Aisha slammed her fist on the table, her eyes glistening with tears.

"Go!"

Omari stood then took the pouch of coins from his bag, sitting on the table.

"I'm sorry," he said.

Aisha looked away.

"Please go, Omari. Please."

Omari left the house. He picked up the items on the list then returned to the stable for his horse.

"That was quick," the stable master commented.

Omari didn't reply.

"Much sooner than usual," the man continued.

"Mind your own damn business," Omari retorted.

He wandered through the city, stunned by what had just occurred. He and Aisha had their differences before, but never about how they felt about each other. They grew up orphans in the streets together. They'd always been there for each other. As their relationship grew into something more, it drew them closer. But the bibi had somehow come between them.

He finally guided his horse to the compound. As he approached the gate, he decided there was only one thing to do.

He entered the kitchen, placing the market goods on the table. He turned to see Haddas staring at him. He was used to her unpleasantness, but this new look made him reach for his sword.

"The bibi wishes to speak to you," she said, her voice trembling.

"What does she want?" he asked.

"Ask her yourself," Haddas replied.

Omari went to Mariama's bedchamber. The bibi sat on the edge of her bed, smiling like he'd never seen before.

"Omari!" she said. "You were gone longer than normal."

"The merchants were stingy."

"Come, sit beside me," she asked.

Omari went to Mariama. Before he could sit, she pulled him down then pressed his hand against her stomach.

"I'm pregnant!" she said.

Weakness swept Omari and he swayed. He steadied himself with his free hand before responding.

"Pregnant? How?"

Mariama laughed. "How do you think?"

The bibi seemed to sense his mood.

"Don't worry. You will not be a husband," she said. "As fond as I am of you, that would be impossible. But you will be a father, and a child needs its father."

"What are you saying?" Omari asked.

"What I'm saying is that your position here has become permanent."

"Thank you?"

Mariama frowned. "I would think you would be grateful. There are many who would kill to be in your position."

"I am . . . grateful," Omari replied. "It just that it's so much in such a short time."

"You strike me as a person than can handle such things."

Omari forced a smile. "Maybe you don't know me as well as you think you do."

"Maybe not," Mariama replied. "But I look forward to finding out."

Omari embraced Mariama and gave her a long kiss. She smiled as their lips parted.

"Now that is what I expected."

"I'm truly happy for you, and for us," he said. "Now if you don't mind, I have chores."

"Not today," Mariama said. "Today you will spend the day with me in the city."

"What's our destination?" Omari asked.

"We have none," she replied. "We'll ride through Sati-Baa and see what happens."

Mariama was truly joyous, but Omari's mood was just the opposite. Aisha's rejection and discovering he would soon be a father put him in a disposition he struggled to decipher.

He walked in a daze to the compound entrance to summon Mariama's wagon. Chuk rolled up, a curious look on his face.

"The bibi has decided to spend the day in the city," Omari said.

"What for?" Chuk asked.

"To celebrate the fact that she's pregnant," Omari replied.

Chuk's curious gaze left him, replaced by fear.

"You once said you could leave when you wanted," he said. "Now is the time."

"What are you talking about?" Omari asked. "Why would I want to leave now? The bibi is pregnant with my child."

"That is exactly why you must flee!"

"I don't understand."

Chuk grabbed Omari by his shirt then pulled him so close their noses almost touched.

"Listen to me. When you return from your trip, pack your things and go. Get off the compound; better still get out of Sati-Baa. And take your woman with you. Neither of you are safe!"

"What are you two talking about?"

Mariama walked toward them, a suspicious look on her face. Chuk let go of Omari's shirt then bowed.

"Nothing, bibi," he said. "Just a minor disagreement."

"It didn't seem minor to me," she said.

Omari smiled at the mother of his child.

"It's as he said. Are you ready?"

Mariama glided by Omari then climbed into the wagon.

"I am now."

Omari climbed in then sat beside her. Chuk reined the horses and they were on their way to the city. Mariama was unusually silent, a grin on her face as she looked about the city. Omari's face was calm, although inside a tempest brewed. Chuk's words didn't make any sense. Mariama was ecstatic about the pregnancy and she seemed to be planning for him to have a bigger role in her life. He felt solemn for a moment; being the father of the bibi's child meant he would have to end his visits to Aisha, at least until the child was old enough not to need their constant supervision.

"Chuk," Mariama said. "Take us to the wharf."

Chuk jerked his head around, the look of shock on his face.

"Where, bibi?"

"You heard me. Take us to the wharf."

"Yes, bibi."

Chuk's eyes narrowed as he looked at Omari. Something was wrong.

"What's at the wharf?" Omari asked Mariama.

"My ship," she said. "I think I want to go sailing today."

"Don't you think it's hot to be on the water?"

Mariama laughed. "What do you know of sailing?"

"Nothing," Omari said.

"Then relax," Mariama said. "It will be fun."

Chuk guided the wagon through the streets to the docks, looking back to meet eyes with Omari. Omari couldn't understand his worry. Mariama looked about, occasionally waving at other dignitaries out for a ride. The smell of the lake finally reached them, the sound of seabirds blending with those of the city. They crested a small hill then descended toward the lake. The massive waters filled the horizon. Omari rarely ventured to the lake edge; the merchants were secretive and brutal to anyone they thought trying to steal their goods. Chuk braked the wagon as they descended toward the waters.

They finally reached the docks. Chuk stopped the wagon before a ship that resembled a merchant dhow, but what did he know of such things? He climbed from the wagon and went to Mariama. She waved her hand.

"I won't be getting out," she said. A sly smile came to her face and Chuk's warnings finally became clear. Omari didn't need to look, he just ran. The angry voices behind him told him his reaction was unexpected.

"Don't let him get away!" Mariama shouted.

Omari didn't know the wharf like he knew the city. He could only run back the way he came, hoping his pursuers weren't as fleet of foot. The closer he came to the city, the more confident he felt of escaping. His confidence disappeared with his consciousness as the throwing club struck the base of his skull.

* * *

The world rocked. Muted voices floated about, the sound of footfalls descending from above. Omari winced as he opened his eyes to darkness. The back of his head throbbed; his hands and feet were tied.

"He's coming to," someone said.

"Good," someone else answered. "Fetch him something to eat."

A torch was lit, and Omari found himself staring into the face of a Sati-Baa nyana.

"We finally got you," the man said.

"You must be mistaken," Omari replied. "I'm the servant of Bibi Mariama."

The nyana grinned. "You used to be."

The other man returned with a bowl of stew. He placed the bowl on the floor beside Omari then looked at the nyana.

"Untie him," the nyana said. He revealed his throwing club, patting it against his open palm while the other man untied Omari's hands and feet. He sized up the nyana then decided against attacking him. Even if he was able to overwhelm him, he had no idea what waited on deck. He never made a move unless he had full knowledge of the situation.

The stew was bland but edible.

"Who are you?" he asked the nyana.

"Akwesi Juma, Nyana Mkuu of Sati-Baa."

Omari put down his stew. This was very serious.

"Why am I talking to you?"

"I was requested by Bibi Kansoleh Dembele"

"What's happening?"

"You're being sent away," the nyana said. "Bibi Mariama couldn't allow you to remain in Sati-Baa with the child coming. There would be too much of a chance that it would discover who its father was."

"Our relationship was no secret," Omari said.

"That which cannot be confirmed never occurred," the nyana replied.

"No matter where you take me, I can return," Omari said.

"If you do the life of your friend Aisha is forfeit," Akwesi replied.

Omari hesitated. He endangered his own life every day, but he would not cause harm to Aisha. He ate another spoonful of stew. It tasted of bitterness.

"So where am I going?"

"Kiswala."

"The merchant islands? What use would I be there?"

"The Mikijen are always recruiting," the mkuu said.

Cold fear streaked down Omari's back. He threw the bowl aside then attacked the mkuu with the spoon, stabbing him in the eye. He howled as he fell away grabbing his damaged orb. Omari grabbed the throwing club from the floor then struck the man hard in the head before finding his way to the stairs leading to the deck. Serving the Mikijen was a death sentence. He would rather take his chances than be delivered to such an inevitable fate.

He charged onto the deck and was momentarily blinded by the sunlight. Shouts and curses cleared his vision; a group of baharia and nyanas ran toward him. Omari looked to the bulwark. He had no idea how far he was from shore but he would take that chance. He ran to the bulwark then scrambled onto it. Someone grabbed his leg and he struck behind himself with the club. The person yelped and released him. He jumped over the side into the warm waters. Crashing into the waves stunned him; it took him a moment to swim. Omari was not a good swimmer, nor a strong one. After only a few moments he was floundering, fighting to keep his head above water. So, he would drown. So be it. He opened his mouth and sank below the surface.

* * *

Omari awoke to disappointment. He was ashore, and he was alive. He opened his eyes to the wounded mkuu. A cotton patch covered his eye and bandages were wrapped around his head.

"I should kill you," Akwesi said. "But I've been paid well to keep you alive."

Omari was shackled to the deck. The senior nyana called out and three more nyanas surrounded Omari, throwing clubs and swords at the ready. Akwesi unshackled him then jerked him onto his feet. They led him down the gangplank to a man wearing some type of uniform, a blue turban on his head. As he neared Omari noticed tentacle tattoos on the man arms. Despair washed over him. This man was a Mikijen.

The mkuu walked up to the man, then handed him Omari's chain.

"Complements of the bibi," Akwesi said.

The man jerked Omari closer.

"I hope he's better than the other ones," he said. "They barely lasted six months."

"He's a street rat," Akwesi said. "He's tougher than most."

The man grabbed Omari's chin then lifted his head.

"What's your name?" he asked.

"Omari Ket," Omari answered.

"Welcome to the Mikijen!" the man said. "I know things seem bleak to you right now, but they are far from it. You have been recruited into the best fighting force in Ki Khanga. The Kiswala are good employers, they pay very well. If you follow orders, you'll end up with a very good life. If you survive."

The man laughed as he turned and strode away, pulling Omari behind him. Omari turned his head, glancing at the ship and the nyanas as they boarded. There was nothing behind him now; his life rested on the bosom of Eda. He prayed she would protect him as she did in Sati-Baa. He lifted his head, following the Mikijen officer to his fate.

A BETTER DEAL

The landing barge careened sideways as the boulder crashed nearby, spilling the sailors manning the upper deck into the churning blood-stained sea. The men inside moaned in unison, their stomachs roiling from fear and motion. Omari Ket retched for a third time then cursed the ancestors. He glared at the rowers, wishing they would row faster. If he had to die, let it be on the sandy beach with a sword in his hand, not in the belly of this retched boat ankle deep in water and vomit.

He finally had enough of it. He pushed his way to the ladder leading to the upper deck then clambered into the sunlight. Arrows riddled the dhow, some of them pinning dead sailors to the deck and the masts. He gazed over the horizon and frowned. The other barges were fairing no better. If he had been of senior rank, he would be on a good horse in the forest behind the city, waiting for the signal to launch the secret attack from the rear. Instead he was atop a floating coffin heading for the stone citadel showering them with arrows and stones.

A crashing sound drew his attention to the bow of the barge. Broken clay lay about, a thick green liquid oozing over the wood.

"Damn it to the Cleave!" he exclaimed.

He ran for the bulwark as flaming arrows rained down on his barge and the others. He leaped as the arrows struck the deck, igniting the liquid which exploded into a roaring fire, singeing the bottom of his boots as he hit the cold ocean waters.

The screams of his fellow Mikijen reached his ears while he swam underwater toward the beach, coming up briefly to gulp air. Finally reaching the shore, he lay still next to a dead Mikijen. If he was lucky an arrow would pierce his head once he stood, ending this terror. As Fate would have it, no such thing occurred. He ran across the beach as fast as he could, not toward the ladder bearers charging the fortress wall, but toward the tangle of bushes and stunted palm trees offering refuge.

Omari grinned as he neared the foliage; the grin faded as a squad of citadel defenders sprang from the bush, waving their swords and yelling.

"Shit!" he said. Omari drew his sword and dagger then plunged into their ranks. His sword bounced off the blade of the nearest man as he drove his dagger into his gut. He spun to his right and ducked as a blade meant for his neck whizzed by. He punched the man before him with his sword hilt then dodged a spear driving for his throat. Omari spun, slashed, stabbed and hacked until all the attackers lay dead or dying. He continued running until he was well within the bush, then dropped to knees out of breath. He looked briefly at his grim handiwork then peered beyond the dying pile to the beach. As the scene evolved before him a bitter taste filled his mouth. What he suspected was proved true as the second wave of landing barges approached, supported by cover fire from Kiswala warships. The first wave was a decoy designed to draw the citadel's fire and exhaust its arsenal. The second wave met much less resistance, landing on the beach easily. Waves of Mikijen stormed the wall, their ladders slamming against the stone under the cover of arrows and manogel fire from the warships.

Omari's anger was brief; he survived and that was all that mattered. His objective now was getting inside those walls. As a Mikijen he would be paid a few cowries and service beads if he survived, but the real payment was the booty he could collect after the city fell. He took a hard biscuit from his provision bag and ate as he watched his comrades fight their way onto the ramparts. By the time he washed down the bread with a swig from his water gourd the ramparts were secured. Omari emerged from the bush then jogged across the sands to the walls. He waited in line with the others then climbed the ladder into the city. Once on the ramparts he squatted and studied the situation. The Mikijen were flooding the space between the walls and the city, meeting strong resistance from the city garrison. In the city people were fleeing to the opposite walls, their cries and screams rising over the clashing of wood and steel. Omari squinted at those walls. Grappling hooks rose over the edge and fell onto the stone. The Mikijen horsemen had arrived and were attacking the rear gates, cutting off any escape. Omari frowned as he recognized the black uniforms and shrouded faces of the first warriors over the wall, the Shuru. The Kiswala had sent their personal soldiers to locate whatever wealth the high merchants of the city had gathered and deliver it to their hands. Omari looked into the city and found their objective, a cluster of wide compounds with high towered homes. If he hurried, he could beat them.

He joined a group of Mikijen running across the rampart to the stairs leading to the field. He broke away as soon as they reached level ground, skirting the wall to the right until he reached the outskirts of the main city. Citizens ran toward the gates, some of them screaming when seeing him, other glaring yet none brave enough to approach him. Omari rushed through the winding roads, finally finding his way to the merchant district. The merchants were frantically loading their wagons, protected by their personal guards. Omari hid behind a nearby building, looking for the house he'd targeted from the walls. He was trying to figure out how he would get through the numerous guards when the answer came in the form of the Shuru. They attacked the guards, drawing them away from their masters. Omari sprinted toward the house unnoticed.

Two guards stood before the door, weapons in hands as they looked toward the fight taking place nearby. Omari was upon them before they realized, killing both men with quick slashes of his blade. He charged into the compound, running through the veranda to the stairs leading to the merchant's wealth. Hurrying down the hallway to the main room, he slammed his shoulder into the door. The door broke open, revealing a bearded man holding a gleaming silver sword, his trembling hand wrapped around the gold inlaid ivory hilt. It was a weapon meant to be admired, not used. The man's fearful expression faded, replaced by a knowing smirk.

"You are not one of them," he said with a coarse voice. "You are a Mikijen."

"Where is the gold?" Omari demanded.

A grin creased the man's face. "I could give you what gold I have here, but it is nothing compared to what waits beyond these walls."

Omari rushed the man, pinning him against the wall, his sword at the merchant's neck.

"The gold. Now!"

The man laughed. "Kill me now and you'll get a pittance. Get me out of here. If you do, I promise you more gold than you can imagine."

Omari said nothing. This was not going as he planned.

"Make up your mind, Mikijen. The Shuru will be here soon and they won't be happy to see you."

Omari turned then walked out the room, dragging the merchant behind him.

"Wait!" the man shouted. He broke away from Omari then ran back into his room. Omari was about to pursue him when the man returned with a bag slung over his shoulder. He tossed a pouch to Omari; Omari caught it, opened it and grinned. It was stuffed with gold.

"A down payment," the man said. "Now get me out of here."

Omari peered out the front door. The Shuru were on the opposite end of the street conducting their thorough looting.

"Come on," Omari said. The merchant slipped behind Omari and the two of them ran up the street toward the wall. The Shuru ropes still dangled from the ramparts.

"Can you climb?" Omari asked.

"Look at me," the merchant said. "Do you really have to ask that question?"

"Shit," Omari spat. "Follow me."

Omari worked his way along the wall, hoping to find a secret gate. They edged closer and closer to the main fighting.

"Mikijen!"

Omari flinched then turned. Three Shuru marched toward him, swords drawn. He didn't have time for this. He grabbed the merchant by his collar then dragged him along.

"What is the meaning of this?" one of the Shuru said.

"I caught this one escaping the merchant quarter," Omari said. "I was taking him to your dhows."

Omari snatched the gold bags from the man's shoulders then handed them to the Shuru. The men looked into the bags and were satisfied with what they saw.

"Don't bother taking him to the dhows," the man said. "Kill him."

Omari nodded as the Shuru turned about and hurried away. As soon as they were out of sight the merchant pulled himself free.

"Why did you give them my gold?" he shouted.

"Because if I didn't, they would kill you and take it,' Omari answered. "They would have taken mine, too."

"I needed that gold," the merchant fussed. "There will be others that will demand payment along the way."

"We'll make do," Omari said. "Now be quiet and look captured."

The merchant lowered his head and shuffled before Omari, who kept a tight grip on his collar and his sword to his back. They pushed through the front gate with the other prisoners.

"Go right," the merchant said.

Omari jerked him to the right, following a path that ran along the wall. They neared the rear of the citadel where the road turned left into the forest. Omari forced the merchant down the road, keeping his grip on the man's collar until they were out of sight of the fort. He let the man go then sheathed his sword.

"Thank you," the man said.

"This is not a favor," Omari replied. "If there's no gold where we are headed, I'll be more than happy to follow the Shuru's orders."

"Don't worry," the merchant said. "There will be more than you can carry."

Omari smirked. "You'll be surprised what I can carry."

The man took the lead.

"This way."

They ambled the road in silence, venturing deeper into the forest. Omari's mood darkened the farther they travelled. The sun was setting low on the horizon; it would be night soon. The longer he was away, the more likely he would be missed. Desertion was not an issue; Mikijen disappeared frequently, especially during military campaigns. It was the reason for the constant recruitment, that and attrition. But Omari's service with the mercenaries was a sentence in exchange for his life. If he was suspected of desertion, his life would be forfeit.

"How much longer?" he asked.

"We'll be there by nightfall," the man said.

Omari grunted.

"My name is Khamasi," the merchant said.

"There is no reason I need to know your name," Omari replied. "Merchant will suffice."

"I thought it would be good if we became familiar with each other since we will be . . ."

Omari grabbed Khamasi by his shoulders then spun him about.

"As I said, there is no reason for me to know your name. We are not building a relationship. This is business. You are merchant, I am Mikijen."

"As you wish . . . Mikijen."

Khamasi turned his back then continued leading the way.

"There is a river we must cross," the merchant said. "The ferryman will charge us to take us across. It is too deep and filled with mambas and kibokos. To swim would be foolish."

"I doubt if you could make it," Omari said.

"I doubt it as well," the merchant replied. "But I also doubt we'll have enough gold to pay for passage."

"Why? It's just a ferry."

"Supply and demand," the merchant said. "Since your masters decided to sack our city, I'm sure the crossing fee has increased considerably. I am not the only one that knows of this route."

Khamasi's suspicions became reality as they neared the river. The sounds of shouting and arguing reached Omari's ears; the woods thinned into a clearing battered by hundreds of sandaled feet. A crowd gathered at the riverbank, people waving their hands and shouting in the same direction.

"Get behind me," Omari ordered.

The merchant did as he was told. Omari unsheathed his sword. The sight of him caused many of the people to flee, some of them jumping into the river and swimming for their lives. As soon as did they entered the mambas appeared, clamping the hapless people into their jaws and tearing them apart. The morbid sight changed the minds of others considering the same thing. The rest stood still and glared at him. Omari knew what they were thinking; if they had the right resolve they could eventually overwhelm him. But many of them would die before he did, and they seem to sense that as well. They stepped aside, clearing a path to the ferry. A bare-chested man wearing loose fitting green pantaloons stood before the ferry, a scimitar tucked in the red sash around his waist. The man was as tall as Omari but much bulkier and was obviously not intimidated by him. Two wide-eyed polemen stood on the ferry behind him. Omari sheathed his sword.

"That is not the ferry owner," the merchant whispered.

"I figured as much," Omari replied. "Most likely a bandit taking advantage of a desperate situation. Something I would do given the circumstances."

Omari walked up to the man.

"I need passage for two," he said.

The man grinned then held out his hand. Omari took the pouch from his belt, opened it and took out two cowries. The man laughed.

"You can keep them. The rest in that pouch will get you across the river."

Omari kicked the man as hard as he could between the legs. As the brute fell forward, he punched him across the jaw for good measure. No sooner had the man fell into the mud did the crowd rush the ferry. Omari pulled his sword and the throng stopped.

"Get on," Omari told the merchant. The man scurried on board as Omari held everyone at bay. He boarded soon afterwards and the pole men pushed the ferry away from the riverbank. One of the pole men smiled and nodded at Omari.

"Thank you,' he said. "I am Chandu. This is my ferry."

Omari shrugged. "You may not be so thankful when you return to the other side. There's no one stopping them from taking this ferry from you now. I suggest you don't go back until your friend revives. You'll need him."

Chandu's smile faded.

Omari gave the ferryman the two cowries he offered the bandit, which eased his worry somewhat. They disembarked then set off down the trail.

"We'll have to make camp," Omari commented. "It will be dark soon."

"We can wait until we reach our destination," the merchant replied. "It's not that far."

They walked another mile before the merchant stopped then studied the forest.

"Here," he said. He stepped off the road into the bush. Omari hesitated. Common sense told him unfamiliar bush was not the place he wanted to be in darkness. But the man slowly fading away was his payday, so he had to follow him. He proceeded into the bush then stumbled, his foot striking a large stone. Omari looked down as he grimaced; the stone was no natural rock. It was definitely shaped by human hands. He encountered more stones as he followed the merchant until he saw his benefactor standing before a decayed structure, a triumphant smile on his face.

"We're here," he said.

"Where is here?" Omari asked.

"I'll tell you when we get inside. It is almost dark and we need a fire."

Omari and the merchant gathered whatever wood they could find then carried it inside. The fire they built was small, smoky yet effective, casting a dim light on their surroundings. Omari took out strips of dried meat given to him as provisions and shared it with the merchant.

"Thank you," the man said.

Omari shrugged. He had to keep the man alive and in good spirits until he received his reward. After that, he would make no promises.

"This is not bad," the merchant said. "The Kiswala are not as frugal as I was told."

The merchant finished the meat strip then burped his satisfaction.

"You're probably wondering whose temple this is, and how it can remain hidden when it is so close to a major thoroughfare."

"No, I'm not," Omari said.

"No one comes to this temple because they fear it," the merchant continued. "It is an ancient building, one that has been in existence since before the Cleave."

Omari looked at the merchant and almost laughed.

"Nothing existed before the Cleave," Omari said.

That's where you are wrong, Mikijen," the merchant replied. "Ki Khanga thrived before Daarila dropped his ax upon it. This very temple was built in his name. People traveled many strides to pour libations in his honor. Back then he was not known as Daarila. Back then he was simply 'Daar.'"

"And how is it that you know this and no one else does?"

"Everyone here knows the story of the temple, which is why everyone stays away."

"Except you," Omari said.

The merchant grinned. "I was never one to indulge in matters of faith. I only believe in what I can see and feel. But there was one part of the story that was true."

Omari chewed another meat strip, waiting for the merchant to reveal the temple's secret. After a long silence he realized the merchant had no intentions of telling him unless he asked.

"And what part is that?" he asked.

"There is a guardian of the temple, a creature that will kill all that approached the temple of which it serves."

"So, we should be dead by now," Omari said.

"I haven't shared the end of the story," the merchant said.

Omari rolled his eyes. "Go on then."

"One day a man with nothing to lose ventured to the temple. His circumstances were so desperate he decided that whatever treasures hidden within the temple were worth the risk. He entered it during the day in hopes that whatever creature lurking about would not stir during the light. He was almost wrong. He was approaching the entrance when a strange sound caught his attention. The man took out his sword, searching about until he found the source of the sound. It was a creature unlike any he'd ever seen. The creature looked at him as a voice filled his head.

"I am injured," it said. "Help me and I am yours to command."

"So the desperate man gave the creature the last of his food and water. The creature's reaction was immediate. It sprang to its feet, its eyes meeting the man."

"Ask what you wish and it is yours," the creature told the man.

"I wish that which is in the temple," the man replied.

"So be it," the creature said. "Take what you need but nothing more. I will insure that no one other than you can possess it."

Omari stopped chewing, his hand moving slowly to his sword.

"And who was this man?" he asked.

The merchant answered with a grin.

Omari didn't know where, but he knew he had to move. He crouched and raised his sword just as the bush exploded before him. Something slammed against him and sent him tumbling through the trees. His only satisfaction was the painful howling in the distance.

"Kill him!" the merchant shouted.

Omari stayed on the ground; his ribs aching as he frantically searched the darkness for the thing attacking him. There was no way he could find it, so he would let it find him. He struck his sword against at nearby sapling; moments later he heard branches above him cracking. He rolled onto his back the pointed his sword upward. A dark shape fell toward him, its body resembling that of a simba, except for the expansive bat-like wings protruding from its back. The creature saw Omari's sword then veered away at the last minute, barely missing the blade and preventing Omari from being crushed by its bulk. It was close enough for Omari to see now, near enough for him to have a fighting chance. He rushed the beast as it turned toward him and swung out with its right paw. The paw smashed against Omari's shoulder and sent him tumbling head over heels until a tree stopped his awkward flight. His sword flew from his hand, leaving him unarmed . . . except for his hand cannon.

Omari frantically poured power into the barrel then jammed the barrel with shot as the beast stalked him. He whispered thanks to Eda that the beast's eyesight seemed just as poor as his in darkness, although he knew it had other senses to compensate for its weakness.

"Where are you, violator?"

The question appeared in his mind so suddenly he jumped, almost dropping the hand cannon. A piercing shriek caused him to stumble backwards. The creature charged at him so quickly he barely had time to raise the hand cannon and light it. The beast slammed into the hand cannon, wrapping its forelegs around Omari, its nailed digging into his back and its hot breath in his face. There was a muffled explosion as the hand cannon went off. The beast howled then pitched backwards; Omari reeled away then crashed into the ground. His back bled, his breath coming in painful waves as his lungs pushed against his bruised ribs.

"I can't believe you killed it!" he heard the merchant say. "Impressive."

Omari saw the man appear over him, a smug smile on his face.

"Thank you for bringing me here unscathed," he said. "It's unfortunate that you won't be able to . . ."

Omari kicked the man's feet from under him. He winced as the man landed on top of him; he grimaced more as he raised his legs then locked the man into a strangle hold. The merchant flailed at Omari but his grip was like iron. He held the merchant until he fell limp. Omari held him a few moments longer until he was sure the man was dead before tossing his body aside.

"The Cleave with you!" he spat.

Omari closed his eyes, preparing for what was to come next. It began as a warm sensation at the small of his back, spreading rapidly throughout the ngisimaugi tattoo across his back, down his legs and arms to his hands and feet. The warmth gathered where his wounds were most severe then became intense heat. Omari clenched his teeth, holding back the scream that might bring other creatures from the night to finish him and feed off his flesh. Just when he thought he could take no more the burning subsided to a pulsing heat. He knew without looking his wounds were healed, but it would be some time before he could travel without pain. He rolled over then stood. Grunting with each step, he staggered into the ruined temple. Omari stumbled over branches and bones, dried blood and feces until he reached the opposite side of the temple. Taking a cannon fuse from his belt, he struck it against the stone floor. It flared, lighting the room before him. Omari forgot his pain as the light revealed Khamasi's treasure. He leaned against the stack of gold then kissed it before slumping to the floor and falling asleep.

Omari awoke with the morning light. He stood, stretched then quickly assessed his predicament. There was no way he could carry all the wealth before him, and there was no way he could arrange an escape with it. He picked his way through the fortune, finding those items that were convenient and valuable then hiding them in various places in his garments. He took a few valuables then stuffed them in his pouch; this was the type of loot he would be expected to have. He emerged from the temple to a grisly sight. The scavengers had arrived, vultures and carrion eaters gathered about the carcass of the merchant and the beast. Curiosity overtook him for a moment and he attempted to get close to the beast. The fisi pack feasting off its flesh was not amenable to his attention; they turned on him, warning him with their laugh-like voices. Omari shrugged then worked his way back to the main road.

By midday he'd reached the river. The ferry was mid-river, its passengers the last people Omari wished to see; the Shuru. Omari attempted to jump into the bush.

"Mikijen!"

Omari hunched his shoulders as if hit by a stick across the back. He ran toward the riverbank, a smile on his face.

"Thank Eda you are here!" he exclaimed.

The Shuru surrounded him, their hands on their sword hilts.

"Why are you here?" one of the Shuru asked.

"When we attacked the city, I spied a merchant escaping. I followed him here, thinking he might be seeking to warn others of our attack. Instead I found this."

Omari took the pouch from his hip and opened it, revealing his recently pilfered gold. The Shuru's eyes widened.

"Is there more?" the ranking Shuru asked.

"Yes," Omari replied. "Much more."

Omari led the Shuru to the temple. The merchant's wealth caused them to gasp. The Shuru left two of their men to guard the treasure; Omari returned to the city with the remaining men to gather the wagons to carry the treasure. They returned to the dhows triumphantly, Omari riding with the Shuru as he munched on an orange. The other Mikijen looked at him with various expressions, the most dominate confusion. As they reached the Kiswala treasure dhow, Omari bid the Shuru farewell.

"Wait," the Shuru leader said.

Omari stopped then turned to face the man. "Yes?"

The Shuru leader rubbed his chin. "So, you just chose to follow this man out of the city and discovered all this?"

Omari nodded his head. "What can I say? Eda smiles on me."

The Shuru spat. "I think you're lying, Mikijen. I think you had your own deal with this merchant and only decided to take us to the treasure because you had no choice."

"That may be true," Omari replied. "But what does it matter? You have what you came for."

"And you have what you deserve," the Shuru commander said.

Omari answered him with a grin.

"Be off with you," the commander said. "Make sure I never see you near such a fortune again during a campaign."

"You can be sure of that," Omari said.

He sauntered back to the Mikijen dhows, his pockets filled with the jewels he kept. Once back in Kiswala he would convert them to more manageable wealth and give himself a little celebration. Being a Mikijen was not a bad way to live, he mused. Not bad at all.

MILTON J. DAVIS

SECOND CHANCE

Omari stood naked on Nyambera's balcony observing the raucous scene in the streets below. He raised the dagga pipe to his lips, took a long pull then exhaled smoke from his nostrils. Whale oil lamps luminated drunken, rowdy Mikijen and their companions staggering between the flickering gauntlet, their boisterous singing and cursing rising into the star-studded sky. Tomorrow they would board the war dhows and set sail, their objective another city-state bold enough to challenge the Kiswala monopoly of the coastal trade. For many of them this was their last living moments. It was a reality that usually didn't bother Omari, but that evening was different. It was the reason he sought out Nyambera's company instead of trying to drown himself in a bowl of beer.

Nyambera ambled onto the balcony then wrapped her slender arms around his waist, pressing her breasts against his back. Omari grinned as he reached back with his left hand then palmed her butt.

"You smoke too much," she said.

"You wouldn't think so if I was paying for it," he replied.

"Oh, you're paying for it," Nyambera replied. "Next time I expect money."

Nyambera stepped away then turned him around to face him. She looked into his eyes and a frown marred her comely face.

"What?" he asked.

"If I didn't know any better, I would suspect you're thinking."

"Can't a man be reflective sometimes?"

"Yes, a man can, but not you."

Nyambera took the pipe from his hand, took a drag, then sat it on the beam.

"What's troubling you?"

Omari tried to reach for the pipe but Nyambera slapped his hand.

"Talk to me."

"Tomorrow we sail for Zeru," he said.

"And?"

"What do you mean and? I could be killed!"

"It hasn't happened yet."

"I shouldn't have come here."

Omari tried to walk back into the room but Nyambera blocked his way.

"I'm a priestess and diviner. Mikijen come to me for advice all the time, but never you. Something must be really troubling you."

"I've served for five years," Omari said. "Most muster out after two, if they live long enough."

"So why do you remain?"

"I have my reasons," Omari said.

"So, you choose to stay," she said. "I still don't see what's troubling you."

"It's a feeling," Omari said. "I can't quite explain it. The truth is I should have died three times over, but for some reason I've always found a way to survive."

"Eda smiles on you," Nyambera said.

"Zeru will be bad," he said. "The Kiswala waited too long to respond to their threat. Their city is fortified, and they've formed alliances with the neighboring villages."

"You'll win," she said. "You always do."

"I'm not so sure this time."

Nyambera took his hand then led him inside. "Come. Let me do a divination."

Omari pulled his hand free. "No. I'm well aware of your skills. If something bad is to happen I'd rather not know."

"Are you sure?" Nyambera asked. "If you know, then you can do something about it."

Omari didn't answer. Instead he walked to his clothes, rifling through them until he found a simple necklace, a rough piece of amber hanging from a worn leather cord. It was the only item remaining from Sati-Baa, a present his mother gave him when he was a boy.

"I want you to keep this," he said.

Nyambera smiled like a child. "Really?"

"If I die looters will take it off my body," he explained. "I'd rather you have it than them. Of course, if I survive, I'll want it back."

Nyambera frowned. "I knew it was too good to be true."

Omari looked puzzled. "What?"

Nyambera sighed. "Never mind. Sit down."

Omari sat. Nyambera took the necklace then draped it over her head. The stone rested perfectly between her breasts, blending well with the color of her skin. She laid on her back then pulled Omari on top of her.

"Now let's get back to working on your payment," she said. "That moment of introspection is going to cost you extra."

"How much?" he whispered in her ear.

"I'll tell you when it's enough," she whispered back.

* * *

The sun barely kissed the horizon as Omari strolled back to the base. The streets were mostly empty except for sweepers and merchants setting up for the early market. Other Mikijen joined him in the walk back, staggering from the previous night's celebrations. Some of them wore layers of beaded necklaces, each strand representing a successful campaign. Omari glanced at his own. Fourteen necklaces rested on his shoulders, each one a symbol of Eda's blessing. Every time he boarded a dhow he was always scared, which was why this particular campaign worried him. Fear did not enter his mind this time, instead a sense of inevitability walked with him to the barracks. As he entered, his servant Thimba met him with a concerned look on his face.

"Bwa, where have you been?" he asked. "I waited all night for you!"

"You didn't have to," Omari said. "Are my weapons ready?"

"Of course, bwa," Thimba replied. "Are you ready?"

"Your duty is to take care of my weapons, not me," Omari snapped.

Thimba fell to ground, prostrating behind Omari.

"Forgive me, bwa!"

Omari grabbed Thimba by the back of his shirt, lifting him to his feet.

"I told you not to do that. I'm not your master."

"I'm sorry, bwa!" Thimba said.

Omari shook his head as he walked to his bunk. His weapons lay on top of his sheets, gleaming and well oiled. His hand cannon was cleaned as well, the powder and shot pouches filled.

"Where did you find the powder?" he asked.

"There is a dhow from the east in port," Thimba said. "I traded them your high boots for it."

Omari nodded. He didn't need the boots, at least not in this weather, so it was a good trade. Thimba had proven himself again.

"Tell the men to get ready," Omari said. "I'll be there soon."

"Yes, bwa!"

Thimba scurried from the room. Omari sat on his bed, rubbing his forehead. He'd been promoted to *soli,* with twenty men under his command. He didn't ask for the promotion; he earned it by attrition. He was barely responsible for his own actions, let alone those of others. The good thing was that the position came with better pay and rations. Better still was that he no longer had to be among the first wave during an assault. He and his men were seasoned shock troops. Let the young ones take the brunt of the attack; veterans like himself earned the privilege of bringing up the rear.

When Omari entered his unit's barracks they were armed and ready.

"Soli Ket," one of the men called out. "Who are we killing today?"

The men laughed. Omari managed a smile.

"Zeru," he replied. "It seems the Zerubu forgot the seas belong to the Kiswala. They've been running dhows east, trading with the Jewel and Spice Islands. It's time we put an end to that."

The warriors nodded in approval.

"Conditions are as always. You'll receive an extra ten cowries if you return; you get to keep ten percent of any booty you collect."

He looked at one of his warriors, a man with a dirty gray beard and yellow eyes.

"If you are caught with any unauthorized booty, you will be whipped and demoted to landing party. Is that clear?"

"Yes, soli," the men said except for the man he stared at.

Omari walked up to face the man.

"Is that clear, Omba?"

Omba shuffled his feet as he looked away.

"Yes, Soli Ket," he said.

Omari singled out Omba not because he tried to steal, but because he always got caught. He could care less what the warriors were able to skim; he always took more than his allotted share, and the Kiswala made more than enough. But a *jambazi* among his warriors reflected negatively on him, and that he would not tolerate.

Omari walked among the men, making a final inspection. Satisfied, he strode toward the waiting dhows. His men fell in behind him. Together they marched to the beach, joining the other units as they loaded onto the dhows. They would sail in the *manowari*, the war dhows, only loading into the landing dhows when they were in sight of Zeru. The small city-state had become a hair in Kiswala's eye, raiding their *bahglahs* as they sailed between ports and competing for trade with the eastern islands. For a time the master merchants tolerated the losses, but time had run out on the greedy Zerubu and their allies. Kiswala was sending a large force, more than enough warriors to subdue the Zerubu. They were making an example of the raiders, sending a message that would not be soon forgotten.

As the dhows sailed to Zeru, the Mikijen spent their time gambling, boasting or fighting. Omari was normally in the midst of such mischief, but not during this voyage. He spent his time on the deck smoking the dagga he stole from Nyambera and gazing into the distance, contemplating the circumstances that led him to this moment. His life had not been easy, yet somehow he managed to find some joy, however brief. But this voyage just seemed wrong. The sense of dread that settled into his mind long ago still lingered, no matter how much dagga he smoked.

He dumped his pipe contents into the sea then headed below deck. Mikijen spoke to him as he passed by, but he didn't reply. He kept walking through the innards of the ship until he reached the room he sought. A man sat in the room against the bulwark surrounded by Mikijen. They all turned when he entered, a few of them with shocked looks on their faces. Omari said nothing as he sat. The man against the wall smiled then continued to speak.

"This is the world that Daarila created," the man said. "It is a world of chaos and uncertainty. It is the way he deemed it to be. If not for the benevolence of Eda, we would not exist. It was she who saved us from Daarila's wrath, and it is she who will protect you when we land in Zeru."

One of the Mikijen, a woman who wore no campaign beads, raised her hand. The man acknowledged her with the tilt of his head.

"I do not doubt your words, sonchai," she said. "But when we land, many of us will die, even some of us sitting in this room. How is that possible if Eda blesses us?"

"Know that if you are in Eda's favor, you can rejoice even in death because you will be with her."

The woman smiled as the others nodded.

The man waved his hands as if swatting away flies.

"Go now," he said. "I must rest."

The others stood and walked out of the room, leaving Omari and the sonchai alone.

"Soli Ket," the man said. "What brings you here?"

"Curiosity, Kamali," Omari replied.

"You don't need my wisdom," Kamali said. "You often boast of being Eda blessed."

Omari laughed. "It is surely a boast. It's a phrase I picked up long ago from an acquaintance who would always shout it when he won a bet. He's dead now, so I guess he wasn't so blessed.

"We all die," Kamali said.

"Not like he did," Omari replied. "He was strolling down the street after wining a stack and a mule kicked him in the forehead. I guess Eda was distracted when that happened."

Kamali frowned. "So why are you here?"

"A feeling," Omari replied. "A bad feeling."

Kamali reached into his pouch then took out a string of white beads.

"Wear these," he said.

Omari took the beads then draped them around his neck.

"What will this do?" he asked.

"It depends," Kamali said.

"On what?"

"On whether Eda decides to truly favor you. Now that you wear her beads, you are in her sight. She will judge you and maybe she won't get distracted."

"Will it keep me alive?" Omari asked.

"That I can't answer."

Omari ran the beads through his fingers then shrugged.

"It can't hurt," he finally said. He stood to leave.

"Soli," Kamali said. He gestured to a gourd sitting before him filled with cowries. Omari rolled his eyes.

"So, we must pay the spirits for their blessings?"

"No," Kamali replied. "You must pay me for the beads."

"Fair enough." Omari reached in his pocket and took out a handful of cowries. He dropped them into the gourd then walked away.

"Eda bless you!" Kamali shouted.

"I hope so," Omari replied.

* * *

The Kiswala manowari dropped their anchors at dusk, just out of sight of the Zeru watchtowers. They would wait until nightfall to move into attack position, guided by the bright night lanterns of the city. Rowers took their benches below deck, making sure the dhows would not be impeded by a dead calm. The Kiswala took no chances; the rowers were hired professionals trained for the task and experienced with sea war. They were paid more than the Mikijen, for their skills or lack of could mean the difference between victory or defeat. The light mood that had dominated the Mikijen during the voyage was gone, replaced by a fatalistic seriousness. Warriors checked and rechecked their weapons, while the baharia handed out arrow shields. Omari took a shield then slid his left arm through the straps. The shield covered his entire body and was designed to interlock with the warriors that would be on either side of him during their assault on the beach. But it never worked that way. Most warriors sprinted across the beach alone, easy targets for the archers defending the city. If they were Haisetti archers, the consequences were devastating. Zeru possessed no such assistance that they knew of, so it would pay to prepare. One of the few things Omari trained his unit to do was hold formation, at least until they reached the walls. If they were lucky the manowari catapults would have breached them. If not, then climbing the walls would pose another challenge altogether. As he contemplated the various ways he could die just reaching the city he sank back into his dark mood. Omari shook his head to clear his mind; he was here and there was a job to be done. He had no choice but to do it. Omari found a clear spot among his unit then curled up to sleep. He would need every bit of rest for the days to come.

He woke to the drumming of the rowers' cadence. The manowari surged toward Zeru, their armored prows slicing through the rough sea. Omari worked his way to the dhow's prow; Zeru rapidly increased in size as they drew closer. They would be in catapult and manogel range soon. It was time to get his unit to the landing dhows. Omari trotted to the bulwark where the boats waited, their winching crews in position. As the warriors assembled, the catapults and manogels were secured and loaded. Moment later the deck shook with the launching of the large stones and arrows. Omari took a look ahead, watching the stones crash into the walls. He couldn't see the defenders from the distance, but he knew they were there. It would have been simpler for the Zerubu to surrender. The Kiswala were harsh yet fair, and under their rule an industrious Zerubu could make a very comfortable living. But people would rather die than be subject to others, even if their way of life would change little. Omari never understood such thinking. He was a product of the streets of Sati-Baa, and the one lesson he learned was how to adapt. For the powerless, it was the only skill that mattered.

The manowari captain blew the landing whistle. Omari and his unit climbed into their landing dhow with their rowers. The Kiswala barrage took a heavy toll on the walls, beating them down significantly while not yet breaching them. That was good enough for Omari; it meant fewer perches for the archers. Making sure all his warriors were accounted for, Omari waved his shield. The landing dhow plummeted downward, slowing just before touching the sea. As soon as the boat reached water the rowers and steerer took command. There would be nothing left to do until they reached the beach.

Instead of ducking before the protective shields, Omari stood at the prow observing the progress of the attack. The Zerubu seemed to be conserving their strength until the Mikijen were close, which meant a bloodbath for both sides. Omari would make sure his unit would not be in the thick of such nonsense. His goal was to get inside the city and secure as much loot as possible before the main army. He would keep his warriors on the perimeter of the battle until he saw an opening, then they would advance.

He watched as the first dhows made landfall. The young warriors high stepped through the surf then ran toward the walls with weapons and ladders. They were met little resistance, which Omari found unusual. By the time their dhow struck the sands, the vanguard had reached the walls and were scaling them. Omari splashed into the surf, his warriors close behind. He kept a slow pace, looking closely at the assault. Something wasn't right. For a city that ravaged Kiswala shipping for years, he was expecting a much stronger battle.

"Soli, why are we moving so slow?" one of his warriors asked.

"Because I said so," Omari replied.

"The others are already entering the city," another warrior said. "We will get nothing!"

Omari ignored them. He kept a slow pace until he saw the ramparts cleared and the gates swing open. Still he hesitated.

"This is not right," he whispered.

His warriors had enough of his tardiness. They surged by him, running and yelling toward the gate. Though he still had his doubts, as soli he could not let his warriors enter the city without him. He ran and caught up with them, then took position before them as they entered Zeru.

As Omari entered the city, he knew something was definitely amiss. The city defenders had been rounded up and sat on their haunches, a resigned look on their faces. One glance and Omari knew they were not warriors. As he investigated the faces of the Mikijen commanders he saw their suspicions too. He and the others gathered about Commander Abasi, a tall man with skin like ebony and a severe expression.

"Something is wrong," he said. "This is a token force. We've been deceived. Call back you warriors immediately. We're leaving."

As Abasi uttered the last words attack horns blared beyond the city walls. Omari ran toward the gates; his warriors close behind. His eyes went wide as he saw the warriors at the gates running toward him. Over their shoulders he saw hundreds of Zerubu warriors emerging from the forest. He stopped his men as they reached the gates, waiting for the other Mikijen to come inside. As soon as they were inside, he gave his order.

"Close the gates!"

Omari helped his men push the gates close then secure them. The rumbling from the distance caused him further worry. He climbed the ramparts, joining the other commanders. The Zerubu army had emerged from hiding and surrounded the city. The Mikijen fleet was under fierce attack, swarmed by Zerubu fireboats and raiders. The Mikijen knew the Kiswala captains would not risk losing their dhows. They would pull up anchor and abandon them. Dhows were worth more than people. The dread that Omari felt for weeks crashed onto him with full force.

Skull masked Zerubu warriors stood at attention around the city. In the harbor the Kiswala manowari burned; those that did not were speeding away under sails and oars pursued by the Zerubu fireships. Omari slumped to the ground, his sword in his hand. If they were not killed in the assault, they would be starved to death by a long siege. He looked at Abasi; the commander seemed to be thinking the same as Omari. Their eyes met briefly, confirming Omari's suspicions.

"Look," one of the solis said.

Omari came to his feet, peering over the ramparts. He watched as the ring of skull masked warriors parted. A massive warrior stepped from their ranks, his bare chest decorated with golden tattoos that radiated against his umber skin. His arms rested on a large sword balanced on his shoulders, his lower body covered by a blood red kanga. His bald head was lowered to hide his face but it didn't matter. Omari recognized him the moment he stepped into the open.

"Yacine," he whispered.

Yacine raised his head as if he heard his name spoken. A smile formed on his hard face.

"Mikijen!" he shouted. "It seems you are surrounded."

Commander Abasi peered over the ramparts. "We have no time for banter. What do you want?"

"We want you to die," Yacine said. "But I have a proposition."

Here it comes, Omari thought.

"I offer you and your men free passage to the nearest Kiswala port. Go back to your masters and tell them that Zeru is generous in victory."

"And what do you want in return?" Abasi asked. "More gold that we can afford?"

Yacine shook his head. "We don't want your wealth."

"What then?"

"Is there a man among you that goes by the name of Omari Ket?"

Omari felt a thousand eyes on him. Abasi stared at him as he answered.

"Yes."

Yacine's smile grew.

"I want him."

Omari grimaced as if stabbed in the gut. Long ago, when they were young Mikijen, Yacine and he had been friends. But Yacine met a woman who stole his heart, a woman he intended to marry. Unfortunately, Omari met the same woman. They began a torrid love affair behind Yacine's back. When Yacine found out, he was furious. He attempted to kill Omari in his sleep and almost succeeded if it wasn't for his comrades warning him. Yacine was stripped of his rank then expelled from the Mikijen. Rumors occasionally found their way to Kiswala about a disgraced Mikijen who vowed revenge on them, but no one paid any attention until this moment.

Omari stood and checked his weapons.

"You know he won't let you go," he said to Abasi.

"I know," Abasi replied. "But your spat will give us time."

Omari took his hand cannon out of its holster then loaded it.

"Time for what? To pray to your gods?"

"If you can stall him . . ."

Omari laughed. He took a fuse from his pouch then cut it in half.

"Stall him? I plan to shoot him in the face then run as fast as I can for the forest. If I'm lucky I'll cut my way through those skull heads before they figure out their leader is dead. Anything after that it's in Eda's hands."

He took a match from his pouch, struck in on the stone ramparts, then lit the hand cannon fuse.

"Goodbye commander," Omari said. "It's been nice knowing you."

"The Cleave take you, Omari Ket!" Abasi spat.

"Not if I can help it," Omari replied.

Omari clambered down the stairs then strode toward the gate. The Mikijen guarding the portal opened the wooden doors just wide enough for him to exit. Yacine grinned as he approached, taking the sword from his shoulders and swinging it before him.

"At last!

"I see you hold a grudge," Omari said.

"You stole Yasmina from me!" Yacine replied.

"Stole is a strong word," Omari said. "Besides, I didn't know you two were in love. Well, at least you were."

Yacine picked up his pace. "Would it have made a difference?"

Omari shrugged. "Probably not."

Yacine gripped his sword hilt with both hands then ran toward Omari.

"Time to die, bastard!"

Omari reached behind his back for his hand cannon.

"Yes, it is."

He snatched the weapon from the holster, aiming it at Yacine's chest. Yacine's eyes widened in shock as he raised his sword high to cleave Omari in half. But the hand cannon went off first, blasting shot into Yacine's chest and knocking him of his feet. The warrior flew backwards a few strides then landed on his back, his head striking the ground hard. Omari grinned as he drew his sword.

"Time to finish this," he said.

As he neared Yacine's sprawled body the gold tattoos across his chest began to glow.

"What in Daarila's name?"

Blinding light burst from the tattoos. Omari covered his eyes as he stumbled back. The outburst was intense but brief; as the light faded Omari uncovered his eyes to a terrible sight. Yacine stood before him, a wicked smile on his face. There were no wounds on his chest; instead the shot that had struck him rested like pebbles around his feet.

"It took me a long time to find a sonchai capable of duplicating the ngisimaugi," Yacine said. "If you ask me, she did a better job."

The two men circled each other, swords on guard. Omari glanced down at the white beads around his neck. Apparently, Eda had chosen to abandon him.

"Let's finish this properly, shall we?" Yacine said.

Yacine was faster than his bulk revealed. Omari barely avoided his first swing. He raised his sword to block a back slash and regretted it. Yacine's powerful blow shook Omari to the shoulders and knocked him off balance. Omari was stronger than most men, but Yacine's strength was way beyond his. Blocking his blows was not prudent for it would wear him down. Omari shuffled and dodged Yacine's onslaught, blocking only when necessary. His furious attack gave Omari almost no time to retaliate. Instead he found himself putting up a defense that was destined to fail.

Yacine's blade nicked his shoulder and his ngisimaugi flared. Omari hit back with a stab to Yacine's thigh that sent him scrambling backwards as the glowing tattoo healed him almost instantly. There was absolutely no way he could kill this mad brute except for a wound to a vital organ or decapitation, and with what he'd seen that would be doubtful. He was losing strength; fatigue creeping into his arms and legs, his breath labored. Yacine fought as if he knew no bounds. Omari raised his hand then lowered his sword.

"Stop," he said. "I can see how this will end. At least let me die with dignity."

Yacine grinned. "So, you wish a warrior's death. For what you did to me, you don't deserve it. I'd rather hack you to bits, feed you to the fisu and listen to them laugh as they chew on your bones."

Omari turned his back then sank to his knees.

"I will fight you no longer," he said. "Take your revenge."

The Mikijen yelled in protest, knowing that they would be next. Omari ignored them. He listened as Yacine ran toward him, imagining that massive blade held high over his bald head.

"To the Cleave you go, Omari Ket!"

Omari's timing was almost perfect. He jumped to his feet then spun to his right as Yacine slashed down with his blade. The sword nicked Omari's right shoulder but did not stop his momentum. He kept turning, grasping his sword hilt with both hands. His blade sliced through Yacine's neck, the brute's head tumbling to the ground. Moments later his body fell forward. Omari stopped himself then staggered, blood running down his arm to his hand. He spat on Yacine's trembling body. A cheer rose from his brothers in Zeru.

"Hah!" he shouted. "Heal that!"

The golden tattoos glowed. Yacine's head stirred then slid toward his body. Omari's shock lasted only a moment before he ran to the head then kicked it as hard as he could. It sailed toward the Zerubu ranks, bounced off the ground then rolled up to the feet of one of the skull warriors. The warrior looked down, impaled the head with his spear then tossed it behind him. The light from the tattoos dissipated.

As much as he wanted to celebrate, Omari knew his troubles were only beginning. The Zerubu ranks parted and their real leaders stepped forward, their swords raised. There was no way he was going to fight his way through these warriors. There were too many. As the leaders lowered their swords to signal the assault, Omari turned and ran toward the city. His ears filled with the chants of the Zerubu as they marched behind him, the ground trembling under his feet. He was halfway to the city when the gate swung wide and the Mikijen came pouring out yelling and waving their weapons. Commander Abasi had made his choice. The Mikijen would fight. Omari turned toward the advancing Zerubu then waited for his brethren to surround him. He ran with them, his eyes darting about as he searched for an opening between the Zerubu ranks. This was a fruitless attack. They were outnumbered with no way to get back to Kiswala. As a group they were doomed, but if Omari could somehow stay alive long enough to get through the Zerubu ranks and into the woods he stood a chance.

The armies crashed into each other. Omari twisted to his right to avoid the spear thrust from the skull warrior attacking him then squatted. His attacker's momentum rolled him onto Omari's shoulders. Omari sprang up and tossed the man behind him. He drove his sword into the belly of the next man, letting his arm relax as he pulled the sword free to meet his next attacker. For a while he was making progress toward the woods until the enemies' numbers stopped him. He fought in the midst of the storm, cutting, kicking, slashing and biting the warriors that kept coming like a human torrent. Then an opening appeared before him, a clear path to the forest. He ran through the gap with hope. With only a few strides between him and freedom, that hope was crushed by a second wave of Zerubu warriors marching through the trees. Omari stopped, his mind working feverishly for a solution. There was only one way out. It was a long shot, but with nothing to lose, he would take it.

Omari charged the advancing Zerubu. He ran up to the closest warrior and instead of blocking his spear, he let it plunge into his gut. The pain was worse than he imagined; his outcry real. He collapsed as the warrior pulled his spear free and marched away. The others stepped over or around him as he lay bleeding. The wound was severe, but Omari was betting the ngisimaugi would heal him in time. As he grew weaker, he realized he had miscalculated. Maybe he should have let Nyambera divine his future; he would have seen that this was a bad idea. So, he would die in the bush, with no hope of seeing Sati-Baa again. Mariama would be pleased, not that she would ever know. To her he was already dead. A moment of sadness touched him when he thought of Aisha. He reached up and grabbed the beaded necklace as his vision faded.

* * *

Something tugged at Omari's left leg. He opened his eyes to see a boy wearing a dingy loincloth and a beaded necklace pulling his boot. Omari jerked his foot free then kicked the boy in his stomach. The boy fell onto his butt, a startled look on his face. He jumped to his feet then ran away.

Omari took his time rising to his knees. His gut was still sore and he was weak, but his wound had mostly healed. The Zerubu were trickling into their city from the forest. Looters pilfered the dead Mikijen, while others dragged the stripped bodies away and dumped them into a mass grave. A sudden pain made Omari reach under his back. It was his hand cannon. His other weapons were still with him as well. Except for the boy, the other looters had yet to reach him and the dead sprawled around him. He gathered his weapons then crawled deeper into the woods until he could not see the city. Omari stripped naked except for his baldric and hand cannon holster. After fleeing for a few miles he came across a small village. He hid until dusk, then snuck into the town, stealing clothes and food. That night he slept in the forest, letting the ngisimaugi do its work. By morning Omari was almost to his normal strength.

Omari abandoned the woods, stepping out on a small trail. The rising sun gave him a sense of direction. East would take him to the coast. From there he could work his way north to the nearest Kiswala city. West would take him to the interior. As far as anyone was concerned, Omari Ket had died in Zeru, killed when the Mikijen force attacking the city was wiped out to a man. His sentence had been fulfilled. No one would come looking for him; no one would care. He contemplated his options as he played with the white beads about his neck. Omari turned west with a smile on his face and strode toward a new life. He always said he was Eda blessed. Maybe he actually was.

THE SKIN MAN

(ORIGINALLY PUBLISHED IN SKELOS 2)

Omari Ket watched as Dessella bent her head forward and draped her beaded braids over his face. She swayed her head in sync with her wide hips as she eased onto his lap in time with the distant drumming from the marketplace. He smiled so hard he thought his teeth would shatter.

She tossed her hair back with a jeweled hand, kissed him then pulled back as she licked her lips.

"Now what was that nonsense you were saying about leaving?"

Omari chuckled. "Good try goddess. Your performance will get you another twenty minutes but nothing more. You love me well, but you don't pay me well."

Dessella snarled then slapped him. "I hate you!"

Omari rubbed his cheek. "No, you don't."

Dessella climbed off his lap then stomped across the room. She leaned against the door then glared at him.

"I wish I did hate you. I wish I could."

Omari stood, picked his clothes off the tiled floor then dressed. He sauntered to his weapons resting at the foot of the bed. His time in port had been fun, but his money and his patience were running low. Paying jobs were few and far between for a former Mikijen, and the opportunity waiting for him was just too lucrative to pass up, even for the bronze vision of loveliness pouting at him.

After making sure all was secure, he ambled to the door where Dessella waited. Omari snaked his left arm around her narrow waist then pulled her close.

"I'll be back," he whispered. He attempted to kiss her, but she yanked his beard and bit his lip.

"Ow!"

"No, you won't," she fussed. "If you were any other man I would believe it. But not you. You don't have to come back. I'm sure there are many other women waiting for you to fulfill that promise."

She was right, but he wasn't going to admit it. He took a silver dagger with a jewel encrusted hilt from his belt.

"Here," he said. "A guarantee that I'll return."

Dessella's eyes widened. "For me?"

"Until I return," he said.

She flung herself on him then kissed him.

"I'll be waiting."

Omari pushed her away. "Okay. Now will you please get out of the way?"

Dessella stepped aside, blowing him a kiss as he exited. The knife he gave her was expensive but of no consequence. It had been given to him in gratitude of a tryst with a woman whose name he didn't remember. When Dessella finally realized he wasn't returning her feeling would be soothed by the stacks she would make from selling it. Either that or she would keep it in hopes that he would return and she could stab him with it.

Omari shrugged as he rubbed the scar on his forearm. It wouldn't be the first time.

Omari stretched as he took in the view from Dessella's third story porch. They built high on Ors, for land was at a premium on the small island embedded in the belly of Lake Sati. He could turn full circle and see bustling shoreline in every direction. It was a tiny, busy, dirty little isle, a way station for those travelling the full length of the massive lake down the center instead of hugging the shoreline.

He descended the stairs, musing on how he'd fallen so far in such a short time. The first few years of freelancing had been a heady rush of fat, easy contracts. Somehow, he always found himself on the bad side of his employers, so much so that the word has spread that he was Cleave tainted. It probably had something to do with the occasional indiscretion with a wife or daughter, but he was a man with appetites and women were quite fond of him. So now he haunted the shadows of port towns hoping to get work, sometimes accepting pay for more nefarious purposes. But Omari was a child of the streets, and if he knew anything he knew how to thrive in the shadows.

He sauntered through the dilapidated central market, buying a couple of redfruit that seemed in reasonable shape. He ate them as he approached the warehouses of his current employer, a tall dark man from Mali who had little humor and strange taste for merchandise. Whatever the task he planned, it was bound to be unsavory.

Omari met the man at the docks near his dhow, the only possession he kept in immaculate shape. The men waiting with him were not mercenaries. They were stout men with dangerous eyes, carrying ropes, hooks and shackles.

"Slavers," Omari spat. "Damn them to the Cleave!"

The biggest of the slavers, a bald man with hiero-glyphics tattooed on his cheeks stepped up to Omari. He was almost as tall as the mercenary and twice as wide, his muscles seemingly carved into him with a sculptor's care. He glanced at the ngisimaugi on Omari's bicep then scowled.

"Mikijen," he growled, and then spat on Omari's boot. Omari back-handed the man so hard he tumbled backwards into his cohorts and they all collapsed into a cursing pile. By the time they regained their feet Omari pointed his hand cannon at them, holding a lit match-stick over the fuse.

"Who's first?" he asked.

Haben Bajinet, their employer, stepped between them. Haben was clothed in traditional Malian garb de-spite the island's temperate weather, a white turban loosely wrapped around his head and a flowing white shirt that hung to his knees covering his loose green pants. A takouba hung from his shoulder encased in a jewel-crusted leather baldric.

"Enough of this silliness," he said. "My dhow is ready to leave and my client is impatient."

"The deal is off," the slaver said. "I won't work with a Mikijen."

"Former Mikijen," Haben corrected. "Omari Ket is a fisa's ass but he's very good at what he does."

Omari cut his eyes at Haben then shifted his hand cannon slightly toward the man.

The slaver pressed a thick finger into his cheek. "You see these marks on my face? I got these beauties in a Kiswala prison. Guess who put me there?"

"It obviously wasn't me," Omari replied. "I never took a thief to the stockade. I killed them."

"See!" the slaver yelled. "Step aside, Bajinet!"

"Silence!"

Haben's command reached into Omari's throat, gripping his vocal chords. He dropped his hand cannon then clawed at his neck. The slavers did the same, their terrified eyes locked on Haben.

"I paid all you half of what you asked," Bajinet said. "No one is leaving. I expect you back in two weeks. If you are not, you will forfeit the remainder of your earnings. Do you understand?"

Omari and the others nodded.

"Good," Haben said. "I wish you a successful journey, if not a pleasant one."

Haben's invisible grip faded as he strode away. Omari rubbed his neck, making a note to investigate his clients better in the future. The slavers glared at him as they massaged their throats.

"Cleave damned sorcerers!" the slaver said. "Come on then. I guess we're stuck with you."

"And me with you," Omari said. He picked up his hand cannon then shoved it into the holster at his waist. Securing his packs, he followed the slavers onto the dhow.

Once on board Omari set up a place on the deck. As protector he needed to be prepared to fight boarders so the deck was his lair for the trip. The crew introduced themselves, each man and woman experienced with the ways of the lake. They seemed happy to have him aboard. Pirates were rare in this part of the lake, but as they neared the shore the chance of encountering them would become more likely. Though he knew the crew was experienced fighters it always helped to have a professional on board.

He was helping the crew raise the sail when the big slaver approached him. Omari stepped away from the crew and took a stance.

"I mean you no harm," the man said.

"Really? Such a drastic change of heart in such a short time."

"Don't get me wrong. When this job is over you and I will have a conversation. But for now, we work together."

The man extended his hand. "I am Lolega."

Omari took his hand which Lolega immediately attempted to crush. Omari's tight grip surprised the slaver.

"Looks can be deceiving," he said with a grin.

"I see," Lolega replied, a hint of respect in his voice.

Lolega let go of his hand then folded his arms. "We will meet after sundown on the deck. You should join us."

"I will."

Lolega nodded then strode away. Omari went back to helping the crew.

"You're going to have to kill that man," one of the crew said.

"I know," Omari replied.

The following days on the lake were uneventful. Omari helped with the dhow chores, ingratiating himself with the crew. It was essential he establish a relationship with them, especially with the slavers' sour attitude. After a satisfying meal of lake fish and water greens Omari sat among the crew on the third evening as they played a noisy game of oware. The ship's nahoda, Samwati, was a master of the game, moving his palm nuts skillfully to the frustration of his crew. After sending another man away in defeat he cut a gaze at Omari.

"What about you, Mikijen? Willing to test your skills and make a wager?"

Omari shook his head. "I'm no fool. I'm here to make money, not lose it."

Dufu, a big fellow with arms like masts patted Omari's shoulder so hard he winced.

"You're a smart man. So where do you go after this?"

Omari shrugged. "I'm not sure. Back to Sati-Baa I suppose, then maybe east. There's always work in Haiset."

Dufu nodded. "Those Haisetti live to fight. They're a bad lot."

"Be careful," Samwati said. "Our slavers are Haisetti."

Omari's attention was distracted by movement on the horizon. The nahoda noticed him then looked as well.

"Looks like we're coming into mist," the nahoda said.

Omari looked up. "That's unusual. The sky is clear."

"It happens," Dufu replied. "Sometimes it drifts from the land, especially if we're near a river."

"But we're not," Samwati said, suspicion in his voice.

Omari stood. "I would advise you to get your weapons. That is no natural mist."

The baharia ran to claim their weapons. Samwati stood by Omari, both of them squinting.

"What do you think?" Samwati asked.

"Pirates, most likely. They probably have a sonchai raising the mist. Make sure you're wearing talisman if you have it."

"We're baharia. You know we do."

Omari walked away. "I'll get the slavers."

He went below to the slavers' cabin.

"Get your weapons and follow me," he said. "Pirates."

"Then do your job," Lolega said. "Protect us."

His foul mood had returned. Omari rested his hand on his sword hilt.

"If you don't get on this deck now when this is all done, I'll come back and kill you all."

The slavers stood in unison. "You can try."

"I don't have time for this shit." Omari snatched out his sword, stabbing the man beside Lolega in the arm. The man yelped then scrambled away clutching his wound.

"He can stay," Omari said. "Now do we have to do this?"

He turned his back and went back to the deck, grinning as he heard the slavers gathering their weapons to follow. The mist had enshrouded the dhow, obscuring the baharia. Omari pulled his hand cannon free, packing it with gunpowder and lead shot then loading the fuse. He stood in the center of the deck.

"Everyone to me," he ordered.

The baharia surrounded him, their crossbows in hand. The slavers came moments later with their lances, glaring at Omari.

"Why are we standing here?" Lolega asked.

"Be quiet," Omari snapped.

Omari strained his ears, but it wasn't the sound than warned him. He smelled the pirate ship before he heard it creak close to the dhow. Grappling hooks fell over the bulwark, their barbs biting into the wood as they were pulled tight by unseen hands. The crew ran to them, machetes in hand. They were about to cut the ropes but Omari raised his hand.

"Wait."

He listened to the grunts of the pirates as they strained to pull their dhow closer. There was loud creaking then a plank slammed on the bulwark. Omari positioned himself before the plank as it shook with the footfalls of the pirates. He lit the hand cannon's fuse. The first pirate's face appeared as the fuse disappeared into the cannon. The explosion was deafening; the pirates screamed as lead shot riddled their bodies.

Omari jammed the cannon into its holster then drew his swords. He climbed onto the plank then looked back to the others.

"Kill anyone that gets by me. I'll be back."

He ran into the mist and across the plank. He only had a few moments, and unlike the old days he had no fellow Mikijen supporting him. A pirate emerged from the haze, stopping before Omari as his mouth dropped open in surprise. Omari dipped low, ramming his shoulder into the man's thighs. He stood and the man fell onto his back then bounced off the plank into the lake. The second man saw Omari then turned and ran away.

"Mikijen!" he shouted.

Omari stabbed the man in the back then shoved him aside. He fell onto the pirate ship deck in a crouch, a crowd of crossbow bolts sailing over his head. The pirate deck was clear of the mist as he suspected. A quick scan told him everything he needed to know. He dropped his sword then yanked free a throwing knife from his waist belt, his target the sorcerer standing in the center of the deck, his arms raised as he chanted the mist spell. He threw the knife with all his strength. The knife smacked into the sorcerer's forehead, the impact sent the sorcerer reeling across the deck then over the side.

Omari picked up his swords then dashed for the door that would take him below deck. The pirates finally regained their senses and attacked. Bolts peppered the deck around him as the pirates massed before him. Omari continued running at them until the last moment, then he dropped to the deck, flinging his body parallel to them. They tumbled over him as he rolled through then sprang back to his feet.

He pounced through the door then clambered below deck, his destination the ballast room. The pirates pursued him, yelling and waving their swords He encountered a few terrified men who jumped out of his way. They were apparently slaves that wanted nothing to do with the crazed man attacking their ship single-handed. Omari burst into the ballast room then smiled when he saw the barrels of pitch used to keep the hull waterproof. He threw a handful of gunpowder at the barrels then tossed a lit fuse on it. The men chasing him saw the lit fuse. They turned and ran, shouting as they fled.

"Fire in the hold! Fire in the hold!"

Omari ran faster than he ever had in his life up the stairs and back on the deck. The pirate deck burned from the flaming arrows fired from his ship. Pirates jumped over the sides, no longer concerned with Omari. His sprint for the plank ended abruptly when he realized it was gone.

"Shit!" he shouted. Omari backed up to the opposite side of the ship, took a deep breath then ran across the deck. He jumped, his hands flailing over his head. As the bow of his ship came into view he reached out with both hands. His palms hit the bulwark and he gripped the wood as tight as he could. His body slammed against the dhow and he lost his grip.

"Cleave . . ."

Hands grabbed his left arm, halting his fall. He threw his right arm up and his comrades caught it. His saviors dragged him over the side and he fell onto the deck. As he rolled onto his back the pirate ship exploded, the concussion causing the dhow to sway.

Samwati plopped down beside him.

"Not bad," he said.

Omari grinned. "It's why I'm here."

He looked up to see the slavers staring down at him, their scowls replaced by slight smiles.

Omari stood then shook his head.

"Show's over," he said. "Let's get back to business."

Fatigue finally caught up with Omari as he massaged his lower back. The nahoda and crew patted his shoulders and hugged him, a few shoving coins in his hand. They had encountered a pirate dhow and not lost a man. At supper each person shared their meal with him; afterwards they formed a circle, the darkness held at bay by lightstone torches suspended from the masts. They passed a huge gourd of beer to one another, each man taking a long drag with his own reed straw before passing it to the next then spitting the chaff onto the deck. Omari was tired, but he knew better than to bypass this ritual. The expedition was officially bonding, which could mean the difference between life or death depending on what waited for them. It also meant he didn't have to worry about the slavers anymore. Killing them would have meant no pay, and Omari needed every stack he could get.

"Tell us about Kiswala," Samwati asked.

"I can tell you about that cesspool," Lolega inter-jected. "It's a string of islands filled with greedy, deceit-ful people that will cut off a hungry man's hand for stealing a piece of bread, or throw a man in jail for trying to feed his family."

"Is that true, Mikijen?" Dufu asked.

"Pretty much," Omari replied. "The islands would be beautiful if it wasn't for the people who live there. The Kiswala were driven out of Aux hundreds of years ago for betraying their own during the Kashite in-vasion but they moan about it as if it happened yester-day. They do love their money. But it's also a place where an ambitious person can earn a comfortable life, honestly or dishonestly."

"So, you went to jail for feeding your family?" Samwati asked Lolega.

Lolega took a sip of beer. "Yes. What could I do? My children were starving. Three years for a bag of yams. A bag of yams!"

"Who did you steal it from?" Omari asked.

Lolega hesitated before answering. "Baraza. Sal-imu Baraza."

Omari whistled. "Then be lucky you're still alive. I've seen him stab a man for looking at him cross. And those men who locked you up? Baraza owns them. They wear the tattoo but they're not Mikijen. They are far worse."

Omari took the gourd, sipping more beer. "I still can't understand why he didn't kill you."

"He took my wife and children in exchange for my life," Lolega said, his eyes distant. "He might as well have killed me."

Dufu's face grew angry. "You gave him your fami-ly to save your own life?"

"I had no choice," Lolega said. "It was the ruling of the Kiswala elders. They had tired of Salimu's killings and considered it a compromise."

The circle fell silent. Samwati placed a comforting hand on Lolega's shoulder and the slaver shrugged it off.

"I don't need your pity," he barked. "All I need is Haben's money. Then I will return to Kiswala and buy my family back."

Omari decided to change the subject. "How much longer to our destination?"

"We should reach the end of the lake in two weeks," Samwati said. "Then it's another week down the Mambezi."

Omari calculated the distance. "We're headed to Kongo?"

"Yes," Samwati revealed.

A chill swept through Omari. "For what?"

Lolega grinned. "Ndoko."

Omari grasped his forehead. "Shit!"

* * *

Three weeks later the dhow maneuvered down the narrow Mambezi River. The banks were covered with thick forest, the highlands rising over the canopy appearing closer than they actually were. Omari struggled with his emotions from the moment he learned they were after Ndoko. The slavers stood on the deck with their tools, staring eagerly into the trees. Omari moved closer to Lolega.

"You know the Ndoko are not animals, right?" he said. Lolega glared at him.

"I don't care. All I know is if I bring one back, I will be paid well."

"It won't be that easy," Omari said. "The Ndoko are formidable warriors. They are also Eda's children. You should think twice about this. We all should."

Lolega's head snapped toward Omari. "I've had enough of your words, Mikijen. You've been worrying like an old money counter since you discovered our purpose. We'll catch a Ndoko then deliver it to Haben. I will do what I was paid to do and so will you!"

Omari stared at Lolega, shook his head then walked away. If he had known the goal of the expedition, he would have turned the job down. No, he wouldn't have. He needed the money. But he would have prepared better. He would have spent a portion of his advance on talisman and gris-gris, and possibly some healing herbs and pain suppressors. But it was too late now. He took out his weapons, sharpening his swords and knives then inspecting his hand cannon, shot and powder. He was going to need every last one of them. And if everything went well, maybe, just maybe, he would live through it all.

The dhow anchored in an oxbow lake which jutted from the main river. Camp was set up quickly and the slavers took to the bush, Omari walking in the lead with Lolega.

"Do you know where you're going?" he asked.

Lolega nodded. "Bajinet hired Dozu hunters to scout the area for three weeks before organizing this expedition. According to them the Ndoko travel this way frequently, usually alone. There's a creek that divides the highlands from the grasses. We'll set up an ambush there then wait."

"It sounds too simple," Omari replied.

"That's why it will work," Lolega said. "I've captured all types living beings; men, beasts and some things in between. I've learned that elaborate plans result in elaborate failures. The best way is to study the target, find those moments when it is most relaxed, most unaware, then build your trap. Ndoko are most vulnerable when sleeping or drinking water."

Omari had no response. He was a mercenary, not a slaver or a hunter. If Lolega thought his plan would work, Omari wasn't the one to question him.

They reached the creek at dusk. Omari and the others set up camp, and then Omari stood watch as the slavers slipped away that night to set their trap. They returned as the moon rested directly above them, tired yet in good spirits.

"We'll be on our way home tomorrow," Lolega said. "The creek was perfect for our trap."

He sat before the fire then leaned back on his hands. "Haben's money is as good as in my hands. I will see my family again, Mikijen. I will!"

The next morning, they broke camp then headed for the trap site. As they neared, they heard loud grunting and cries.

Lolega and the other slavers ran ahead, smiles on their faces. Omari followed more cautiously, studying the surrounding bush as he made his way. By the time he reached the clearing his senses were on full alert. This was not right.

He stepped to the edge of the clearing. The slavers gathered around the creek edge, beating their prize to submission with short thick clubs. Lolega turned toward him, a victorious smile on his face. Omari looked at their captive in terror. It was not a Ndoko, but a local mountain nyani.

"Let it go," he shouted. "And get . . ."

The bush exploded on the opposite bank. Twenty Ndoko burst from hiding, their war howls filling the air. They leaped the entire expanse of the creek, ripping into the men as they descended with their wrist blades, slashing them into a bloody mess in moments. Only Lolega remained with a sword and club in his hands, surrounded by the Ndoko. They knew he was the leader; his death would not be pleasant. Omari did the only thing he could do. He turned then ran, Lolega's screams fueling his haste.

He halted as something dropped from the trees above and landed before him. It was a Ndoko warrior, his wrist blades stained with fresh blood. Omari whipped his hand cannon around, trying to light the fuse; The Ndoko lunged, knocking Omari and the gun into the bush. Omari rolled free of the gun then came to his feet, just as the Ndoko slash at him with his blade. Omari managed to raise his sword and the metal rang as the blades clashed. Omari's arm went numb with the impact and he dropped his sword. He ducked another blade swing then kicked out hard at the Ndoko's shin. The Ndoko howled then fell to its knees. Omari punched the Ndoko's jaw then winced as a finger snapped. He was about to kick again when he spotted another Ndoko closing on him. He spun, snatching a throwing knife from his belt and throwing it. The Ndoko dodged but not fast enough; the knife buried into its shoulder.

The path before him was clear again, but something gripped his ankle then lifted him. He sailed through air, landing hard onto a clump of bushes. Three Ndoko charged at him as he gained his feet and drew his knives. This was it then; he would die in the bush fighting Ndoko. So be it. Omari rush the trio. He waited until the last moment then dropped to the ground, hoping to trip the middle warrior. It was like slamming into a tree. He slashed at the Ndoko's shins and it jumped away. Another Ndoko lifted him by his shoulders and he kicked it in the face. It dropped him, but he never touched the ground. The third Ndoko caught him, lifted him over its head then slammed him on the ground. Omari rolled despite the breath being knocked out of him. He couldn't win this fight. The Ndoko were too strong and too damn quick. As he struggled to his feet, his finger and ribs broken, his breath ragged, the Ndoko ceased their attack. A net fell over him, its weight dropping him to his knees. A new Ndoko strode up to him then threw something his way. It was Lolega's head. The Ndoko squatted before Omari.

"Mikijen," it said. "You keep bad company."

Omari was too tired to answer.

The Ndoko said something in a language Omari didn't recognize. He felt a sharp pain at the back of his head, and then everything turned black.

* * *

Omari awoke cradled in a basket of leaves. He lay on a wooden platform suspended high above ground, surrounded by thatch and bark tree houses, the Ndoko clan's village. He was naked and smelled like shit. Based on the beating he took it was probably his shit. He craned his neck for a closer inspection then realized he was covered in some type of paste. Everywhere it touched him, his skin tingled. He wasn't sure if he was being healed or poisoned. He proceeded to wipe it away when a grunt made him freeze.

A Ndoko, the last one he remembered seeing before he almost died, descended before him.

"Don't touch it," he said. "It will help you heal."

Apparently the Ndoko were not familiar with the healing powers of his ngisimaugi. If they didn't know, he wasn't going to tell them.

"And why should I heal?" Omari asked.

"Because you are valuable," the Ndoko said.

Omari held back a spit. So, he was to be sold.

"The others were valuable as well," he said. "Yet you killed them."

The Ndoko grabbed his arm, twisting it to reveal his tattoo.

"But you are Mikijen. You have something I need."

Now the conversation is getting interesting, Omari thought.

"Everything comes with a price," he said.

"I've paid the price," the Ndoko said. "You're alive. You owe that to me."

"What is it I have that you desire?" he asked.

"You have the Mikijen ways," the Ndoko replied. "I wish you to teach them to me and my clan."

Omari laughed and his side ached. "If you're referring to fighting, I believe the Mikijen could stand to learn a thing or two from you."

The Ndoko made a gurgling sound Omari assumed was laughter. "You will learn our way of fighting. My warriors will not take orders from you unless you can defeat them in the Game. I will teach you how to play, and you will teach me how the Mikijen fight."

So they would eventually beat him to death, Omari concluded.

"How about I tell you what I know and you set me free?" Omari suggested.

The Ndoko shook his head. "I will need you for a long time, until I've accomplished my dream."

"And what dream is that?"

"To unite the Ndoko. To build a kingdom like the Kiswala and the Haisetti."

Omari shivered. He once heard an old Haisetti warrior say he hoped the day would never come that the Ndoko formed a kingdom. Ki Khanga would never recover. What the Ndoko clan leader wanted from him was tactics and strategies. He wanted to learn how to wage war.

"I can't help you," Omari replied.

The Ndoko stood, towering over the prone Omari, his fists held at his side.

"You have a choice, Mikijen. You can give me what I want and have a chance to live, or refuse me and die now. Because you fought so bravely, I will make sure your death is quick. But you will die."

Omari decided at that moment that he owed Ki Khanga nothing. Life under Ndoko rule probably wouldn't be so bad, especially if he was second to its potential ruler. He looked at the hulking Ndoko then smiled.

"My name is Omari Ket. What is it you wish to know?"

* * *

Omari winced as he slammed into the banana tree then cried out as a large bunch of the ripe fruit plummeted toward him. He rolled from harm then ducked the flurry of punches meant for his already bruised head. Instinct took over as he whipped out his right leg and tripped his opponent. He spun on his back then lifted onto one arm before landing upright on his feet then immediately swayed to the vocal rhythms and chest thumping of the surrounding Ndoko. One Ndoko stood away from the circle, watching the Game with intensity.

Boda rolled to his feet, his jerking gestures signaling his anger and embarrassment. It didn't take Omari long to decipher the Ndoko language, an interesting combination of broken Kiswa, body and hand gestures, and an old Ki Khanga tongue Omari might have never heard if not for his education under his wealthy patron Mariama. Those days seemed a lifetime ago as he squared off again with Boda while Dumi, the Ndoko who spared his life, looked on.

They were tied, each with a takedown. One more round would determine which of them would serve as Dumi's second. In reality Omari's purpose would not change no matter what the outcome. He was to teach Dumi tactics and strategy in exchange for his eventual freedom. But in order for the other Ndoko to follow him, he had to gain rank among them. And to gain rank, he had to beat them in the Game. Omari would have been happy with a lower rank, but his fighting proved better than he expected. If he defeated Boda, he would be eligible for a high rank.

Boda launched into a cartwheel that was too slow to be convincing. Omari danced to his right but didn't attack. The frown on Boda's face proved his move was a feint for a more destructive blow of which Omari had no clue. Omari gave up trying to learn all the intricate Ndoko fighting moves in such short time. He picked up a few techniques then adapted them to every situation.

Boda twisted to face him then launched into a whirlwind of kicks and punches. Omari kept away, side-stepping and weaving, waiting for his chance. It came moments later when Boda's run ended. Omari jumped at the Ndoko in that brief hesitation, landing a crushing elbow to Boda's jaw while driving his knee into his groin. He punched the falling Ndoko across the jaw for good measure.

The vocals and beating ceased. The Ndoko looked at Omari in shock and satisfaction. As Omari sank to the ground Dumi entered the circle.

"Please no," Omari said, raising his hands in defeat. "I have nothing left. Kill me now and be done with it."

Dumi grabbed his arm then pulled him to his feet.

"No time for rest," Dumi said. "You must teach us formations."

Omari glared at Dumi. "You must be crazy."

Dumi smiled. "You must be crazy speaking to me that way. But I guess it is earned, *pili*."

Omari's eye widened. Dumi had made him his second-in-command. He looked at Boda sprawled in the grass then realized he'd won. He didn't feel like it.

"Right. Formations. Follow me."

The Ndoko lined up behind him.

"*Ngozi mtu*,' they said in unison.

Omari looked at them puzzled. "Skin man?"

Dumi patted his shoulder, which hurt like the Cleave.

"They have given you a name," he said. "You are one of us now."

Omari tried to smile but that hurt, too.

"Ngozi mtu it is."

Omari hobbled off into the brush, the Ndoko close behind.

* * *

Fire swept through the forest canopy, forcing the hiding Ndoko to the ground. Some fell in their haste, tumbling through burning limbs then crashing into the hard ground. Those who survived the fall were rounded up by their attackers, helmet wearing Ndoko covered in leather armor and armed with long bladed spears. They herded the wounded, healthy women and children into a waiting pen. The men joined those who had fought them, their fates uncertain. The warriors raised their spears and shields in triumph. Another village had fallen.

Omari stood beside Dumi, looking almost comical in his oversized armor. Dumi raised his war club in unison with his Ndoko, his smile broad.

"Another victory, Ngozi mtu!" he shouted. "The forest falls before our might!"

Omari nodded. When he began teaching Dumi and his band Mikijen tactics and strategies he thought they would never catch on. They were too stubborn and too traditional, challenging his every word. But after the first victory they relented. The Skin Man's wisdom was valuable. Victory after victory proved his worth.

"Come," Dumi said. "We must seal this victory."

Omari trudged behind Dumi to the pen holding the male Ndoko. The Ndoko leader waded through them, picking out the young men. They would be trained to fill his ranks. He also selected a few older males, those who showed fear. They were malleable; he would make them servants. The others he looked on with disgust.

When he turned his back the slaughter began, his warriors killing everyone not selected. The females and women wailed as their fathers, husbands, uncles and sons were decimated.

Omari strode away until he was too far to see or hear the massacre. He snatched the helmet from his head then threw it has far as he could. Omari was not a squeamish man, nor was he unfamiliar with cruelty. But never had he experienced it at such a level. Worst of all, he was the one who had made it all possible.

He heard Dumi before he saw him.

"Why are you here, *pili*?" the Ndoko asked.

"I've done enough," Omari answered. "Let me go."

"Not yet," Dumi answered. "There is more to do."

"I have nothing left to teach you," Omari said. "You have learned well . . . too well."

Dumi came closer. "The killing bothers you?"

Omari hesitated. "Yes."

"It is our way," he replied.

Omari stood, his mind resolved. "If you will not let me go, then I'll leave."

Dumi's head tilted. "You will what?"

"I'll leave."

Dumi unsheathed his wrist knives. "Don't make me do this, mtu. I have come to think of you as a brother."

"And yet you'll kill me if I try to leave," Omari replied.

Dumi's smile faded. "Yes. You are my *pili*. The warriors follow both of us. If you leave, they will have to choose who to follow."

"I don't want them to follow me. I wish to go my own way."

"But they will do it. At least some will. It is our way."

Omari unsheathed his swords. "After today they will follow only you."

Dumi sprang at Omari so quickly his plan almost failed. By the time he'd dropped his swords and swung his hand cannon about Dumi loomed over him. He fell back as he lit the fuse then waited what seemed like an eternity before the blast deafened him. Dumi fell onto him and Omari braced himself for the pummeling he expected. Instead, Dumi lay still. Blood ran warm onto Omari's neck and face as he struggled to heave the Ndoko away.

Omari stood, wiping blood from his eyes. Dumi lay on his back, his face unrecognizable.

"By the Cleave," Omari whispered. He had only meant to wound him. Instead Dumi lay dead.

Omari backed away, ignoring his swords. The voices of Dumi's warriors grew louder as they responded to the blast. Omari looked upon Dumi one last time then ran for his life.

Omari could not stop running. He learned from experience that he needed all his strength and stamina to fight a Ndoko. Sometimes he would sit up late into the night, contemplating escape but he knew the only way he could do so was to fight or run. But now the decision had been made for him.

Dumi's warriors would linger at his body, for how long Omari did not know. But he did know that once their mourning was complete they'd come for him. So he continued to run.

Their voices reached him as he fought his way up a steep hill. Omari was tempted to run faster, but he fought the urge. The Ndoko were strong and fast but they were not known for stamina. But then neither was he, at least not recently. As an orphan on the streets of Sati Baa running was the difference between life and death. As a Mikijen running was a part of the constant training routine, a regimen that honed the mercenaries' stamina and made them a formidable fighting force.

Arrows whizzed by his head as the Ndoko made his name a war chant.

"Ngozi mtu! Ngozi mtu!"

Omari kept running. As he reached the hill's summit a war club smashed into his back, knocking him forward. He rolled down the hill for a time then sprang back to his feet in full stride. Once he reached level ground, he picked up his pace. The Ndoko voices faded with each step; soon they were drowned by the cacophony of the forest.

But he did not stop running. His legs ached, his back throbbed, his chest burned but he kept moving. The sun descended below the tree line before him, but he kept running. Staggering was a better description. When the sun returned, he was still on his feet, limping into the clearing which lead to the lake dock he'd disembarked from almost two years ago. The landing was in terrible shape, the forest reclaiming what had been taken years before. Omari stumbled into the dilapidated buildings, seeking some type of weapon to defend himself just in case the Ndoko still pursued him. What he eventually found was much better. A single dugout canoe floated against the wrecked dock. There was no paddle, but Omari didn't need one. He fell into the canoe, pushed it away from the dock then stroked with cupped hands into the lake. He was about a mile from shore when he heard it.

"Ngozi mtu! Ngozi mtu!"

The Ndoko stood at the edge of the lake, shaking their weapons and loosing arrows that had no chance of reaching him. Sadness overwhelmed him; these warriors threatening his life had once been his cohorts. He lay down, the lake flow carrying him further out. There would be a time he would have to figure out how he would survive, but at that moment all he could think of was rest. So he slept . . .

. . . and awoke on the deck of a merchant dhow. A shirtless boy wearing a dingy loincloth squatted beside him, staring into his eyes.

"He's alive!" the boy shouted.

A thick brown man with a grizzled face shoved the boy aside.

"Good thing you opened your eyes, Mikijen," he said. "We were about to cut you up for bait. Lake eels love human flesh."

The man turned to the boy. "Bring him some water and some food."

Omari sat up, groaning with every move.

"What's your name?" the merchant asked.

"Omari . . .Omari Ket."

"Welcome to the Mzuri," the man replied. "I'm Abasi, nahoda of this beautiful dhow. The way I see it you owe me for saving your life."

Omari was in no mood to argue. "I do?"

The boy brought him a water gourd and a bowl of fish stew. Omari ate and drank with gusto.

"I figure that's about six months' worth of food you're eating." Abasi said.

"That's mbogo shit," Omari replied. "Get me to Ors and I'll pay you for this and much more."

The nahoda laughed as did the boy. Omari placed down the bowl then sprang on the nahoda, snatching the sword from his belt as he punched him unconscious. He looked at the boy.

"Bring me more food," he said.

The boy backed away, his eyes filled with fear. "Yes, bwa, yes!"

The boy scampered away.

Omari settled before his food. This was his dhow now, at least until they reached Ors. He gazed back at the dwindling forest. He closed his eyes, imagining the furious Ndoko still calling his name.

"Ngozi mtu," he said under his breath.

"What did you say?"

The boy had returned with more food, a puzzled look on his face.

Omari smiled. "Nothing. Nothing at all."

*   *   *

Salimu Baraza arrived at his sprawling farm chasing the sun into the western horizon. Two of his servants greeted him at the entrance of his tabby stone home, one helping him from his horse, the other opening the gate to the expansive grounds. He crossed the courtyard, sweeping his eyes across the smaller homes of his wives and the even more modest homes of his concubines. He was a wealthy man by any standards, which was why his brother merchants put up with his incongruent behavior. The thick layers of *tobis* he wore and the jeweled rings gracing his thick fingers displayed his wealth to all. It was only a matter of time before he became Grand Merchant of Kiswala. No one doubted his eventual ascension. They waited only for the announcement to be made.

The merchant knew something was wrong as soon as he stepped into the grand foyer. Malek, his door servant, did not greet him as he entered; nor was Lobi, his personal servant, waiting to herald his return. Instead there was silence and a thin trail of blood leading to the stairway.

Salimu drew his sword then cursed. Robbers were constantly trying to break into his homes; this one had progressed more than most. Salimu's only thoughts as he climbed the stairs were how bad his servants were injured and how long it would take him to dispatch another witless thief.

He reached the top of the stairs in total darkness.

"Lobi? Malek? Where are you?" he said.

The man who stepped out of the shadows was neither. Salimu tried to defend himself but the man disarmed him with his sword then pressed the tip against his neck.

"Who are you?" Salimu asked.

"It doesn't matter who I am," the man said. "What matters is how you answer my next question. There is a woman whose husband was named Lolega. Where do I find her?"

Salimu grinned. "She is one of my concubines. You can have her if you let me live."

The man's fist slammed into Salimu's face. Pain blinded him; he lost his balance then tumbled down the stairs. He was barely conscious as he lay sprawled on the dirt floor. The interloper took his time walking to him. When he finally arrived, he placed the sword once again at Salimu's throat.

"Where is the woman?" he said.

"I'll take you," Salimu said. Whatever bravery Salimu possessed fled on his way down the stairs. This man cared nothing for his status or his wealth.

"Stand up," the man ordered.

Salimu groaned as he stood.

"Turn around," the man said.

Salimu shook. "I said I'll take you!"

The bandit punched him again, knocking Salimu to his knees. He struggled back on his feet.

"Turn around!" the man growled.

Salimu turned his back to the man. The man pulled his arms back then tied them together at the wrist.

"Take me to the woman," he said.

Salimu led the man out of the compound then to the concubine's house.

"Call her," the man said.

"Husna!" he shouted. "Open the door! Quickly!"

Long moments passed before he heard the door lock slip aside. No sooner had the door open did the man shove Salimu inside. Husna squealed in fear as he tumbled by her then landed on his face.

* * *

Omari Ket grinned as Salimu's face hit the packed dirt. He turned his attention to the woman. He could see why Salimu claimed her; she was beautiful in a simple way, with large eyes that seem to penetrate secrets. He looked over Husna's shoulders; three children hid in the darkness.

"Are you Lolega's wife?" he asked.

Husna's large eyes grew larger at the mention of the slaver's name.

"Yes, I am his wife! Are you his friend? Did he send you for us? Where is he?"

"I'm not his friend," Omari said.

Husna's eyes glistened. "Then why are you here?"

Omari didn't answer. He took a dagger from his belt then handed to Husna.

"Do what you wish," he said.

Husna screamed as she jumped on Salimu's back then stabbed him over and over. When she stood her hand was covered with blood. Omari extended his hand and she gave the dagger back to him.

"Now what?" she asked.

"You and your children will walk in front of me," Omari said. "We'll go to Salimu's barn and take a wagon. Then we'll go to the main house. Do you know where he keeps his gold?"

"Yes," Husna answered.

Omari grinned. "Good."

They took the wagon then looted Salimu's home. Omari ordered Husna and the children to do most of the work as he kept watch, his sword in hand. Once the wagon was filled they fled the farm. They were miles away by sunrise.

Omari stopped the wagon. He took one of the horses free then saddled it.

"If you continue west for another three days you will reach Mombu," he said. "You can buy your way on a passenger dhow to Ki Khanga. Once on the mainland head to Sati-Baa. It's a big city; easy to get lost in. No one will ask any questions."

"The Kiswala will come after us!" she said.

"They will come after me," Omari replied. "I'm sure Salimu's servants and wives told the story of a bandit that killed their master then stole his concubine and his gold."

Husna didn't seem convinced. Omari placed a gentle hand on her shoulder.

"We are well beyond Kiswala influence, so we have nothing to fear."

Omari took enough gold to lay idle for at least a few months. He climbed onto the horse and nodded goodbye to Husna and her children. He would ride northeast to Haisetti to seek more work.

"Wait," Husna said. "What happened to Lolega? Where is he?"

Omari shared a sympathetic smile Husna. "He was killed by Ndoko."

Husna beamed. "Then I am free of both of them."

Omari's eyes widened. "I thought you loved him. You almost cried when I told you he was dead."

"I almost cried because I thought you were going to try to return me to him," she said.

Omari laughed.

"Farewell then, Husna," he said. "Enjoy your freedom. May Eda keep you."

"I'm sure she will," Husna replied. She sent you."

Omari frowned. "I doubt that."

"Then why did you come for us?"

Omari didn't answer. He reined his horse then rode away, forcing his mind to think of other things.

THE NGOLA'S PROMISE

The gamblers gathered around the table, their covetous eyes expectant. Piles of cowries sat before them, their boasts and curses filling the smoke-stained air. Each took his turn betting against the patron and each took their losses in stride. Everyone, except Omari Ket.

"Curse it to the Cleave!" he shouted. The stout man sitting before him chuckled as he took Omari's last cowries. A tear formed in the corner of Omari's eye as he watched them disappear into the man's pouch. A night with no food and sleeping in the street awaited him. At least it was dry season.

The man standing behind him patted his shoulder.

"My turn," he said.

"Wait," Omari said.

"Wait for what?" the man replied. "Your luck is terrible and your pockets are empty. Get out the way!"

Omari jumped to his feet then punched the man in the throat. The man staggered away gasping as he clutched his damaged neck. The room fell silent, the patrons staring at Omari. What was once a jovial atmosphere had become tense. Omari sat back in the chair then rustled through his belongings. A smile came to his face; he pulled out his hand cannon then slammed it on the table.

"This!" he shouted. "I'll bet this!"

The opponent looked at the hand cannon while scratching his head.

"What in Daarila's name is that?"

"It's a hand cannon!" Omari replied. "The most dangerous weapon in Ki Khanga. It speaks like thunder and can slay a hundred men with its voice. It has saved my life many times."

The gambler picked up the hand cannon, examining it carefully.

"One stack," he said.

"One stack? One stack! It's worth at least three."

"I'm not a fighter," the man said. "I have no use for weapons."

"Maybe I can help."

Omari turned to the woman who spoke. A smile slowly formed on his face as he studied her. She was an umber skinned woman dressed in an extravagant robe that conveyed her wealth. Dozens of thin jeweled chains encircled her graceful neck. The thin wrinkles at the corners of her brown eyes hinted she was older than Omari, yet her face still embraced her youthful beauty. The woman was flanked by two burly guards wearing sleeveless tunics and pants which ended at their thick calves. Short swords hung from their waist belts. Their countenances were as unpleasant as the woman's was comely.

The woman placed a bag of stacks on the table, and Omari returned her gesture with a generous grin.

"To whom do I owe my salvation to?" he asked.

"An interested investor," the woman replied. She smiled then stepped away from the table.

"Okay, let's go!" Omari said. The others looked at Omari uncomfortably.

"You sure you want to this?" his opponent asked.

"Since when did you become concerned about my well-being?" Omari snapped.

"I could care less," the man replied. "But a stranger just gave you more money than you deserve and you're not wondering why?"

Omari smirked. "I think I know what she wants. And when I win my money back, I'll make sure she gets it. Now let's play!"

* * *

The tavern had long since emptied. Omari sat alone at the gambling table in shock and denial. There was no way he could have lost so much money in such a short time, yet he did. He was too drunk and too stunned to slip out early so when the woman and her guards approached his hand fell to his sword hilt. He hadn't expected to have to fight his way out of the situation, but he had no choice.

"Seems things didn't go well," the woman said.

Omari jumped to his feet, his sword drawn. The woman shook her head.

"There's no need for all that. You do owe me a lot of money, but I don't want your life in return."

Omari stayed on guard, his eyes darting back and forth between the guards. Neither of them made a move for their weapons. Omari relaxed, lowering his sword.

"What do you want?" he asked. "Me?"

The woman laughed. "An interesting proposal, but you're much too young for my taste. I do have a task that your skills would be ideally suited for."

"How do you know what skills I have?"

"You are a former Mikijen, are you not?"

"Yes," Omari answered.

"And you still wear the ngisimaugi?"

Omari's eyes narrowed as he glanced at the black tentacle running down his left arm.

"Yes."

The woman smiled. "Fascinating. Then you'll do fine."

The woman turned then walked away.

"Come with us," she said. "First you need a good night sleep, then we'll discuss what I want. Does that sound reasonable?"

It didn't, but Omari was too inebriated and broke to argue.

"Sure," he finally said. "Lead the way."

Omari followed the woman and her men to a waiting wagon. He climbed in and the men sat beside him. One of the men offered him a beer bowl.

"Thank you," Omari said. He took a long sip. This was good beer. He took a longer sip. This was very good beer. He was in the middle of his third pull when the world went dark.

* * *

Omari could barely keep his eyes open. Whatever the woman slipped into his beer lingered. He had no idea where he was or how long he'd been there. He tried to move his arms but his hands were chained together. He attempted to stand but was pushed back down to his knees. He looked to either side and saw the woman's bodyguards standing beside him, the amicable expressions gone from their faces. He was kneeling beneath a large ancestor tree before a lavishly dressed woman flanked by two armed warriors. The woman sitting before him was definitely beautiful and regal; the warriors flanking her no less attractive. All three bore countenances of serious intent. They did not seem impressed by him at all, which hurt his feelings somewhat.

"What is this you bring me, Mayele?" the seated woman said. "I hope you aren't wasting my time again. I told you before I'm not interested in your pretty men, although this one is prettier than most."

"I wouldn't waste your time, Great Ngola," Mayele said.

The mention of the woman's title cleared Omari's head. He was kneeling before the ruler of Matamba, and the women standing beside her were Mino, some of the fiercest warriors in Ki Khanga. He was in serious trouble.

"This man is no consort," Mayele continued. "He is a former Mikijen."

"So you bring me a hired sword." The Ngola smirked. "You more than anyone else should know I need no warriors." The Ngola glanced at her fighters and they grinned in return.

"The reputation of the Mino is unmatched," Mayele agreed. "But still there is one thing they have not obtained for you. This man may be able to do so."

Mayele's pleasant smile evaporated as he looked at Omari and the men holding his chains.

"Stand him up and turn him around!" she commanded.

The men yanked Omari to his feet then spun him about.

"He still bears the ngisimaugi." Mayele announced.

The Ngola smiled, the Mino grinning as well.

"What is your name?" she asked.

Omari raised his chest and kept a stoic demeanor.

"Omari Ket."

"You've done well, Mayele," the Ngola said. "Very well. Unchain him."

The men unchained Omari then stepped away as the Mino advanced on him, their spears lowered.

"I have a task for you, Omari Ket," the Ngola said. "Accept it and once the task is complete you may go free with as much wealth as you can carry. Refuse and my Mino will kill you and feed you to my mambas."

Omari looked at the Ngola, the Mino standing before him and his captors on either side of him. Under normal circumstances he would try to fight his way out, placing his fate in Eda's hands. But the promise of payment was tantalizing and much better than the very good chance he would die where he stood.

Omari smiled. "I accept."

The Ngola smiled back.

"Excellent!"

She looked to her warriors. "Take him to Izegbe. She will prepare him."

The women bowed then prodded Omari with their spears. Omari walked away, cutting his eyes at Mayele.

"I will see you again," he said. "This I promise."

"I doubt it, Mikijen," she replied. "May Eda bless you."

Omari smirked. "She does."

Omari marched away with the warriors. As they neared the palace he noticed how the men of the city looked away from the women, a hint of fear on their faces. The reaction of the women was just the opposite. They smiled warmly at the Mino, a look of pride on their faces.

The Ngola's palace was a large rectangular building, the stone walls covered by white stucco painted with images of war and sacrifices. The warriors led him to the entrance where a man dressed in a long robe and conical hat waited.

"Take him to Izegbe," one of the warriors said. "She will know what to do."

The man prostrated before the warrior. He rose then glared at Omari.

"Follow me," he ordered.

Omari stepped into the palace. The interior walls were painted white as well, intersperse with expensive and rare fabrics from throughout Ki Khanga. The man led him to a room at the end of the wide corridor, the beautifully carved doors closed.

"Kiswala," Omari said.

"What?" the man replied.

"Those doors are from Kiswala," Omari said. "They are very expensive."

The man frowned. "This is the Ngola's palace. What did you expect?"

The man knocked then dropped to the floor, pulling Omari with him.

"What are you doing?"

"Prostrate, or Izegbe will kill you," the man said.

Omari reluctantly prostrated, touching his head on the stone. He heard the door open.

"What you want, Odion?"

"Honored mother, the Great Ngola has sent this man to you. He is to be sent on the journey."

"Leave us," Izegbe said.

Odion crawled backwards for a distance before standing and backing down the hall.

"Stand up," Izegbe said.

Omari came to his feet, looking Izegbe directly in the eyes. She was broad shouldered and firmly muscled in a way that impressed and aroused him. Her bronze plain face bore ritual scarifications on her cheeks. Unlike the warriors that escorted him to the palace she wore leather armor draped with chain mail. A sword and dagger hung from her waist.

Izegbe looked him up and down then smiled.

"Interesting," she said. "Turn around."

Omari turned slowly, his arms outstretched. When he faced Izegbe again her eyes were wide.

"Very interesting," she said.

She drew her knife then stabbed Omari in the gut.

"Wh-What?" he groaned as he fell to the ground. He grimaced as he bled; moments later his ngisimaugi warmed on his back. Izegbe stood over him, watching as the tattoo glowed, Omari clenching his teeth. The wound slowly closed, the bleeding reducing to a trickle.

"So the stories are true," Izegbe said.

"You could have just asked me," Omari replied.

"I would not have believed you," she said. "There have been others who claimed to have what you possess. They are dead. With this you might stand a chance."

Izegbe grabbed his arm then dragged him into her chambers. She lifted him onto her shoulders, carrying him across the room then dropping him onto a hard bed. Omari grimaced.

"How long does it take?" she asked.

Omari lifted his head to take a look at the wound.

"Two days at the most," he said. "It would help if it was bandaged."

Izegbe ignored his request.

"Are you immortal?" she said.

Omari shook his head. "A wound to the head or the heart is fatal. If a limb is severed it won't grow back. You can bleed to death if it's a severe wound or if there are many wounds."

Izegbe folded her arms across her chest.

"Not as good as I expected," she said.

"Sorry to disappoint you."

"Still, it may help."

The woman strode toward the door.

"I will send a healer. Once you are well, we will be on our way."

"To where?" Omari asked.

"You'll see," Izegbe said. She exited the room, slamming the door behind her.

The healer arrived a few moments later, a thin, bare-chested man wearing a bark cloth kanga with dozens of gourds hanging on his person. Omari lay still as the man poured various ingredients into a stone mortar then mashed them together. He scooped the resulting paste into his hands then spread it on Omari's wound. The paste numbed his belly and Omari sighed.

After inspecting the application, the man gathered his gourds and proceeded toward the door.

"No bandages?" Omari asked.

"No," the man said. "The poultice with dry to a coating. The kipande in your tattoo will help. Do not move until you are healed."

Omari lay on his back then closed his eyes. He fell asleep immediately, the stress of his predicament finally overwhelming him. He dreamed of Sati Baa, of the life he once had there and was forced to abandon. He awoke to gentle nudging and the smell of lilacs. Opening his eyes, he spied the first friendly smile he'd seen in weeks.

"I have come to feed you, Mikijen," the woman said. "Can you sit?"

Omari struggled to a sitting position, watching the poultice as he did so. Surprisingly the coating did not crumble. It moved with the flexibility of his skin, remaining attached as he leaned to the woman to take the tray on which she brought his food. The woman dipped the spoon into the stew but Omari grasped her hand.

"I can manage," he said.

"It seems you can," she replied, her eyes inspecting his body. "I have heard many stories about the Mikijen."

"They're all true," Omari said. "Except the bad ones. Those are lies."

The woman chuckled. "No, I believe they're all true. I can look at you and tell you have done good and bad things."

Omari didn't reply. He ate his stew, ignoring the truth in the woman's words.

"My name is Nourbese," the woman said.

Omari smiled "It's a beautiful name."

"I'm glad you think so," Nourbese replied.

"I'm Omari. I've been summoned by your Ngola to find a treasure for her."

Nourbese giggled. "You're a liar as well."

Omari laughed as well. "I had to try."

"You would like to lay with me. That is why you lied."

Omari smiled. "Yes to both."

"That is not possible," Nourbese said. "You belong to the Ngola. If you were to lay with anyone, it would be her. But you don't want that to happen."

"Why?"

"Because she kills any man she lays with," Nourbese said. "She only does so when she wants a child. Lucky for you she does not need one, for you are a well-built man and would make good children."

Izegbe entered the room, a frown on her face.

"Nourbese, why are you talking to him?"

"I was just..."

"You were to feed him. Nothing more. Get out."

"Yes, Izegbe."

The woman gathered her items then left the room.

No sooner did Nourbese exit did Izegbe begin to take off her clothes.

"Undress," she told Omari. A sly grin came to his face.

"I thought I belonged to the Ngola."

Izegbe grinned.

"The Ngola does not want you, nor is she here."

"I could tell her," Omari teased.

"If we survive this journey, you can tell her anything you want. For now, be quiet and take off your clothes. You're wasting time."

Omari obliged.

* * *

Omari awoke alone. There was a bowl of water, a large towel and soap beside his bed. Apparently Izegbe was one for cleanliness. He washed up then began donning his clothes as Nourbese entered with his morning meal. The large tray was filled with fruits, meats and grains with a jug of beer.

"Good morning Omari," she said. There was sadness in her voice.

"Good morning, Nourbese."

Omari sat at the table and Nourbese served him.

"This is a large breakfast," he said.

"Izegbe wanted to make sure you were well fed," Nourbese said. "She said you would be tired."

"I take it she is pleased with me," Omari said.

"She can't stop talking about it. She was actually humming this morning. Humming!"

Izegbe entered the room and terror filled Nourbese's face. She scurried from the room with her head lowered and shoulders hunched as is if expecting a blow. Izegbe followed her with her eyes until she was out of the room.

"Finish your food then get dressed," she ordered. "Our bulls are waiting."

"Bulls?"

If Izegbe was pleased with him, she showed no signs of it as she waited for him to finish his meal. Omari dressed, grabbed his weapons then stood for Izegbe's inspection. She nodded her approval and they marched from his room to the stables where their bulls waited. The bovines were similar to wild nyati but apparently much more docile. They mounted the large beasts and were quickly on their way. Omari maneuvered his bull beside Izegbe.

"So where is this talisman we seek?" he asked.

"In the Sati Swamp," Izegbe replied.

"Which is why we are riding the nyati."

"Yes," Izegbe replied. "They will get us to the pine islands. Once we arrive the way is less certain."

"How so?"

"We have a map, but it is old. The recent maps were used by the others."

"Who never returned," Omari said.

Izegbe said nothing.

They traveled the remainder of the day, reaching the forest edge at nightfall. Izegbe set up camp and they ate from the supplies they brought with them. That night Izegbe visited him again. This time they had sex until daybreak then slept away most of the day. It was afternoon before they set out again, Izegbe humming the entire day.

The swamp was in view as they camped for the night, the forest evergreens giving way to tall cypress trees and marsh grass. Omari set up camp as Izegbe went off with her hunting bow, returning with three swamp rabbits and some local vegetables. They prepared the meal together, cooking a savory stew.

"How did you become a Mikijen?" Izegbe asked him as he chewed on a leg bone. Omari almost choked.

"I didn't think conversation was allowed."

He was surprised again when Izegbe smiled.

"Answer my question," she said. There was softness in her voice.

"It wasn't my choice," Omari said. "It was either become a Mikijen or die."

"What did you do? Were you a thief? A murderer?"

"I was in the wrong place at the wrong time," Omari said.

Izegbe rolled her eyes. "I think you did something wrong."

"In a way, I did," Omari said.

"Men are always doing stupid things," she said.

Omari nodded. "Which is why I'm here."

Izegbe shrugged. "When we reach the swamp we must be wary. Many of the Ngola's enemies live there. They will try to kill us."

"How did they come to live in the swamp?"

"The Ngola exiled them. They defied her rule and were defeated. Then there is the Frog Hag."

Omari put down his stew. As a boy in Sati-Baa he grew up with the legend of the Frog Hag. Most parents would warn their children of her, usually when they were misbehaving.

"You keep stealing and the Frog Hag will come for you!"

"Go to bed now or the Frog Hag will take you from your bed and eat you!"

"Talk back to me one more time and I'll send you to the Frog Hag!"

Omari had heard the warnings so many times as a boy the threat lost its sting. If there was a Frog Hag, he'd be long dead. Apparently his skepticism showed in his expression.

"You do not believe in the Frog Hag?"

"When I see her, I'll believe it," Omari replied.

"If you see her, it will be the last thing you see," Izegbe said.

Omari shrugged. "Anything else we need to be mindful of?"

"No," Izegbe said. "If we make it through the wild tribes and the Frog Hag, you will be free to collect the talisman."

"What exactly is this talisman?"

Izegbe looked unsure.

"I don't know. You will know it when you see it."

"How am I supposed to find something and I don't know what it looks like?"

"You will know."

Izegbe placed down her bowl then crawled to her sleeping mat.

"It's late. We must rest."

Omari laughed.

"You have no intentions of resting."

"Neither do you," Izegbe replied. "Hurry up."

* * *

The next day they entered the swamp. The nyatis didn't hesitate when they reached the wetlands; they waded into the water, their hooves unimpeded by the muddy foundation. While Izegbe frowned as the warm waters climbed her legs, Omari was unperturbed. He was used to being wet after years serving the Kiswala. What bothered him more was that they were crossing the swamp in the open instead of using the bordering forest as cover. If the Ngola's enemies were fair to good archers, they were done for. On the other hand, traveling through the woods could set them up for an ambush. It seemed there was no good way to travel where they were headed, so he cleared his mind and took in the scenery.

They were halfway across the open water when they heard the cries coming from all around them. Masked warriors burst from the woods waving throwing spears and brandishing loaded bows. Izegbe looked at Omari, her expression all the answer he needed. If they had to run and fight, they might as well run in the direction closer to their goal.

"Hita!" Izegbe shouted as she slapped her nyati's neck. The beast bellowed then charged forward as Izegbe released her lance from its saddle sheath. Omari did the same, his bull keeping pace with Izegbe's. It was a formidable advance, but the masked warriors before them did not move. Instead they raised large shields and slammed them into the ground. Omari grinned; this was a disaster waiting to happen. He kicked his bull, spurring it to run faster.

The bull bellowed as its head and horn hit the shields. Instead of breaking the wooden barrier and the men behind it, the bull's head bent at an awkward angle. Omari went soaring over the barrier, a shocked look on his face that turned into a painful grimace when he splashed down into mud and water. He lay stunned for a moment before regaining his feet. Izegbe learned from his mistake; she turned her bull aside and fought with spear and sword against the warriors swarming around her and the bull like lethal bees. Omari ran towards them, loading his hand cannon. He reached the edge of the fray as he lit the fuse.

"Ago!" Omari shouted.

The warriors looked his way just as the hand cannon fired. Three men went down, the loud blast stunning the others. The hand cannon's voice had another devastating effect; Izegbe's nyati flew into a frenzy, flinging warriors aside with its head and horns and kicking others airborne with its rear legs. Izegbe dropped her weapons and clung to the bull with its head and horns. Omari jammed the cannon into its holder then took out his sword, working his way through the stupefied attackers until he reached Izegbe and the now calm bull. Omari scanned the scene; the other warriors were running toward them, high-stepping through the water. He climbed onto the bull with Izegbe.

"Get us out of here!" he yelled.

"Hita!" Izegbe shouted.

The bull splashed through water and grass, carrying them into the forest. Once on solid ground it ran fast and confidently through the short trees and open grasses, the warriors falling far behind. Izegbe continued to push the bull until darkness forced them to stop. Omari slid off the bull, rubbing sore butt. Izegbe fell off the bull and lay still on the ground. The bull laid down as well, breathing heavy.

Omari finally found his way to Izegbe then sat beside her.

"You could have warned me about the shields," he said.

"I didn't know," Izegbe replied. "They were not ordinary shields."

"Charmed by a powerful sonchai most likely," Omari said.

Izegbe gave him a sideways glance.

"Thank you for coming back for me."

"You had the map," Omari said.

Izegbe grinned. "I should have known."

"Should we expect more surprises like this?"

Izegbe sat up. "I don't know. We are in Eda's hands now."

"In that case, we should be fine. Eda is my patron."

Izegbe cut her eyes at Omari. "Is that so? Then you must have done some wrong she is punishing you for."

"Why would you say that?"

"This journey has been a disaster. I'm glad my part is almost over."

"Over?"

"Yes. I return tomorrow."

Izegbe gave him the map.

"The landmarks are clear. You should be able to find the talisman with no problem. If you survive."

Omari took the map. It was too dark to study it, so he put it in his pack. He took out dried meat and yams and they ate as they rested. Once they had their fill, they sat beside each other, listening to the chirps, croaks and squalls of the nocturnal swamp life.

"You are not as bad as most men," Izegbe said.

"I didn't need you to tell me that," Omari replied.

"You are strong, you fight well, and you are not that ugly."

Omari laughed. "I think you're trying to give me a complement."

Izegbe frowned. "It's not a compliment. Just an observation."

"So, what do we do now?" Omari asked. "I'm not sleepy."

Izegbe glanced at him them began removing her clothes. Omari did the same.

* * *

Omari awoke to the rising sun. He opened his eyes to see Izegbe dressed and mounted on her bull. Omari jumped to his feet.

"You're taking the bull?"

"Of course," she replied. "It's mine. You killed yours."

"Not on purpose!"

"Still, you have no bull. According to map you won't need one. Good luck, Omari Ket. May Eda bless you."

Omari gathered his items as Izegbe rode away.

"I will speak well of you to your daughter!" she shouted.

Omari stood dumbfounded.

"My daughter? What? Wait!"

Izegbe laughed as she kicked the bull into a gallop. Omari watched her ride away with a mixture of anger and resignation. He'd heard the stories of the Mino choosing men from the surrounding lands to impregnate them. The men would present themselves during an annual festival, where they would put themselves on display for the women warriors. A warrior would choose her mate then sleep with him that night. The next day the men were driven away; those who refused to leave were killed. Izegbe apparently decided she wouldn't wait until the festival, and since she believed Omari would die he made the perfect mate. That and the fact that he was not so ugly.

There was nothing left for him to do but continue the journey. He took out the map, comparing the drawn landmarks to the reality before him. The swamp treetops peering at him from over the low evergreens resembled a location on the western side of the map, so he packed his gear and headed in that direction. As he traversed the dense forest, Izegbe's word of his daughter distracted him. He thought of Mariama, the reason he was on this quest that might likely end in his demise. He was so distracted that he didn't notice the activity above him, the muted shapes following him in the canopy starting and stopping in time with his movements. It was midday before his head cleared and he picked up the commotion.

His right hand fell to his sword hilt; with his left hand he extracted his dagger from its sheath on his right forearm. Omari stopped walking then looked up. He wanted whatever was pursuing him to know they were no secret in hopes it would discourage them. It didn't work.

The canopy grew denser and lower as the day progressed. Omari could barely see an opening between the trees, indicating a clearing. Whatever followed him would have to act soon if its intentions were to attack him. He braced himself.

"Eda guide . . ."

His prayer was cut off by sudden pressure around his neck. He gagged as he was jerked off his feet. Omari grabbed at the appendage circling his neck and sliced it with his dagger. There was an ear-piercing scream as the fleshy coil released him. He fell to the ground, landing on his feet but falling to his knees as he caught his breath. As he stood to run another appendage grabbed his arm. Before he could cut himself free he was pummeled by bodies from the treetops, his ears filled with yips and cries. Omari slashed with his dagger and struck out with his fists as the unknown horde bit and clawed. He managed to fight himself free and get on his feet, catching a glimpse of his attackers as he turned to run. They were some type of primate, almost as tall as an adult human with faces like a nyani and tails twice as long as their bodies. Some pursued him on foot while the others climbed the trees and chased him from above. He held his sword and his dagger, slicing through any of the creatures blocking his way, determined not to fall under another assault. The creatures seemed less eager to attack with each death of their own.

The forest transformed into an open area of knee-high water and grass. Omari high stepped into the marsh. He took a quick look; the primates did not follow him. Instead they lined the water's edge, pacing from side to side as they shrieked and threw handfuls of feces in his direction. Omari slowed as he turned toward them.

"Daarila's asses," he shouted. "Are you afraid of a little water?"

Omari froze as he realized there was probably a reason the primates didn't follow him into the clearing, and that reason had nothing to do with an aversion to water or the lack of tree cover. He ran again, hoping to get out of the marsh before whatever terrified the primates appeared.

He sprinted by a bare mound to his left, paying little attention to the nondescript mass. A deep croaking sound from behind made his insides shudder; Omari turned to see that the mound had eyes, and they were trained on him.

"Shit!" he yelled.

He took two more bounds before something hard smacked against his back. He jerked, his weapons flying from his hands. Omari dug his fingers into the mud, trying to keep his head above water as he was dragged backwards. A loud cackle made him twist his head about. What he saw would have been humorous to him if it wasn't real. A ragged old woman danced on the head of a giant frog, clapping her hands as she babbled. The frog's pink tongue extended from its wide mouth, ending on Omari's back.

"Frog Ha . . .!"

Omari's fingers pulled free from the mud as he flew into the frog's open mouth. Rank darkness consumed him as a viscous liquid enveloped him. He tried pushing against the frog's insides but the muscles crushed him. Outside, he could still hear the Frog Hag singing his demise. His skin burned, the frog's saliva digested his clothing. The damage to his body ignited the healing properties of his ngisimaugi. It flared and the frog croaked its discomfort. The ngisimaugi became hotter; the Frog Hag's singing ceased and she began to babble again. Omari was losing consciousness when the ngisimaugi flared with heat so intense Omari believed he was on fire. The frog belched, expelling him. Omari flipped through the air landing with a splash into the marsh, the muddy water cooling his back. Sitting up instinctively to avoid drowning, Omari saw the giant frog thrash in pain, the Frog Hag scampering about it waving her mangled staff and shouting in grief. Omari was hurt, but he wasn't going to wait for the Frog Hag to realize he had been regurgitated. He struggled to his feet then staggered across the marsh to a clump of trees ahead. He chose the largest, hoping that the dense cover would protect him from the Frog Hag's ire. To his relief there were no canopy primates, just the heavy organic smell of the swamp and the weak illumination of the dusk sky. As he caught his breath the sound of splashing came to his ears. He looked up to see the primates charging across the water. Some ran toward the Frog Hag and her fallen companion; the others were coming directly for him.

"Damn it to the Cleave!" he spat.

Instead of fleeing he took time to load his hand cannon. He didn't load the fuse; he wanted it to fire as soon as he touched the power. He lit the match then stuck the stem between his teeth before checking the map one more time. After coming this far, he would at least see this talisman before he died.

Omari trotted toward his destination. Running would wind him too much before the primates caught up with him. The canopy rustled with the screaming beasts as they swept through the branches like a storm. Omari ran faster when he saw a small clearing ahead. The beasts reached him as he stepped into it and spun around to face them. They clambered out the trees then shambled toward him on all fours, fangs dripping with spittle. Omari took out his hand cannon then waited. The weapon wasn't very accurate, but at close range loaded with lead shot it was effective against a mob. He took the matchstick from his teeth then grinned.

"The Cleave to you all!" he shouted.

He lit the powder as the beasts leapt at him. The powder exploded and the shot tore into their flesh, the power of the blast throwing them back into their cohorts. Omari dropped the hand cannon, charging into the pack through the smoke with sword and dagger, slaughtering the wounded and dazed beast. The smoke slowly cleared, revealing his grim work. Omari stabbed each animal a final time to make sure they were all dead before moving on.

He entered another patch of woods. According to the map, what he sought was nearby. The stench of death reached his nose as he progressed but he pressed on. Something told him that the scent would lead him to his prize.

He was right. The bush opened to a solitary tree surrounded by a pile of human remains in various stages of decomposition. Omari took a kerchief from his pouch then tied it around his mouth and nose before stepping into the pile to reach the tree. He looked about the base of the tree but saw nothing; it was when he looked above that he spotted his prize. It dandled from the lowest branch, a woven bag with a yellow and blue pattern common among the fetish bags of the sonchai he'd met during his travels. Omari was reaching for the bag when the terrible yet familiar scream broke the morbid silence. He turned to see the Frog Hag scrambling toward him faster that was humanly possible, her arms raised as blue light danced between her fingers.

"You have failed!" she screamed. "I will send your burning body back to that Matamba bitch!"

Omari snatched the fetish bag down then ran. The light between the Frog Hag's fingers coalesced into a broad beam then streaked from her hands, striking Omari in the back. His cries of pain mingled with the Frog Hag's cries of glee as the power consumed him. But a strange thing occurred. Through the unbearable pain Omari sensed the healing powers of his ngisimaugi. The energy grew stronger and stronger eventually matching that of the Frog Hag's attack. He was enveloped by a sphere of competing forces, his senses paralyzed, his body suspended mid-air by the battling forces. The Frog Hag's malevolent energy finally conceded. Omari fell, landing on a hard surface. As the ngisimaugi mended his skin, Omari heard cries of shock. Someone moved him, rolling him onto his back.

"Is it him?" a woman asked.

"Yes!" another woman replied.

"How did he get here?"

"It's like the last one. The Frog Hag sent him. But this one is alive!"

"Does he have it?"

There was a pause.

"Yes! Yes! He has the fetish bag!"

Omari's ears filled with ululations and words of praise. A familiar voice whispered in his ear.

"Can you hear me, Omari?"

It was Izegbe. Omari grinned as he regained his full strength. He sat up suddenly, wrapping his arms around her then kissing her full on the mouth. She struggled for a moment then gave in, kissing him like she did numerous times during the night. When they let each other go, they were both smiling.

"You have done well," Mikijen."

Omari turned to see the Ngola sitting upon her throne, flanked by her guards. The monarch smirked while her guards glared at Izegbe.

"It seems not only have you retrieved our fetish bag, but you have also added to our ranks."

Omari looked at Izegbe and she looked away.

Omari stood. The Frog Hag's attack had burned most of his clothes away. He was healed yet still needed rest. Never had he seen the ngisimaugi protect him as it did. He shouldn't be alive, yet he stood half naked before the Ngola and her audience.

"You have done what was demanded," the Ngola said. "For that I grant you your life and your freedom. What you have brought back is something most sacred to us. What more to you wish, Omari Ket? Ask and if it is within my power, I will grant it to you."

Omari grinned then turned toward Izegbe. The warrior's eyes went wide.

"No! No!" she said. Her sisters howled in anger then advanced on Omari, their spears lowered. The Ngola raised her hand and they halted. Omari walked up to Izegbe, standing so close their noses almost touched.

"Do not do this," Izegbe pleaded. "Do not make me a slave."

Omari smiled.

"Great Ngola," he said. "I want two baskets of cowries, three bags of gold dust and...one riding nyati."

He winked at Izegbe before turning away and approaching the Ngola.

"I would have never let you have her," she said.

"I know. But it was worth it just to see her reaction."

"You are an annoying man, Omari Ket," the Ngola said. "I hope your daughter is different."

Omari glanced at Izegbe. "She will take after her mother; beautiful and fearless. Of that I have no doubt. If Eda's allows, I will see her one day."

"If you return to Matamba you will be killed," the Ngola said. "Goodbye, Omari Ket."

"Goodbye, Ngola,"

The rewards and the nyati were waiting for Omari when he exited the palace. So was Izegbe. She watched in silence as he secured the cowry baskets to the bull. Omari mounted the bull then smiled at Izegbe.

"Where will you go?" she asked.

"I'm not sure," Omari replied. "Wherever it is, I'll be more careful about who I gamble with."

"You are not as bad as most men," Izegbe said. "Maybe you should find a wife."

"I already have," Omari teased. For the first time since he'd met her Izegbe smiled.

"Goodbye, warrior," she said. "May Daarila walk with you."

"Goodbye Izegbe," Omari said. "Tell our daughter about me."

"I will," Izegbe said. "I will."

Omari reigned the bull then set off down the road leading away from Matamba.

ASSASSIN'S CHOICE

The city of Berima lay on the natural boundary between the grasslands and forests of southern Haiset. It was a region of large farms and thriving plantations, the foundation of the incomes of those who lived there. Many Haisetti and others came to the city seeking honest work. Many, but not all.

Omari spun to face the three robbers that trailed him into the inn. He thought the owners would protect him, but they did not want any part of what was about to happen. They disappeared into the back of the establishment while the customers looked away. Apparently, the ruffians were well known and no one wished to be on their bad side. Omari was a stranger that was too loose with his money. No one cared if he lived or died.

The men attacked in unison, their swords drawn. To their surprise Omari spun then ran at them. At the last moment he fell lengthwise to the floor and rolled. The men tripped over him, falling to the stone floor. Omari was on his feet before they could recover, chopping all three men with his sword on the base of their necks, killing them instantly. He crouched, looking for more attackers, his eyes meeting those of the stunned inn patrons. Satisfied that he was safe, Omari searched the dead men for valuables. Apparently, it had been a slow day for their pockets and pouches were empty save for a few cowries. Their swords might be worth something, so he took them then sat at the nearest table. Two inn workers dragged the bodies outside. A nervous woman came to his table.

"What will you have? she asked.

"Beer," Omari replied. "And a bowl of sorghum if you have it."

The woman seemed to want to ask him another question but thought better of it. Omari reached into his pocket. He was running low of money and his prospects for employment were few. Haiset was a rural land with few people needing his skills. At least he was in Berima. The region held a number of prosperous farms with owners wealthy enough and hated enough to need protection. The fight might be a good omen, he mused. Word would spread how he handled the thieves and would probably result in an offer. He would take any that came, for he needed the cowries.

The woman returned with the bowl of beer and a smaller bowl of sorghum. She placed down the items then lingered at the table.

"What is it?" Omari asked.

"My...my master would like to know how you were paying?"

Omari gave the woman one of the swords.

"He can sell this. I'm sure it will suffice."

"Thank you, bwa," the woman said. She took the sword then hurried away.

Omari wasn't sure if it would cover the meal, but he was sure that the servant and the owner were too afraid to argue with him. The beer was weak and the sorghum was adequate. He finished the meal then left the building, searching for a safe place to sleep for the night. He was inspecting an alleyway between two family compounds when he heard someone approaching him from behind.

"Stranger?" the person said.

Omari turned to see a short man dressed in a red robe that fell to his knees. His head was shaven on one side, indicating that he was a messenger.

"What do you want?" Omari asked.

"I have been sent by Bwa Danjuma to invite you to his home. He has business he would like to discuss with you."

Omari smiled. "If you don't mind, I was about to sleep for the night. I will meet with Bwa Danjuma in the morning."

"The bwa has authorized me to offer you shelter for the night," the messenger said. "I know whatever the bwa has will be more comfortable than your current arrangement." The servant peered over Omari's shoulder into the alley.

Omari grinned. "Lead the way."

He followed the messenger through Berima to an impressive compound resting on the top of a hill overlooking the city. The base of the hill was surrounded by fields of sorghum, yams and fruit trees. They trailed a winding road to the crest of the hill, entering through an elaborately carved gate. Omari recognized the design. The gates had been created by Oyo craftsmen, a sign of the bwa's wealth. The cost to have them carved then transported such a distance was substantial. The messenger led him into the home and to a room within the veranda. As the messenger promised, it was a much better arrangement. The modest space contained a small bed with a worn head rest. There was a nightstand at the head of the bed and a chest at the foot. A wax candle, pitcher of water, wash cloth and black soap rested on the nightstand.

"Excuse me while I announce your arrival to my bwa," the servant said. He scampered away, entering the bwa's house. Omari inspected the room while he was away, testing the bed and looking about for any valuables that might have been left by the previous occupant. His inspection was interrupted by the return of the servant.

"Since you have accepted the bwa's hospitality, he has decided to delay your meeting until the morning. He wishes you a good night."

Omari nodded. "I wish him the same."

Omari dropped his gear then stretched out on the bed. The bwa most likely heard about his fight in the tavern and wanted to make use of his skills. If all went as planned, this room would be his home for the foreseeable future. He'd stay long enough to earn enough to travel to Mali where he was sure to find more work. Fez and Mali were always at odds, which meant constant employment for a skilled mercenary. Omari washed up with the pitcher of water on his nightstand then settled in for the night.

The morning came too soon. Omari woke groggy and sore. He was massaging his shoulders when a servant entered his room. The woman wore a white tunic with a thick beaded necklace that matched the beads adorning her braided hair. She shared a pleasant smile with Omari."

"The bwa has requested your company for breakfast. He will meet you on the veranda."

Omari nodded then waved the woman away. He dressed then proceeded to the veranda, leaving his weapons behind. Bwa Danjuma sat at the table, his hands pressed together in morning supplication. Omari waited until the bwa finished before clearing his throat. Baw Danjuma looked up and smiled through his voluminous beard. He stood; the man was a head taller than Omari and just as wide. He wore an emerald silk robe that covered his strong shoulders and hung loose about his body.

"Welcome, Omari Ket," he said with a deep voice. "Please, join me."

Omari took a seat at the table. Servants swooped in as if perched nearby, filling the table with plates piled with savory meats and delicate pastries. Omari could barely recalled sitting before such a feast.

"I think you were expecting more dignified guests," Omari said.

"Not at all," Danjuma said. "As you can see, I am not a small man, nor is there anything small about what I do. Your presence will prevent me from overindulging. Please, eat."

Omari obliged, trying to pace himself but failing. Everything was delicious; even the water seemed to be better than water should be.

"So, Omari, how did a man such as you find himself in our humble city?"

"What do you mean by 'a man such as me?'"

"I heard about your exploits in the inn. It's obvious you're no ordinary loiterer."

"I wish there was a good answer," Omari said. "I go wherever there is an opportunity."

"Then you must be lost," Danjuma said.

"I wouldn't say that," Omari replied. "I am sitting before you."

"A most fortuitous circumstance. If not for your altercation at the inn you would be sleeping in the alley."

"Eda blesses," Omari said, his mouth stuffed with pastries.

"Let's get down to business. You seem to be a man that is good with weapons."

"I am," Omari replied. "Who do you need protection from?"

Danjuma took his time eating a pastry before answering.

"I don't need more bodyguards," Danjuma replied. "I need a special talent for a special task."

Omari drank the last of his water, wiping his mouth with his sleeve.

"What do you require?"

"I need you to kill a man," Danjuma said.

Omari placed down his cup.

"You have the wrong person," he said. "I'm no assassin."

"You just killed three men," Danjuma said.

"I was protecting myself," Omari replied.

"And I'm sure you killed many more during your time as a Mikijen . . . for pay."

Danjuma glanced at the tendril of his tattoo than ran to his wrist. Omari started to object, but Danjuma had a point.

"That was my work," he said. "I have never hunted down a person to kill them."

"This is more difficult than I expected," Danjuma said. "Let's get to the core of the matter. I will pay you one thousand miquils of gold; five hundred up front, the rest when you return with the man's head."

Omari picked up a piece of bread and chewed it slowly to hide his shock. One thousand miquils! With that much gold he could return to Sati-Baa and buy his safety.

"Who is this man you want killed so badly?" Omari asked.

"Yohance!" Danjuma shouted.

The servant that brought him to Danjuma's compound appeared with a rolled-up parchment. Danjuma nodded toward Omari and Yohance handed him the parchment. Omari unrolled the document revealing the sketch of a man's face. There was nothing that stood out about him, except a small scar over his left eye.

"Who is he?" Omari asked.

"Atika Sanusi," Danjuma said.

"What did he do to warrant such a high price for his death?"

"Does it matter?" Danjuma said.

"It does if you want me to consider your offer," Omari replied.

Danjuma sighed. "He stole from me."

"And for that he must die?"

Danjuma jumped to his feet.

"He stole my daughter!"

Danjuma shook with rage, veins popping in his neck as he gripped the sides of the table. Omari watched as he regained control of his emotions then sat.

"I'm sorry. It has been five years since I've seen Samira. In truth I'm not sure if she's still alive."

"How did this Atika end up with your daughter?"

"Atika came to me as a slave," Danjuma said. "He was a good worker and a loyal man, or so I thought. I allowed him into my home and around my family. That was my mistake. Unbeknownst to me Atika had taken a liking to Samira, and she to him."

Danjuma stopped to take a drink of water.

"When I discovered what had occurred, I reacted immediately. Atika was chained and beaten. I contacted the local slave merchant to arrange for his sale. Two days after his beating he was gone, as was my daughter."

"Are you sure she did not leave on her own accord?" Omari asked.

"You ask insulting questions, Omari Ket," Danjuma said. "Of course, she did not leave on her own. Even if she did, it would be unacceptable. My daughter must come home if she is alive and Atika must die."

"Do know where he might have gone?" Omari asked.

"I sent men in every direction," Danjuma replied. "None could find them. It was if they rode away on an impundulu's back."

Omari worried his chin. This land was unfamiliar to him, and if people who lived there all their lives could not find the errant slave and the slave master's daughter his prospects weren't much better. Danjuma had to be desperate to ask him.

"I accept," Omari said. "I'll stay here a few days to get my bearings then I'll set out. How long do I have?"

"As long as it takes," Danjuma said. "I will cover your expenses. Send a runner when you are in need and I will supply it."

This deal was getting better every second, Omari thought.

"Just give me my payment and I'll begin," Omari said.

"Yohance!"

The servant appeared once again. He carried a bag which he handed to Omari. The weight alone told him what he needed to know; he opened the bag and grinned at the pile of miquils inside. Omari counted them out to confirm. Satisfied, he closed the bag then stood.

"The next time I see you I will have the head of Atika Sanusi," Omari said. "This I promise."

"I hope so," Danjuma said.

Omari left Danjuma's house, bouncing on the balls of his feet. This was his best payment in months. He would look for this Atika for a few weeks. If he did not find him he would be on his way. Five hundred miquils was more than enough for his needs. He could care less if Danjuma never saw his daughter or Atika again.

Omari went back to the inn. The owner scowled as he entered.

"I will not serve you!" she shouted.

"You don't have to," Omari replied. "I came here to ask a few questions."

He reached into his bag and took out a gold piece. He tossed it on the counter. The innkeeper's eyes went wide as she scooped the nugget into her hands.

"What do you wish to ask?" the innkeeper said, never taking her eyes off the nugget.

"Where do I find the slave merchant?"

"He lives on the east side of the village. It is easy to find, it's the only large house in the district. That and the smell."

Omari nodded then set out for the eastern district.

The slave merchant's compound was easy to locate as the innkeeper had said. The stench of human captives was overwhelming, so much so that Omari was forced to cover his nose and mouth as he neared. He hoped he could meet the merchant without seeing his hapless captives. Although he knew that slavery was a reality of Ki Khanga, he despised it. He knocked on the compound gate. The sound of the gate being unlatched was followed by the squeaking of its hinges as it opened. A bald man with ragged teeth wearing dingy clothes stuck his head through the gap and glared at Omari.

"What do you want?" he asked.

"I'm looking for the master merchant."

The man maneuvered his head to look behind Omari.

"Where is your wagon?" the man asked.

"I'm not here seeking slaves," Omari replied. "I'm . . . "

"Then go away!" the man said. "We're a business establishment. We have no time for empty banter!"

The man was about to close the gate when Omari grabbed the beads around his neck then dragged him through the gap. The man squealed like a trapped wart-hog.

Omari slammed the gate against the man's head, knocking him silent.

"I'm here to see your master and you will take me to him, understand?"

The man shook his head clear. Terror twisted his face as he recognized Omari.

"Help me! Help me!"

Omari heard the clatter of men with weapons approaching the gate. He shoved the gatekeeper to the ground then extracted his weapons. This assignment had barely begun and he was already in trouble. He thought of returning the miquils to Danjuma, but he couldn't imagine giving up such a large sum. So, he waiting for the attackers to come through the gate. When they did, he had to fight to keep from laughing. The gatekeeper's rescuers were a collection of elders carrying rusted swords and spears. They burst through the gate then stopped abruptly upon seeing Omari. They looked at the gatekeeper sprawled on the ground with a growing lump on his head then back to Omari.

"We don't have to do this," Omari said. "All I want is to meet with your master. Your friend decided to be difficult. Look where it got him. But at least he's still alive. I can't promise the same for you."

The rescuers looked among themselves, waiting for someone to speak for them. Finally, the youngest of them stepped forward, his spear shaking in his quivering hands.

"What do you want with our master?" the man asked.

"I'm looking for someone, an escaped slave. I think your master can assist me."

"Come with us," the man said.

"No!" the gatekeeper said. He sat up, rubbing the knot on his head. "You must protect the compound!"

The man glared at the gatekeeper.

"We are," he said. "We are taking this man to Bwa Tippo before he kills all of us."

The men formed a sorry escort as they led him into the compound. To his dismay Omari walked between pens of captive humans. Their conditions were deplorable. The fact that there were so many meant business was not going well for Bwa Tippo. They crossed the compound then entered the veranda. Bwa Tippo was working in his garden, gathering fruit from his pomegranate trees.

"Bwa Tippo?" the man said.

"Did you kill the intruder?" Bwa Tippo asked without turning around.

"No, bwa," the man replied.

"Well did you at least capture him? He might sell well in Watandu."

"No bwa," the man said. "He is standing here with us."

Bwa Tippo back straightened, the fruit falling from his hands. He turned about slowly to see Omari standing before him.

"Ahhh!"

Tippo dropped to his knees.

"Please do not kill me, Mikijen!" he pleaded. "I will give you all that I have!"

"I'm not going to kill you," Omari finally said.

Bwa Tippo jumped to his feet, a relieved grin on his face.

"Them maybe you'll consider working for me," he said.

"A bit too late for that," Omari replied. "I've been employed by Bwa Danjuma."

"Curse that man to the Cleave!" Tippo said. "He is the spawn of Daarila if ever there was one!"

Omari wasn't interested in what Tippo thought of Danjuma.

"I have a question for you. If a slave were to escape, where would they run?"

Tippo shrugged. "It depends. Many think they can hide in the nearby cities, but I always find them. Others will try to run to Sati-Baa. It's a better chance they could hide there, but it is very far. But now many go to Kenja."

"Why?" Obaseki asked. "Isn't that where many are captured?"

"It used to be until that witch Nubia appeared," Tippo said. "She and her damned militia have made business most difficult."

This was going to be harder than he imagined. The thought of taking the 500 miquils and heading south crossed his mind again. But if he was heading south he might as well take a look in Kenja.

"Is there any place in particular an escaped slave in Kenja would go?"

"Bashada," Tippo asked.

Omari knew Bashada well. It was a Kiswala city with a bad reputation. He normally would steer clear, but not only would anyone most likely not recognize him there, if they did, they wouldn't care.

"Thank you for your time," Omari said. He walked away.

"Wait!" Tippo shouted. "A journey as arduous as the one you are about to take would be much easier with servants. I happen to have a few that would be most helpful to you."

"No thanks," Omari said. "I'll manage."

"You'll think differently if you run into Nubia."

Omari smirked. "I'll take my chances."

Omari was relieved to be away from the slave compound. He returned to the inn, renting a room for the night. He made sure to secure his door well; the owner had more than one reason to kill him in his sleep and rob him. His sleep was restful despite the threat.

Omari woke the next morning, paid the innkeeper then went to the local stable and purchased a decent horse before setting out for Kenja. He stopped in a small village just outside the borderlands to replenish his supplies then crossed into the country known for its verdant farmland and vulnerable people. He followed the main road to the first village he encountered. As he rode past the first farm, the farmers immediately ceased their labors and ran toward their compound. Omari chuckled; they probably thought he was some slaver. Soon afterwards he heard the clanging of a bell and his mood changed. He knew when a warning was being sounded, which meant warriors would appear soon afterwards. Omari reined his horse about and galloped away until he reached thick brush. He dismounted then ran into the bush. The horse was on its own; it was too big and too noisome to hide.

Omari pushed as deep as he could into the bush. His pursuers appeared moments later armed with spears and swords.

"There's his horse!" a man shouted.

"He must be in the bush," another answered.

Omari watched the men approach the bush and his hands tightened on his swords. The man who was the leader stopped them.

"No," he said. "We will wait for Nubia."

"We don't need her," one of the others said. "She has trained us. We know what to do."

"Still, we will wait for her," the leader said. "There's no reason to risk our lives when she is nearby."

Omari had no idea of Nubia's skills, but he was not about to wait to find out. The horse had not strayed far; if he could fight his way through the warriors he could ride away before Nubia arrived. He crept to the forest edge then burst from hiding, swords drawn. He bowled over the man before him with his shoulder, stabbing him as he slammed into him. By the time the others recovered he was halfway to his horse. A spear struck the ground beside him as he reached the horse; he jumped up and landed on the horse's back. The startled animal

snorted then ran before he was secured in the saddle.
Omari clambered around the horse as throwing spears
whizzed by. He finally settled onto the horse then dug
his heels into its sides to speed its escape. Something
hissed by his ear; he turned to see a woman holding a
long bow taking aim at him.

"Shit!"

Omari kept his eyes on her, hoping his timing
would be precise. The woman released the arrow and
Omari dipped. The projectile streaked over his torso. He
decided at that point that if the man he was seeking hid
in Kenja, he would remain hidden. Just then his horse
lurched and Omari flew over its head. He twisted about
in an attempt to roll but slammed against the ground,
losing his breath. He lay on his back for a moment, gasping for air then struggled to his feet. The horse lay on its
side, an arrow protruding from its body. The woman
rode toward him, followed by other riders. Omari took
out his swords, having no time to load his hand cannon.
By the time they reached him he had regained his
breath. He dodged the woman's attempt to run him
through with her spear then grabbed the bridle of the
horse of the man closest to him. He jumped onto the
beast's back, unseating the rider at the same time. As he
turned the woman was coming for him, her sword
drawn. They clashed and Omari was immediately impressed. The swing of his sword arm was known to dis-
arm most men or at least unnerve them; this woman
deftly deflected his blow then stabbed at his face. They
battled as their horses circled, each seeking an advantage but finding none. Exhaustion claimed them both
and they disengaged. The other riders charged Omari,
their lances drawn. He was a dead man; he didn't have
the energy to fight them off.

"Stop," the woman ordered.

The men pulled up short, their spears only inches away from Omari's body. She maneuvered her horse close to him before speaking.

"You are no slaver," she said. "If you were, you would have been dead by now."

"No, I'm not," Omari replied.

"Then who are you, and why are you in Kenja?"

"I am Omari Ket," he said. "And I've come seeking a friend."

"Was your friend a slave?" Nubia asked.

"Yes, as I was," Omari lied.

"Then you are both free,' Nubia said. "There are no slaves in Kenja, and those who come to enslave end up food for the fisi."

"You are Nubia?"

The woman nodded.

"Then maybe you have seen him."

Omari gave Nubia the drawing. She took it and studied it before passing it to her men.

"I do not recognize him. Why would you have a drawing of him?"

"We were very close," Omari replied.

Nubia's eyes narrowed. She was about to speak when one of her warriors interrupted.

"I know him," the man said. "His name is Atika. He was here but left a few months ago."

Omari smiled with mock joy.

"It's good to know he is still safe," Omari said.

"He was travelling with a woman. She was not his wife, but they loved each other. Her name was Samira."

"Why did they leave?" Omari asked as if he cared. "They were safe here."

"Men came from Haiset hunting them," the man said. "We killed them, but Atika was still afraid. He and Samira left."

"Do you know where they went?" Omari asked.

"To the coast." the man answered.

"Thank you so much," Omari said. He looked at Nubia.

"I must go to him," Omari said. "I know the person that seeks him. It is his former master. Samira is his former master's daughter."

Nubia's skeptical countenance faded.

"You are skilled with weapons," she said. "Why?"

"I was my master's bodyguard," Omari said. "He had me trained to fight, but my skills surpassed those of my trainers. When I heard Atika had escaped I vowed to follow him. I killed my trainers and escaped. I'm sure they will come after me, just like they came after Atika."

"They will find nothing but death here," Nubia said. "Just like the others."

Nubia sheathed her sword.

"Go find your friends, Omari Ket. May the ancestors grant you a safe and successful journey."

Omari bowed. "Thank you, mama."

He bowed to the others before setting off down the road. It was a close situation, but he survived. He would walk to the next village and steal a horse if there was one available. He considered abandoning the hunt again. He shook the pouch with his payment; it was more than enough. But he was intrigued. Atika had fled south, to Bashaba most likely. It would be easy to hide there, or catch a dhow to another country. Bashada possessed a Mikijen outpost, which might cause Omari some issues if he entered but he would deal with that once he arrived. He would follow Atika to the port city, asking question along the way.

At the third village Omari finally came across a horse worth stealing. The draft horse was big, making mounting it difficult. Luckily for Omari it wasn't particular about who rode its back, so he was able to ride away with little fanfare. He was well away from the farm before daylight.

Six days of travel brought him to the outskirts of Bashada. Omari needed to ask questions, so he went into his pack for his old Mikijen uniform. It was wrinkled and fitted tight in some places, but it would work against those who didn't stare too long. He would have to make sure to avoid any other Mikijen. Some would notice his old uniform and most likely question him which would lead to someone getting killed. Omari was sure that someone wouldn't be him.

He rode through the tea plantations on the outskirts of the merchant city. So far, he drew no attention; the people he encountered either preoccupied with tending their fields or struggling with the whims the marketplace. He was relieved when he reached the city. Despite its size a person that wanted to be invisible could get their wish in Bashada. What Omari hoped Atika hadn't done was catch a dhow out of the city. There was no way he could find the man and his bride if he had done so. He decided he would check the plantations along the way before going into the city, just in case the two decided to seek work in the fields.

Omari ambled up the road of the first plantation toward the main compound. He couldn't tell if the workers were hired or slaves, for their clothing was poor yet not ragged. A few of the workers glanced at him, but most paid him no mind. He was halfway up the road when he spotted commotion at his destination. A group of men emerged from the compound. The man in the center walked briskly, followed by three others with spears and swords. Omari sighed; he wasn't in the mood for a fight. The man in the center began shouting.

"What are you doing here? I paid the other man!"

So the Mikijen are earning extra income, Omari thought.

"I' m not here for cowries,' Omari shouted back. "I'm looking for someone."

Omari and the shouter stood face to face.

"And why should I help you?"

"My friend will be back if you don't."

The man spat at Omari's feet and Omari punched him in the face. He grabbed his mouth as he staggered back then fell on his ass. He glared at his bodyguards and the two stood still with fear in their eyes. The man struggled to his feet, holding his hand over his bleeding mouth.

"I'm going to remember you," he said. "I'll remember you all when Raheed returns!"

Omari snatched out his dagger then pressed it against the man's throat.

"Never threaten a man unless you have good protection," Omari said. "Now, have you seen this man?"

Omari handed him the drawing.

The man looked at it then grimaced.

"What did he do to cause so much trouble?"

"What are you talking about?"

"You are the third man to come looking for him."

Omari lowered his knife. "Third?"

"Yes. The first man took the woman. That's when I told him he had to go. Then the second man came looking for him. I told him the same thing I'm telling you. I don't know where he is and I don't care."

"Did he go to the city?"

"Maybe. I don't know. As long as he was away from me."

Omari sheathed his knife.

"How much did you pay the other Mikijen?"

"You should know."

Omari took out his knife again.

"How much?"

"One hundred cowries."

Omari held out his hand.

"I'll need twenty more."

The owner reached into his bag and took out a leather pouch. He threw it at Omari.

"Now leave my property!" he shouted.

Omari nodded as he turned and walked away. He opened the pouch, counted forty cowries then smiled. It enough to get him good lodging for the night and a decent meal without dipping into his own. He decided to take advantage of the other planters, stopping by their farms and demanding information on Atika. By the time he was done he collected one hundred and twenty cowries. Added to what he received from Danjuma he had no reason to find Atika. But his curiosity was piqued. He would find the man then decide if he would kill him.

Bashada had changed little since his last visit so it was easy for him to find the hostels. He paid for a good room and a good meal and received both immediately. The hostel owner offered to find him someone that would share his bed for the night; Omari was briefly interested but declined. He took off his Mikijen uniform and was naked when the chambermaid arrived with his bath water, accompanied by two burly men who carried the ceramic tub filled with steaming water. The three offered to bath him but Omari waved them away. Despite days on the road he wanted to be alone. The bath was soothing and refreshing. Too awake to sleep, he donned less conspicuous clothes then strolled about the city, working his way toward the landing beach. If Atika had been refused employment on the plantations, he would most likely seek work with the merchants. The monsoons were blowing west, which meant there were many dhows arriving at Bashada and many laborers needed to unload them. He wandered to the area where the food kiosks were set up then waited, Atika's image in his hands. The break bell rang not long afterwards and the workers walked in single file to the food vendors. Omari studied them as they came, comparing faces to the one in his hand. A half an hour had passed when he saw a lanky man saunter into view, a weary look on his face. Omari looked at the drawing then smiled.

"Atika," he whispered.

He watched the man purchase bread and stew then retreat to a wall on the opposite side of the beach. He ate alone, which meant he hadn't been working long enough to make friends. By the look on his face Omari guessed he wouldn't make many. The man was miserable; killing him might end up being a kindness. Whatever he decided to do, it wouldn't be at the dock beaches. He doubted anyone would miss him, but murder was murder, and the local constables would investigate.

"Are you going to buy something?"

Omari turned to look into the face of a nearby food merchant. The woman squinted at him, her hands on her narrow hips.

"No," Omari replied.

"Then move along! You're scaring away my business."

Omari grinned then ambled away, keeping his eyes on Atika. He knew where the man was; now it was about being patient. He returned to the city and the market place. There he bought a finely made chest with sturdy locks, a box large enough to hold a man's head. He had no intentions of bringing back the man alive then killing him before Danjuma; a head and some object the planter would recognize would be enough. After haggling with the merchant for the box he went to the herbalist for herbs that would preserve the flesh. He would probably have to smoke the head to keep it from decaying quickly. He didn't look forward to doing so, but it was necessary.

Omari found a merchant selling coffee. He bought a cup then took a seat by the cart. After a second cup, he returned to his hostel, burning away the rest of the day by playing oware with the locals. He wasn't good, but he wasn't bad either, which made for a few good games.

The shadow of dusk crept into the hostel, letting Omari know it was almost time. He went to his room to gather his weapons then came down and paid the hostel owner. He had changed into his Mikijen uniform. He worked his way to the landing beach just as the workers were returning to the city. It didn't take Omari long to spot Atika. He worked his way toward the man, the others clearing the way when seeing his uniform. Atika was oblivious to the commotion. He trudged toward the barracks where most workers slept, oblivious to Omari's approach. Omari reached the man. He grabbed him by the shoulders then spun him about.

"You're coming with me," he said.

Atika said nothing. He turned with his hands behind his back. Omari tied them together then led him away. They walked until they reached the outskirts of the city. When they stopped, Atika dropped to his knees.

"Finish it," he said.

Omari was caught off guard.

"Why do you think…"

"Because a real Mikijen would have told me why I was being arrested and then taken me to their compound. So finish it."

Omari lifted the man's face as he drew his sword.

"Why shouldn't I," he asked.

"You were paid to kill me," Atika said. "If you are an honest man, you will do it. Danjuma wants me dead, just like his daughter."

Danjuma's daughter was dead? This was news to Omari.

"Did you kill her?" Omari asked. If he did, it would make his task easier.

"No," Atika said. "The second man Danjuma sent did. Danjuma said she was ruined, that no worthy man would be willing to offer a decent loloba for her now since I had soiled her. He said she was better off dead. That's why we ran away. No matter what he thought, she was my queen. I would have never harmed her."

"And you just let him do it?" Omari asked.

"He Danjuma changed his mind about his daughter. He was sent to take her home, nothing more," Atika said. "She didn't want to go, but I insisted. Our life was too hard. After a few days I changed my mind. I went after them, vowing to fight for her. I found her body on the side of the road, not far from Bashada. He killed her and left her like she was nothing."

Tears ran down Atika's cheeks. Omari stood over the man, speechless. A man that would kill his own daughter . . .

Atika wiped the tears away then glared at Omari. "What are you waiting for, assassin? Do it! I'm tired of running. Get it over with. This is the only way I can be with Samira in peace."

Omari took out his sword, then raised it over his head.

* * *

The pounding on his bedroom door dragged Danjuma from a sound sleep. He sat up in his bed then rubbed his eyes.

"What is it, Yohance?"

The banging continued. Danjuma grabbed his robe from the bedside then tied it around his naked body. By the time he reached the door he was angry. He grabbed the golden handles then snatched the doors open.

"Yohance! What . . ."

Danjuma stared into the smirking face of Omari Ket.

"What . . . What are you doing in my house?"

Omari strolled by the man, a square box under his arm. Danjuma's anger seeped away as he imagined what the box held. He placed the box on Danjuma's bed.

"You did it," he said. "You killed Atika!"

"I believe you owe me a few miquils," Omari said.

"Yes! Of course!"

Danjuma would not normally open his safe in front of strangers, but his elation affected his reason. He pushed aside the secret wall then quickly unlocked the safe. He took out the miquils then closed the safe, hoping the assassin did not notice the combination. He shuffled to Omari.

"Here," he said as he tossed him the bag. "Now let me see his head."

Omari opened the box. Danjuma was about to cry out in joy until he recognized the head as Yohance's. He stumbled away in shock.

"What have you done? What have you done?!?"

Omari took his pay then sauntered toward the door.

"Your servant was difficult," Omari said.

"Give me my money back!" Danjuma shouted. "You did not fulfill our agreement!"

Omari turned and smiled.

"Actually, I did."

Danjuma was about to charge toward Omari when another man entered the room. Danjuma stopped in his tracks as his blood went cold.

"Atika!"

Atika stood before him, hate twisting his face. He held a sword in his right hand.

"You killed her because she loved me!" Atika said.

Omari grinned.

"See? I brought you his head. And the rest of him, too."

Omari left the room, closing the doors behind him.

OLD HABITS

(ORIGINALLY PUBLISHED IN GRIOTS: SISTERS OF THE SPEAR)

Kadira tucked her braids under her head wrap for the fifth time, holding back a vile curse. The vendor before the poultry cart waited patiently, for he was used to the worries women suffered with their fashions. Kadira, however, was annoyed beyond concentration. She was tempted to tear off her head wrap and shave herself bald on the spot. She should have never let Nguvu talk her into this silly hair style. She was a warrior, not a trollop.

"What can I do for you, sister?" the vendor asked.

Kadira placed her hand on her wide hips as she concentrated on the various types of edible birds hanging from the wagon. If there was one thing about the Sati-Baa market it was food was never in short supply. The farmers of Kenja kept it well stocked, especially since their new formed militia succeeded in deterring the once frequent slave raids from Haiset. The rumor was that a female priest organized the militia, a woman trained by the

Dogon to heal and to fight. A rivulet of adrenaline coursed through her sword arm and she bit her lip. Those days were done. She was a wife and a mother now. Best she concentrate on the job at hand, which was buying food for her huge, greedy husband and their growing greedy child.

"I can't believe what I'm seeing!"

Kadira grinned then turned. Omari Ket stood with his arms folded across his chest, his head tilted. He was draped in armor and weapons that told of journeys throughout Ki Khanga, an outfit appropriate for a journeyman mercenary. Kadira struck a similar pose.

"Believe it, Snake," she answered.

Omari held his arms open and she hugged him. She smiled until one of his hands found her backside. A quick jab to the stomach sent him stumbling backward.

"None of that," she said. "I'm a married woman now."

"Two shocks in one day!" Omari exclaimed.

Omari assumed his skeptical stance again. "Who's the lucky man?"

"Nguvu."

Omari's face twisted. "I don't know him."

"You shouldn't. I met him long after you and I parted ways."

A wistful look came to Omari's face and Kadira felt embarrassed.

"So what brings you to Sati-Baa?"

"Money, what else?" Omari replied. "I thought that's why you were here."

"Sati-Baa is home now," Kadira said. "Nguvu and I have given up the road. Nguvu is a mhunzi. We make tools and sometimes weapons. We also have a child."

Omari slapped his forehead. "Okay, I understand now. I'm dreaming. No, I'm having a nightmare. Excuse me while I go wake up and find the real Kadira."

Kadira laughed out loud. "You always made me laugh, Omari." She reached out and touched his hair. It was straight like a horse's tail.

"What happen to your hair? It looks like a horse's ass."

Omari slapped her hand away. "I spent some time in Fez. Most of the men there are wearing their hair like this now, and the women seem to like it. You know how I am about pleasing women."

Kadira ignored his words. "Well, it was good seeing you, Omari. Don't get killed."

She turned to leave but Omari grabbed her arm. A pleasant tingle raced from his touch to her chest and she smiled before she realized it.

"Aren't you at least a little interested in why I am here?"

Kadira hesitated. Of course she was interested. The reality was she was terribly bored, despite her feelings for Nguvu and their child. She reluctantly faced Omari.

"Okay, why are you here?"

"A Menu-Kash priest put out a call for all those skilled in weapons to accompany him on a journey to Wadantu. He's willing to pay eighty stacks each . . . if we return."

Kadira's eyes went wide. "Eighty stacks?"

Omari grinned. "Eighty."

She shrugged. "For that much I'm sure mercenaries are falling over themselves."

"True, but none of them have your skills or experience."

"This priest does not need me."

"I need you," Omari admitted. "You're the best archer in Ki Khanga besides that Dogon witch in Kenja and a better sword arm than anyone I know. You would also be the only person I know, and I need someone I can trust."

"Any other reasons?"

"I did have a few others, but they've been dashed to pieces by your news of husbands and babies," Omari admitted.

"Eighty stacks is life changing money, but I have to decline. Besides, Nguvu wouldn't hear of it."

Omari looked shocked. "Since when did Kadira let a man stop her from doing what she wished?"

Kadira pointed out two plump chickens to the poultry seller and he quickly cut them down.

"Since Kadira became a married woman," she answered. "And it's not him stopping me. This is my decision."

Omari shrugged. "I'll be at the Simbala hostel if you change your mind, or if you want to revisit old times."

Kadira smirked. "You have no shame."

Omari winked. "Of course I don't."

Kadira paid for her chickens and headed home. She glanced back; Omari stood watching her, his compelling smile fanning a flame that had recently re-emerged. She was bored and restless but had done a good job keeping it in check. By the time she reached the farm, that flame was a raging fire. She was greeted by the rhythmic clanging of a familiar hammer striking a worn anvil. Kadira crept to the smithy and peered at Nguvu as he worked over a long red hot length of steel. Olea's cradle sat on the opposite side of the cramped shed.

"What took you so long?" Nguvu asked. "You know I had work to do. I had to bring Olea out into this hot shed. I'm surprised she's still asleep."

Kadira placed the groceries on the cluttered table and went to her daughter. Olea stirred as she lifted her from the crib and held her close. The babe instinctively nuzzled her chest and Kadira began to feed her.

"I met an old friend in the market," Kadira said.

Nguvu continued flailing the hot steel. "Really? You have old friends?"

"Of course I do," Kadira replied.

"What's his name?"

"How do you . . . Omari."

Nguvu stopped hammering. "I've never heard you mention his name."

"It was a long time ago, before the war," she said.

Nguvu began hammering again. "So what is he doing in Sati-Baa?"

"A Kashite magic man is gathering mercenaries for an expedition into Wadantu. Omari is going."

Nguvu placed his hammer down, satisfied with his work. He took the steel to his brine barrel and dipped it. Steam rose from the barrel obscuring his face.

"How much he paying?"

"Eighty stacks."

Nguvu whistled. "That's a lot of stacks."

He placed the steel down on the table. Nguvu was a decent blacksmith, but it was not his true trade. He was a killer, a very good one in fact. He was also a rogue, like Kadira. She knew what ran through his mind. He sat on a metal stool he'd built himself then wiped his sweaty hands on his dingy apron. Kadira watched his massive muscles ripple across his bare upper body and grinned.

"You want to go, don't you?"

His question caught her unaware.

"Of course not!' she barked.

"Don't lie. I know you do because I want to."

Kadira looked away from Nguvu, stroking Olea's head as she continued to feed.

"We're not the people we used to be."

Nguvu stood. "Yes we are. We just have a child now."

"Exactly."

Nguvu walked to her. "I think you should go."

Kadira blinked in shock. "What?"

Nguvu folded his massive arms across his chest. "I said I think you should go."

Olea was still feeding, so fainting was not an option. "I can't go. You know that."

"We could hire a wet nurse for Olea," Nguvu said. "She's still young so she won't miss you too much. If she does, you'll have plenty of time to make things right . . .if you come back."

Kadira stepped closer to her man, raising her head to look into his eyes.

"Are you trying to trick me into staying?"

"No," Nguvu answered. "I'm giving you an opportunity to do what you want to do."

She felt the pressure ease from her nipple. Olea was drifting to sleep again so she placed her back in her cradle.

"You seem anxious to get rid of me," Kadira said. "Is there something I should know?"

Nguvu chuckled. "Now that's funny. Kadira is playing jealous."

She rushed him and punched him in the stomach. She hurt her hand, but at least she made her point.

"I would think you would be worried, especially with Omari going along as well."

Nguvu's eyebrows rose. "Should I be worried?"

Kadira massaged her sore hand. "No."

"Then I won't." He hugged her and her arms fell to her side in surrender. She'd fought all her life, confident in her skills. There was no place in Ki Khanga where she was not prepared for danger in any form, but for some strange reason Nguvu made her feel safe.

"We have survived because we trust each other," Nguvu said. "We also know how we feel. You have not been happy here. At first I thought it was because it was such a big place. But it is because you miss the road. I have never seen you this excited since we settled."

He released her.

"You can't tell me you don't feel the same?"

"I don't." Nguvu went back to his stool and sat.

"I was raised to kill," he said. "I deserted and fell in with you because you offered something more. Now that I am away from it completely I've had time to realize how terrible my life has been. This is good for me. You are good for me. But I want you to be happy."

Kadira became nervous. "It's not like I won't come back."

"So you're going?" Nguvu asked.

Kadira looked into her lover's eyes. He was sincere, she knew. But she also knew he wanted her to stay.

"Yes," she finally said. "I'm going."

Nguvu nodded thoughtfully. "Then you'll need weapons, potions and talisman."

"Do we have the money for all that?"

Nguvu smiled. "You don't, but I do, at least for the potions and talisman. We'll have to make the weapons ourselves."

"I still have my bow," Kadira said. "I will need arrows and blades."

"I'll make them," Nguvu said.

"No offense, lover, but I'll need something more dependable."

Nguvu frowned. "You haven't seen my best yet. I'll give you a stack to purchase the best, and I've give you my best. I hope you don't have the opportunity to see which is better."

Kadira couldn't hide her joy. A broad smile cut across her face as she grabbed Nguvu's hand.

"Come inside. The baby's asleep. There are other things I need to store up on before I go."

Nguvu swept her up into his arms. "I should have sent you away a long time ago."

* * *

Olea's hungry wail woke Kadira. She slid from atop Nguvu, dressed then pattered across the floor to the cradle.

"Hello, hungry girl,' she cooed. "You may have my looks, but you have your baba's appetite."

Kadira winced as Olea took to her breast. "I think it's time to put you on solid food."

The statement made her sad. If she went on this journey she wouldn't be the one to do just that. Some strange woman would be taking care of her child . . . and maybe even her man. She had no idea how long she would be gone, or, like Nguvu mentioned, if she would return. It was a sobering thought, one that added weight to her shoulders and forced her to sit. Did she really want to risk this gift?

And it was a gift. Her first pregnancy was unexpected. It was the sickness that alerted her that something was different. She told Nguvu after she was sure and he was overcome with joy. He announced they would settle down immediately, which sparked a three day argument that almost came to blows. Kadira insisted she was still healthy enough to travel but Nguvu wouldn't hear of it. The argument was ended by her increasing sickness. She became so ill she couldn't stand, let alone walk. They settled in a nearby village and Nguvu hired a house nurse to no avail. Kadira miscarried. They both grieved the loss then immediately set out to have another child, this time deliberately. When she announced she was pregnant again they moved to Sati-Baa and became 'normal' folks, as Nguvu liked to say. Now she was tired of being normal. The road's call drowned any protest she could muster. Even as she fed Olea she felt its pull. Seeing Omari was the tipping point. This hunger would not go away until she satisfied it.

"I hope you only have to miss me for a moment," she whispered to Olea. "If not, I hope you'll forgive me."

Nguvu rose from sleep as she lay Olea down. He strode naked across the room for a drink of water, leering at her over the cup as he drank. She wanted to take him to bed again, but there were things to do.

"I'm going into the city for shaft wood and feathers," she said. "I'm going to the Fez bazaar as well."

Nguvu nodded. "You always preferred their potions."

"I think I'll look at their swords, too."

Nguvu's eyes rose. "That's going to be expensive."

"I want to come back home. I'll splurge for the best."

Nguvu strode to her and slapped her butt. "I'm going to make you the best. It'll be a sword as good as me."

Kadira returned the slap. "There's no such thing of a sword that good."

An hour later she walked the wide paved avenue that bisected Sati-Baa, her destination the main market. The Fez bazaar was just beyond the local stalls, tucked down a narrow alleyway. She had stopped to buy a ripe soursop when once again a familiar voice interrupted her bargaining.

"I must be the luckiest man in the world!"

Omari came to stand beside her.

"It's destiny, Kadira. I know it is."

Kadira smirked. "Either that or you're following me."

"Sati-Baa is a big city, but it's not that big," Omari said. "Where are you headed?"

"To the Fez bazaar."

Omari smiled. "That means you're going with us! You always seek out the Fez before you go on the road."

Omari bowed. "I'll accompany you. There are a few things I could use from those sorcerers myself."

Kadira bought her fruit and they headed for the bazaar. An old feeling crept into her head and she smiled. This was good. This was very good.

The vigorous market crowd thinned as Kadira and Omari neared the Fezzan market section. The folk making their way down the street with them were not wives seeking food for the day's meal or children hunting toys and trinkets. These were folks seeking more ominous and powerful items. Kadira frowned as she ambled between stalls of talismans, gris-gris, potions, powders and other charmed items. Her visit was a necessary evil for someone who traveled the road as she had. A skilled sword and intelligence were the foundation of any mercenary, but there were some challenges beyond the physical and one had to be prepared. Fezzan charms were some of the best available at a decent price, rivaled only by those of Menu-Kash but paled in comparison to the wonders of Kamit. But Kashite items were tainted with the evil of the Cleave and Kamitic talisman were virtually impossible to find and expensive to obtain. Fezzan origins were obscure but Kadira didn't dwell on it too long. She used what worked and so far her Fezzan talisman had not failed her.

Omari looked from stall to stall, his face crinkled as if walking through a pig sty.

"I remember why I haven't been to a Fez market. These places reek with dread."

"Don't be so superstitious," Kadira said. "I remember saving you a few times with these dreadful concoctions."

"And I've never forgiven you for it," Omari retorted.

"I'll remember that," she said.

Kadira finally found what she was looking for, the Fezzan armory. Unlike the wooden stalls the armory inhabited a stone structure with an arched entrance. A sturdy metal studded wooden door guarded the entrance. Two nyanas stood at either side of the door, their swords cradled in their arms. They looked at Kadira and Omari suspiciously as they approached. Kadira reached for the door when one of the nyanas extended his hand.

"I am advised by the denfari of Sati-Baa to warn all those who choose to enter this armory that the laws of our city do not extend beyond this door. Once inside this armory you are subject to the customs of Fez. We have no jurisdiction beyond this point."

"I understand," Kadira answered. She walked past the constables then knocked on the door. She looked back; Omari remained behind.

"Are you coming?" she asked.

"I don't need any weapons," Omari answered.

"That's fine. You can wait for me here, coward," she said with a sweet smile.

Omari growled. "I hate you!" He joined her at the door.

The armory door opened to a damp, cavernous dimly lit room. Kadira strode inside, ignoring the long wooden tables stacked with hundreds of knives, swords, shields and various other implements of death. The Fezzani were no different than any other merchants, displaying their cheaper creations to distract an unsuspecting shopper. The real jewels were behind the thick wooden counter which came into view as she walked closer. As she neared a door opened behind the counter. She was temporarily blinded by a bright light escaping from the door. She shielded her eyes; when they cleared a bearded man with tan colored skin wearing a red tasseled conical hat stood behind the counter, his predatory smile bordered by a voluminous mustache and narrow beard.

"Welcome, sister," he crooned in perfect Trade Speak. "How may I serve you?"

Kadira leaned on the smooth counter top. "I'm here for a sword."

The man swept his arm before him. "As you can see we have many weapons of the finest Fezzan craftsmanship."

"I'm not interested in that junk on the table," Kadira said. "I'm interested in what you have behind this counter."

The Fezzani grinned. "I see you have dealt with us before."

It was Kadira's turn to smile. "I have."

The man nodded. "Then I will not waste either of our time."

The man reached under the counter. The sword he revealed rested in a silver scabbard, its handle decorated with creamy ivory and jewels. Kadira grasped the hilt, drawing the sword out partially. She frowned.

"Pretty, but useless," she said. "Stop playing with me, Fezzani. I came here for a real sword."

The Fezzani's eyes narrowed. He reached under the counter again. This time he walked around the counter, approaching Kadira with an object wrapped in a thick woolen blanket.

"I see you are not one to be fooled," he said. He removed the blanket, revealing a sword encased in a simple leather scabbard. He drew the sword and Kadira smiled. The sturdy steel blade emitted the slight blue glow of Fezzani nyama. Omari joined her, his arms full of weapons from the tables.

"This place is a gold mine! I found. . .ooh, what's that?"

"It's what I came for," Kadira replied. Kadira turned her attention back to the Fezzani.

"How long will it retain its nyama?"

"It depends on its use." The Fezzani lifted the blade, running his calloused hand along the flat. "Years if used only against normal blades, less if matched against a similar weapon."

"How much?"

The Fezzani's face grew cold. "A sword of this type must not be just purchased. It must be earned."

He threw the scabbard aside and attacked. Kadira dodged to the left, the blade barely missing her scalp. Omari dropped his armful of weapons and rolled into the darkness. She had her sword out and ready by the time the Fezzani took a second swipe at her but she still dodged. Her sword was not charmed yet; if it clashed with the Fezzani blade it would shatter. She reached in her bag, snatching out a small vial. Sidestepping a quick thrust, she flipped the cork from the vial then spilled the liquid in her hand. The Fezzani saw her move and pressed his attack, but Kadira's dexterity thwarted him. She managed to coat her blade just as her luck ran out. The blades met with sound of metal and the flash of magic. Kadira kicked the Fezzani in the stomach and he stumbled back. To touch a Fezzani with the sole of a shoe was the ultimate insult; the weapon master spat in anger.

"Aziz!" he shouted.

The door behind the counter swung open. Another Fezzani leaped from the blinding light, a battle ax in one hand, a shield in the other.

"This bitch has insulted me!" the Fezzani shouted. "We shall pay her with death!"

Aziz lifted his ax. A sudden booming sound echoed through the room, accompanied by a flash of light from behind Kadira. Aziz jerked up and backwards as if someone pulled him away with a rope then crashed into the wall behind the counter.

Kadira dared to look back. Omari stood with a smirk, a smoking piece of metal in his hand pointed where Aziz had been.

"Hand cannon," he said.

She jerked her head back to the Fezzani. He looked where Aziz had been, his eyes wide. Kadira rushed forward, knocking his sword free. She swept his feet and he crashed to the floor. The impact jarred him from his trance. When he looked up Kadira's sword was at his throat. Kadira took a pouch of cowries from her waist belt and tossed it beside him.

"I'll take it." She kept her sword on his throat as she picked up the Fezzani's sword and scabbard. She backed away, searching for Omari at the same time.

"Omari, where are you?"

"Here!" she heard him say. He peeked from behind the counter then emerged with Aziz's ax.

"This is a damn fine weapon," he said.

Kadira rolled her eyes. She remembered why she left him years ago. He was a beautiful man and a talented lover, but he was a scavenger and a rogue. She hated that about him.

"You have a new toy, now let's get out of here," she said.

They walked backwards until they exited the Armory. The nyanas greeted them with curious looks.

"What happened in there?" one of them asked.

"Nothing," Kadira answered. "I bought a sword."

"And I won an ax," Omari said, grinning.

Kadira and Omari strolled away from the armory, ignoring the glares of the Fezzani merchants. Kadira gave her new sword a final inspection then slid it back into its sheath while Omari spun his ax, playing with the weapon like a new toy.

"Thank you," Kadira said.

Omari shrugged as he twirled the ax. "It was nothing. You've saved my life often enough. It's about time I returned the favor."

Kadira laughed. "You didn't save my life. I would have eventually beaten them both. You just shortened the fight."

She looked at his waist belt at the metal tube he called a hand cannon. "Where'd you get that thing?"

"The East," Omari replied. "The East Islanders are in love with them. They have bigger ones installed their dhows. To be honest, I'm surprised I hit that Fezzani. Hand cannons are very inaccurate. A crossbow is much more reliable."

"So why do you carry it?"

Omari unleashed one of his signature mischievous smiles. "It makes a grand impression. I've escaped quite a few tight spots because of the noise and smoke."

He reached out and grasped her wrist. "Come with me. I did you a favor now you can do one for me."

Kadira snatched her arm away. "You're lucky shot isn't worth that much!"

Omari laughed. "I don't mean that! Unless you're thinking . . ."

"No," Kadira snapped.

Omari frowned briefly then his smile returned. "Since you're here and have decided to go with us we might as well get it settled now. I'll take you to the Kashite."

"Makes sense," she agreed. "Lead the way."

Every nation of Ki Khanga possessed a district within Sati-Baa with the exception of Wadantu. The Baatians controlled the city center and the docks, with the other compounds arranged in order of most to least important to the merchant city. Those closest to the center were considered valuable allies. The district the furthest away from the Baatian center was that of Kash. If the Baatians had their way there would be no Kash district, but the mysterious warrior priests were not ones to offend. Their intrigues had ruined Aux and kept Haiset under constant armed vigilance. A request by Kash was rarely denied. Only Kiswala and Kamit seemed immune to their demands; Kiswala because of a suspected alliance; Kamit because they feared no one.

It was a long trek. The two stopped briefly at a small market to eat and rest, Omari reveling Kadira with stories of his journeys since they parted ways. His words stoked the fires of freedom inside her even more; by the time they reached the Kashite district she was eager to be on her way.

The Kashite wall was a formidable thing, a structure of large granite blocks punctured by a towering metal gate festooned with gold and jewels. Eight heavily armed guards stood on either side of gate, two spearmen on each side accompanied by two-person chariots. The guards edged closer to the gate as they approached. Omari stuck his hand into his pouch then rustled around for a moment. He eventually extracted a flat golden tablet inscribed with Kashite hieroglyphics. The men cleared the way and they entered the district.

Kadira was swept with a sense of dread. She'd only traveled to Kash once, and one time was enough. The episode was one she was not proud of and she'd tried her best to scour it from her memory. Walking down the pale brick streets between the stone pyramid-like buildings brought the memory back in full details. She regretted her decision. She was about to turn away when Omari stopped before a building shaped like a stylized jackal. He showed his tablet to the guards and they waved them inside. Hieroglyphs covered every part of the wall. A man sat in the center of the room in a high back chair before a wicker table, dressed in a simple white robe that bared one shoulder then fell to his bare feet. A snug white cap covered his bald head as he read a papyrus scroll.

"Omari," he said without looking up. "To what do I owe this visit?"

Omari bowed. "I have another person for our expedition, Sebe."

Sebe looked up. "Ah, I see. She cannot go."

"Is there a problem?" Kadira asked.

"Yes. You will be a distraction."

Kadira boiled. The Kashites were known for their strict codes, one which frowned upon women warriors.

"This not Kash," she replied.

Sebe lowered his scroll and looked directly at her. Kadira suddenly felt vulnerable.

"You are right . . . Kadira," he said to her surprise. "This is not Kash, and you are not just any woman. I have no doubt that you are more than capable of protecting yourself. I also have no doubt that some among our group will make you prove your skills. I do not wish to have to replace men unnecessarily."

"So, you will punish me for your men's weakness?" Kadira replied.

"I will speak for her," Omari said. "I will tell the others I am her companion."

Kadira jerked her head toward Omari. "No you will not!"

"It is a good idea," Sebe agreed. "Omari is well respected and the others like him. If he claims you they will not challenge his claim."

"I won't hear of it," Kadira shouted. "I'm not his. I'm married!"

"Then stay home with your husband and child," Sebe said. "If you wish to go on this expedition you will accept the terms as offered."

Kadira fumed, but the prospect of the journey and the pay overruled the insult.

"So be it," she finally said. "But this arrangement is in word only, not action, Omari."

"I could care less," Sebe said. "We leave in three days at sunrise. Meet us beyond the south gate. Do not be late."

Kadira stormed out of the jackal house, Omari chasing close behind.

"That went well," he said.

"No it didn't!" Kadira snapped. "I should have cut that bastard's throat!"

I don't think you would have gotten that close," Omari said. "He's a Kashite priest, you know."

"I would have gotten close with this." She snatched out her Fezzani sword. The blade felt heavier than she remembered, and the blue glow was gone.

"What in . . . That bastard drained my sword!"

Omari slid beside her and placed his arm around her shoulder.

"Okay, it's been a bad day. How about we go to the nearest tavern and drink the rest of it away?"

Kadira shoved his arm away. "I'm going home."

Omari nodded. "That's probably a good idea, too."

"Goodbye, Omari," she said.

"That sounds so final. You are still coming with us, aren't you?"

Kadira didn't answer.

It was nearly dark when she arrived home. Light emerged from the windows of her house; a faint glow peeked from the cooling embers in the forgery. When she entered, Nguvu sat at the table, fussing with an object she couldn't clearly see.

"Did you get your Fezzani sword?" he asked without turning around.

"I did, for what good it will do."

Nguvu turned his head. "What's wrong with it?"

Kadira pulled a chair from the table and plopped down. "Not only did I have to fight for the thing, the damn Kashite priest drained its charm."

Nguvu's eyebrows rose. "Kashite priest?"

"His name is Sebe. He's the leader of the expedition. Omari took me to see him today to confirm my place." She decided not to tell him about the arrangements.

"So you were with Omari?"

Kadira's stomach churned with nerves. "I ran into him on the way to the Fezzan market."

She studied Nguvu's face, looking for some sort of disapproval. She found none.

"Well, since your Fezzani sword is broken maybe you can take a look at mine."

Nguvu turned around completely, holding a beautifully wrought leather scabbard. Kadira stood as she grasped the scabbard and pulled the saber free. The sword was forged Malian style, slightly curved and single edged. It felt perfectly balanced, the hilt fitting her hand naturally. The blade shimmered like a mirror.

"This is beautiful!" she exclaimed.

Nguvu smirked. "Thank you."

Kadira cut a few strokes in the air. "You made this for me?"

Nguvu nodded.

She slid the sword back into its scabbard and placed it on the table. She then straddled Nguvu and kissed him.

"Ask me to stay and I will," she whispered.

"That's your decision," he said. "I won't deny you what makes you happy."

"You make me happy," she purred.

"You love the road. Go. I will be here when you return."

Kadira looked into his eyes. "What if I don't come back?"

"Then I will come find you," Nguvu answered.

Kadira was about to place another kiss on Nguvu's lips when her daughter wailed for attention. She went to the cradle, lifting her into her arms and feeding her. As she took her fill Kadira looked at her closed eyes and her beautiful face. How could she leave this lovely thing? She was a mother with responsibilities far beyond that of a wandering mercenary. What treasure could be worth more than the one she suckled in her arms? Her early life was hard, like Nguvu; she had no rec-ollection of her mother or father, and she did not know what a mother was supposed to do. But she knew she loved her daughter more than anyone or anything, even Nguvu.

"I'm not going," she said. "I can't."

Nguvu stood. "Don't decide tonight. It's been a long day. You may feel different in the morning."

Kadira stayed with her daughter most of the night, playing with her bright eyed child until day-break. She went immediately to bed, falling into a pleasant dreamless sleep. For the next three days she repeated the sequence, making love to Nguvu, feeding and caring for Olea. On the third day she awoke, her mind swirling with confusion.

"Go," Nguvu said.

"I . . ."

Nguvu sat up in their bed. "If you don't go, you will always wish you had."

Kadira faced him. "Why are you so eager to be rid of me?"

"I'm not," Nguvu said. "I want you to get this out of your system once and for all. I need you here totally."

Kadira took a deep breath. "Are you sure you are okay with this?"

Nguvu shook his head. "No. But you must do this."

Kadira went to the water barrel and washed. She woke Olea then fed her. Once she was done she dressed, slowly donning her armor and weapons. When she was done, she searched for Nguvu.

"I'm out here," he said, as if reading her thought.

She stepped outside; Nguvu held the reins of a magnificent red stallion.

"The stable master owed me a favor," he said. An expensive saddle rested on the horse's back and a quiver of throwing spears rested on its flank.

Kadira stood on her toes and kissed him.

"I'll miss you both," she whispered.

"Come back soon or I'll come to get you," Nguvu replied.

"I will."

She kissed him one last time then mounted her horse.

"Wait for me," she said.

"I will," Nguvu replied.

Kadira couldn't bear to look at him any longer. She reined the stallion about and galloped away toward the city walls.

* * *

Kadira knew she was late, but did not spur her mount. She took her time passing through Sati-Baa's busy streets, stopping at each market to purchase last minute provisions. A part of her hoped she would be too late, and then she could return home with an excuse that would satisfy her husband and her conscience. As she passed through the eastern gate she took one last look backward. She knew once she appeared at the Kashite camp there would be no turning back. She was a woman of her word. She would commit to the expedition until it returned.

They were waiting where the Kashite priest said they would be, a gathering of camels, horses, ox drawn carts and men. As she neared she recognized the clothing of almost all the northern countries; the bare chested kilt wearers of Kash, the blue quilted armor and conical helmets of Haiset, the chain mail wearing bowmen of Aux and even the nearly naked frog hunters of the Sati-Baa marshes. Standing out among all of them was Omari. He wore a red robe that challenge the sun in its brilliance, his head capped with a feathered monstrosity that made him resemble a harlot. Yet he was as handsome as a god, which made her smile despite herself.

He kicked his mount and galloped to her.

"I thought you weren't coming! I'm so happy to see you."

"I'm here," Kadira said. "What the Cleave do you have on?"

Omari lifted his robe. "Oh this? It's a long story. The woman who wore it before I removed it wished for me to keep it. It's a memento of our night together."

"And you're supposed to be my companion, showing up to camp in another woman's clothes?"

Kadira slapped him hard.

"What was that for?" Omari rubbed his jaw.

"That was for show," she said, smiling. "Now they'll believe I'm your woman."

When they reached camp the men were smiling, whispering and snickering. Sebe was not amused.

"You are barely here and have already stirred trouble. This will reflect on you, Omari."

Omari nodded. "I have things under control."

Sebe's frowned deepened. "I don't believe you, but we are in Ba's hands."

The Kashite waved his fly whisk. "We must leave. Time is of the essence and we are behind schedule."

Shrill horns blared and the camels replied. The trained beast rose in unison and fell in step behind the lead camel. The mercenaries gathered around Omari and Kadira, a few of the men winking at her. She marked their faces in her mind so she would know who she would have to make an example of.

"Okay warriors," Omari shouted. "Time to go on a stroll!"

The men laughed and fell in behind them.

Kadira took one last look Sati-Baa. She was actually doing it. She was leaving.

The first days of the journey were painfully uneventful. Kadira assumed they would take a dhow to the southern end of the Lake Sati then cross overland to Wadantu. Instead they took the land route, traveling east from the city to the bridge at the Kash River. The route would add weeks to the journey, something that Kadira didn't anticipated. She confronted Omari as soon as she realized the direction.

"You should have asked," he answered nonchalantly. "No one travels to the marshland during this time of year. You've lived in Sati-Baa long enough to know that."

"Apparently I haven't," she retorted. "Enlighten me."

"It's bata season," he said.

"Bata season? What does that mean?"

"I see you spent too much time under that husband of yours," Omari said. He instinctively ducked the punch meant for his face.

"Keep your insults. What in the Cleave is a bata?"

"You mean you never noticed those enormous frog legs hanging in the market?"

"Of course I have. So what?"

Omari smiled. "They're bata legs. I think it would better if you heard it from the source."

Omari cupped his hands over his mouth.

"Kunta, Bangiri!"

The frog hunters ambled over to them. Even miles away from their marshland homes they carried the stench of marsh and fish on their bodies.

"What do you want, pretty man?" Kunta said. The frog hunter was a foot shorter that Omari but twice as wide, all of it hard thick muscle.

"My woman'—he winked at Kadira— 'wishes to know why we won't travel through the marshlands."

Kunta flashed a yellow grin at Kadira. "I wondered that too, pretty woman. The Kashite claims to be a powerful priest, but he trusts no other."

"You haven't answered his question," Bangiri cut in. "The bata are hungry this time of year, pretty woman. They will eat anything they can fit in their mouths. Anything."

Kadira thought back to the size of the legs in the market and she grimaced.

Kunta smiled. "Now you understand. Bangiri and I could take a few, but we would lose some of you. We have only four hands."

Omari grinned. "Now you know."

The two frog hunters lingered, their eyes on Kadira. Omari approached them.

"Is there something else?" he asked.

"Yes," Kunta answered. "We were wondering if you were going to share . . ."

"NO!" Kadira answered. "Don't make me show you what I'm capable of, frog eater."

Kunta grinned. "I was hoping you would."

Kadira's foot smacked Kunta's mouth. Teeth flew into the air as he collapsed onto his back unconscious. Bangiri hustled to his friend's side.

"Make sure you tell him what happened when he comes to," she said. "Tell him it will happen again if he comes near me."

"Yes . . . Kadira. I will tell him." Bangiri answered.

She stalked away, Omari close behind.

"You're not making many friends," he said.

"I'm not here to make friends. I'm here to make money."

"It would go easier if you didn't try to kill anyone who speaks to you the wrong way. Let me handle it."

"Like you handled that?"

Omari smiled. "I'll do better the next time."

"Please do," Kadira warned.

She went back into the tent and began cleaning her weapons. She would give this expedition one more day. If things didn't get any better she was heading home. For good.

The next morning they crossed the Joliba River into Kenja. The Haisetti led them for they were very familiar with the country. The peaceful villages that inhabited the savanna grasslands were frequent victims of Haisetti slave raids. Kadira and Omari rode close to the center of the group near the

Kashites. She smirked at the priest and his entourage; they were obviously not experienced with the rigors of the open road. They resembled more a procession that an expedition with their gaudy headdresses, ceremonial horns, drums and dozens of servants carrying various containers and chests filled with all types of talisman and other powerful items. A good sorcerer would have whittled her list down to a few effective items then relied on the goodness of other mages of the destination for whatever extra needs. But then again they were travelling to Wadantu, a place as mysterious as the Cleave but for different reason. The Cleave was a result of the Daarila's anger toward Ki-Khangans, whereas Wadantu was the result of Eda's love and sympathy. Both were forbidden; what the Kashite priest planned to do could have bad results for an opposite reason.

A fog rose before them as they ventured further into Kenja, a thick moist cloud that eventually enveloped them and clung to their garments. The sudden change in conditions unnerved Kadira but the others seemed not to notice.

"This fog is strange," she commented.

Omari shrugged. "It's almost rainy season."

"Yes, but . . ."

Cries rose from up ahead. Kadira spurred her horse forward, galloping toward the source with Omari close behind. When they reached the front of the caravan a wall of fear greeted them. The Haisetti were dead to a man, each impaled by an arrow to the throat. The others looked about fearfully, shields raised, swords drawn and lances held ready. The Kashites arrived soon afterwards. Sebe in his elaborate chariot flanked by Auxite horsemen, their compound bows loaded. His face was grim.

"What is going here?" he fumed. "Are bandits roaming Kenja now?"

The fog faded quickly after Sebe's words. At first Kadira thought the sorcerer willed it away, but his expression was as perplexed as hers. The mist gave way to a ring of warrior surrounding them, armed men garbed in a variety of clothing and brandishing a myriad of weapons from swords to throwing irons. They were obviously a militia, a fact that made them no less dangerous despite their irregular appearance.

The men parted and a woman emerged from their ranks. She wore a grey pange about her hips, her upper body bare with the exception of a swath of cloth covering her breasts. Her head was bare of hair; she walked calmly to them carrying a massive bow, the arrows bouncing inside her hip quiver. She scanned their party, but her eyes lingered on Kadira.

"Dogon witch!" Sebe shouted. He punched his hand at her and the Auxites fired their arrows. The woman waved her bow, knocking the arrows aside. Just as quickly she loaded her bow with two arrows and fired. The Auxites jerked then fell from their mounts, their necks skewered by her arrows. Kadira was very impressed.

"That's the woman I told you about," Omari whispered.

"What woman?" Kadira replied.

"The woman I said was the only person who could match you with a bow. Nubia."

Sebe opened his mouth then his eyes went wide. He clutched at his throat as he struggled to breathe. Kadira looked at Nubia. The woman's right hand was extended, her fingers gripped tight.

"Apparently the bow is not the only thing she is good at," she said.

Nubia halted before them.

"Your mouth will get you killed sooner than later, Kashite," she said. She looked at Kadira.

"You will come with me and explain why you have trespassed. The others will stay here."

Kadira's stomach churned. "Nana, I am just a hired sword. I have no idea . . ."

"You ride with this group with no knowledge of its purpose?"

Kadira lowered her eyes. "No."

Nubia smirked. "Then you will come with me or you will all die now."

"Go with her already!" Omari urged.

Kadira nodded. Nubia turned her back then sauntered away. Sebe let out a gasp; apparently he could breathe again. Though he glared at Nubia, he made no other gestures.

"Go on then," Sebe said to Kadira. "I hope you are a better diplomat than you are a companion."

Kadira followed Nubia into the swirling mass of mist, hoping that she would live out the day. The warrior woman stopped, grasped her head, swayed then fell. The line broke as the men rushed to her but Kadira reached her first. She caught Nubia then eased her to the grass. Nubia shared a thankful smile.

"The Kashite was more powerful than I expected. I thought I was going to collapse before him."

Kadira took her water gourd from her waist then handed it Nubia.

"Kashites are reputed to be powerful sorcerers. Apparently not as powerful as the Dogon."

Nubia sipped her water then wiped her mouth. "Their nyama comes from a tainted source. It will be their doom."

Nubia stood. One of her warriors, a tall broad man with a natural scowl approached them, his eyes on Kadira.

"You should not take water from her," he said. "It may be poisoned."

"Your warning is too late, Rabana," Nubia chided. "This woman is good. It is why I chose her."

Rabana shared a reluctant smile with Kadira. "What is your name?"

"Kadira."

"Come with us, Kadira," he said. "We go to the village."

The village occupied a shallow valley just beyond a cluster of low hills. A deep moat filled with thorn bushes surrounded the gathering of conical huts capped with pointed thatch roofs. Warriors patrolling the perimeter rushed forward with relieved looks on their faces. Kadira walked beside Nubia, her head filled with a thousand questions.

"You may ask me what you wish," Nubia said.

"Why did you kill the Haisetti?"

"They were leading you to this village," Nubia answered. "We tracked you from the moment you entered Kenja. We would have let you be if you avoided our villages."

"They could have just wanted to replenish supplies," Kadira argued.

Nubia stopped, her eyes suddenly hard. "The Haisetti never come to trade. They come to take. They knew the danger. Your 'companions' probably felt confident with a Kashite priest in their midst. They were wrong."

She had angered Nubia so she decided to hold her questions. She followed the baKenja into the village and to a small hut in the center. The men dispersed to their homes; Nubia went inside the tent then returned with two mats. The women sat before each other.

"Your reason on this journey is different from the others, despite what you tell yourself," Nubia said. "You will find what you seek, but it is not what you expect."

She handed Kadira a scroll. "This map will lead you through Kenja without encountering any villages. There are clearings designated for trade. If you are in need of provisions send a person and someone will come."

Kadira took the scroll. Nubia reached into a pouch on her side and extracted a crudely cut amber piece threaded on a simple leather strip.

"Wear this," she said. "It will protect you when you enter Wadantu."

"I have my talisman," Kadira said.

Nubia sucked her teeth.

"Fezzani magic is useless in Wadantu."

Kadira took the necklace and immediately put it on.

"How do you know all this?" Kadira asked.

"This is my home," Nubia replied. "There are no secrets to me here. Now go. Your companions wait."

Kadira bowed to Nubia then turned to leave.

"One more thing," Nubia called out. Kadira turned to receive her words.

"Trust no one," Nubia said. Her eyes narrowed. "No one."

When Kadira reached the village edge a wagon with provisions waited. She managed to harness her horse and pull the wagon to the expedition. The fog wall persisted but faded as she approached. Omari was the first person she saw.

"Kadira!" He galloped toward her, a brilliant smile on his face.

"I assume the baKenja will let us live?"

"Only if we do as we are told," Kadira replied.

She continued riding to the Kashites, ignoring the stare of the others. Her status seemed to have risen among them because of Nubia's summons. Maybe they would stop leering at her and focus on the journey. She hoped so.

Sebe and the others looked in her direction as she approached. The Kashite sat in his throne-like chair flanked by fanning acolytes and the Kashite warriors. Kadira dismounted and approached. The guards did nothing to impede her.

Sebe looked up at her, his arrogant stare replaced with the hint of worry. This unnerved her. He was the leader of the expedition. If he was losing his confidence they might as well go back to Sati-Baa.

"What did the baKenja witch have to say?" he asked. The bitterness was gone from his voice.

"She knows where we are headed," Kadira replied. "Her quarrel was with the Haisetti, not us. She gave me this map. She said it will lead us to Wadantu and keep us away from baKenja villages."

She took out the map. Sebe looked at it and waved his hand.

"She gave it to you which means she trusts you. You will lead us through Kenja."

Kadira laughed. "I'm not a pathfinder."

The hard look returned briefly in Sebe's eyes. "You are now. Take your place at the lead of this expedition or we all go home."

Kadira bit back her words then turned to walk away.

"Wait," Sebe called out.

Kadira spun about then folded her arms across her chest. "What?"

"What is that you wear?" he asked.

"What are you talking about?"

"The necklace."

Kadira had forgotten the amber necklace. "It's a piece of amber given to me by Nubia." Sebe's eyes widened then he smiled.

"You may go."

Kadira rode back to the provision wagon. The men were helping themselves to the food, Omari among them.

"Omari!" she called out. Omari looked up, his mouth smeared with honey.

"You pick the worst times for conversation," he snarled.

"Sebe wants me to lead the expedition through Kenja and you're going to help."

Omari choked. "Me?"

"Yes, you. Now get that food fest organized over there and make sure everyone gets equal share. We leave within the hour."

If Omari was good at anything it was following orders. Provisions were distributed and the expedition set off immediately. They journeyed through the verdant savanna, surrounded by large herds of gazelles, wildebeests and other animals of the grasslands. Elegant giraffes nibbled at acacia tips as zebras flitted about like nervous flocks. It was a beautiful land, more beautiful than any Kadira had seen. She realized why the baKenja had now decided to fight for it and themselves.

They camped at one of the areas designated on the map. Kadira and Omari set up their tent near the camp edge, building a large fire with gathered wood. Kadira leaned back on her hands, rolling her head to loosen the tension in her neck. A pair of warm hands grasped her shoulders and began massaging them.

"Thank you, Omari" she said.

"You're welcome," he replied. "You've had an interesting day."

"No more interesting than any of us."

"The fate of this journey is in your hands."

Kadira didn't reply. She was lost in Omari's hands, savoring his experienced touch.

"We can continue this in the tent," he said.

His words killed the mood.

"Get your hands off me," she hissed.

"I was just . . ."

"Get your damn hands off me!" she yelled.

Kadira shoved him away and pulled her dagger. "Enough of this farce. I'm taking my own tent."

Omari looked puzzled. "What of our agreement?"

"I'm leading the expedition now. I don't need your cover. Touch me like that again and I'll send you to the Cleave."

Kadira gathered her things and stormed to the Kashites.

"I need a tent," she demanded.

The acolytes smirked then gave her a tent. They sent servants with her to help her set up the monstrosity.

She went inside, spread out her things then sat hard on her blanket, fighting back her tears. She wasn't mad at Omari; she was mad at herself. A few more minutes of his skilled touch and she would have gone into the tent with him. Nguvu deserved better than that. Olea deserved better from her mother. She had to be stronger. She would be.

When Kadira emerged from her tent the next morning Omari was waiting for her.

"I'm sorry," he blurted out.

Kadira's embarrassment showed in her smile.

"No Omari, I'm sorry. I overreacted. You were just being yourself and I was letting you."

"So you won't kill me?" he said. The boyish smile returned to his face.

Kadira smiled back. "No, I won't kill you. But you have to respect my situation now, Omari. I'm a married woman. We had our time and now it's done."

Omari fell to his knees, touched his forehead on the ground then sprinkled his head with dirt.

"Get up!" Kadira shouted. "You're embarrassing me!"

"Yes please, get up, you buffoon," Sebe said.

The Kashite priest stood behind her with his ever present acolytes.

"How far are we from Wadantu?" he asked.

Kadira took Nubia's map from her bag and unrolled it.

"At least two more days, maybe three. The map ends there. There is no route going into Wadantu."

Sebe gave her a sly smile. "Don't worry. We will find our way."

They set out late that day, taking their time breaking camp and enjoying a long, lazy meal. Despite their tardy departure they made good time, arriving at the next map point a few hours early. A shallow river flowed before them and they took advantage of the clear water to fill their gourds. They bathed as well, all except Kadira. She watched them all, comparing each man with the image of Nguvu in her mind. Some were fit, others not. As always Omari stood out, his perfectly proportioned body a gift from the Creator. But none of them possessed the overpowering physicality of her man waiting for her in Sati-Baa. No one would, for Nguvu was bred to be who he was, one of a few that made up the Mansa's Shield, an elite group of shock warriors charged to protect the Mansa of Mali. She remembered the first day she saw them, one hundred men forming an ebony line of muscle and steel. They were magnificent.

Omari strolled over to her naked. *He never quits*, she thought.

"Aren't you going to bath?" he asked innocently.

"No show for you today," she replied. She reached into her bag, took out a pange then tossed it to him.

"Cover up your worm. I'm embarrassed for you."

Omari pouted. "You're mean."

He wrapped the cloth around his waist and stomped away.

The next day the road ended. The expedition stared into a wall of green, a thick tangle of trees, shrubs and grass that gave no hint of entry.

"Wadantu," Kadira said.

"How do we go into there?" Omari asked.

He was answered by the arrival of the Kashites.

"This is where I take over," Sebe said.

His acolytes bowed before him, presenting a small gold trimmed box. Sebe leaned close to the box, whispering to the object reverently. It opened on its own and the priest reached into it and extracting a crystal vial, a small blue chip contained inside. Kadira gasped.

"What is it?" Omari asked.

"A piece of the Creator's Ax," she whispered. "Kipande."

Omari shuddered. "How did he obtain such a thing?"

"It's like Nubia said, the source of Kashite power will ruin them."

Sebe stepped toward the forest wall. The crystal vial glowed. Sebe turned slowly side to side until the vial shined brightly. He raised the vial over his head and shouted.

"Open!"

The forest exploded. Trees shattered then fell away; shrubs ripped from the ground and tumbled to the right and left. Kadira and the others fought to control their mounts until the commotion subsided. When the air cleared a wide ragged road into Wadantu lay before them.

Sebe turned to them. "Follow me."

The Kashites resumed their position as leaders of the expedition. They unhitched the horses from the chariot and saddled them. The path Sebe blasted through the thicket was too uneven for the vehicle. Sebe and his acolytes entered Wadantu as their vanguard, followed by the Kashite spearmen and Auxite archers. The mercenaries brought up the rear with Kadira and Omari leading them. Though the Kashites advanced confidently between the ravaged devastation the mercenaries proceeded cautiously, their eyes trained more on the foliage to either side than on the road ahead.

The power of Sebe's charm was more evident as they advanced. The path ran for miles. Kadira had seen much in her days on the road and at war, but never had she seen such destruction.

"I remember a voyage I took beyond Kiswala," Omari began.

"Beyond Kiswala?" Kadira's eye narrowed. "Are you sure you want to tell me this? I know how the Kiswala guard their trade secrets."

"I am the only Mikijen here," he said. "No one will know, unless you tell."

Kadira shook her head.

"Our destination was a city called Tai on the Eastern Sea. There was a war; by the time we reached Tai it was rubble. The Kiswali were angry of course, so they sent us ashore to see if we could salvage anything of worth. It was the worst destruction I'd ever seen until now."

"The devastation is not what concerns me," Kadira said. "I'm worried about who heard it."

The ragged road finally opened into a wide green field. A group of steep hills rested on the horizon surrounded by small trees and some type of stone columns Kadira could not make out. It was the first sign of men.

"Eyes and ears open!" Omari shouted. "We may have company."

No sooner did Omari utter those words did the sound of hoof beats break the eerie silence. Horsemen advanced on them from either side.

"Archers take the flanks!" Omari shouted. "Horsemen stand behind them!"

Kadira instinctively led a group of riders to the right flank while Omari took his riders to the left. She glanced at the Kashite; they took the same position with the exception that they had no cavalry. The spearmen backed the archers, their spears and shield at the ready. Sebe and his acolytes rested between them. They waited patiently until their attackers were in range.

"Fire!" Omari shouted.

Arrows took flight like startled fowl, arching over-head then falling into the ranks. The riders fell in large numbers but continued to charge.

"Monsters!" someone shouted. "They're monsters!"

Kadira strained her eyes to see what was going on. The archers continued to fire; it was a few moments more before she could see what had un-nerved them. These were not horsemen. They were a terrifying amalgam of man and beast; their bodies that of the great grass antelopes, their torsos man-like, their heads crowned with horns. They bran-dished shields, assegais, bows and arrows like men but they were anything but.

"What in the Cleave are they?" Omari shout-ed.

Kadira's eye narrowed. "I don't know, but they die like men. Riders, prepare to charge!"

The archers let loose one last volley then ran aside. Before Kadira could kick her horse it let out a loud grunt and ran toward their attackers. She put the reins between her teeth, took out her bow and loaded. The man-beasts threw their spears toward her; to her surprise her horse dodged them nimbly without breaking stride.

"Nguvu, what kind of horse did you give me?" she said between her teeth.

Her arrows found their marks, bringing down more of the creatures. Soon she was too close so she sheathed her bow and took out Nguvu's sa-ber. She could see the faces of the creatures now, their angry eyes meeting her stare. This would be a battle with no quarter.

The man beast nearest to her did an unex-pected thing. It leaped into the air, its shield and spear raised. Her mounted did the unexpected as well. It leaped also, carrying her upward. She hugged the horse's neck as it slammed into the man-beast. The man-beast fell first, no match for the horse's bulk. When they came to the ground Kadira and her horse were atop the man-beast. Before she raised her sword the horse began pounding the beast with its hooves.

"By the Creator!" she exclaimed. At that moment she realized what she rode and a wide grin came to her face. Nguvu had given her a great gift. He'd bought her a Malian war horse.

Her glee was short lived. The man-beasts quickly surrounded them and attacked. A second surprise was gripped in the palm of her hand. Nguvu's sword cut spear and man equally, its sharp edge melting wood and flesh. Her war horse fought as well, kicking, butting and biting in precision with her movements. In moments the crowd about them cleared as those beasts still alive sought easier prey. Kadira took a moment to assess the battle; they were hard pressed on either side with more beasts coming from the distance. She looked ahead to the hills. If they could reach them, they would at least have the higher ground.

"To the hills," she shouted "The hills!" She worked her way between the beasts and her cohorts, freeing those on foot to run. The other riders picked up her plan and joined her. The Kashites were already fleeing for the high ground, leaving the Auxites to their fate. Soon they were all running toward the summits. The man-beasts followed; although they seemed to slow the closer they came to the hills. Omari worked his way to her. His right arm was bloody, but he seemed otherwise okay.

"They're leaving," he shouted.

"That worries me," Kadira replied. "They may be driving us into another trap."

Omari laughed. "The only thing in front of us is those hills . . ."

The ground beneath them lurched. Kadira and her horse fell forward; luckily she and the beast were unhurt. Others were not so fortunate. She staggered to her feet.

"What is happening?" she said.

The ground shook again. Kadira looked ahead to the Kashites. They were no longer heading toward the hills; they were heading to the west toward another stand of woods. The ground shook again and Kadira staggered back. The hills were moving.

The ground trembled as she mounted her horse. Omari struggled to keep his still so she rode up him and lifted him onto his horse.

"Ride for the woods as fast as you can!" she shouted.

A deafening bellow emerged from before them. The hill was no longer a hill. It was a beast unlike any either of them had ever seen. It seemed made of earth and stone with a large single tusk protruding from its face. It glowered at them and bellowed again. Nothing else needed to be said. They rode for their lives.

Kadira clung tight to her horse's neck as it bounded across the undulating ground to the woods ahead. The hill beast ran parallel to them, each footfall causing the ground to ripple like water disturbed by a giant stone. She marveled at how the steed kept upright despite the vicious jarring. Others were not as lucky. Her cohorts tumbled from their horses, some killed by the fall, others when hundreds of pounds of horseflesh collapsed upon them. She searched for Omari and found him riding ahead of her. His mount stumbled about, fighting to keep its footing on the quaking earth. Kadira looked back from where they came. The antelope-men were there, following the fleeing interlopers at a safe distance. A few mercenaries fled in their direction, obviously more willing to take their chances against the horde than the stampeding monstrosity. They were met with spears and death.

Omari's horse fell. Omari leaped clear then struck the ground hard. The horse fell awkwardly, thrashing about for a moment before lying still. Kadira guided her horse toward Omari.

"Omari!" she shouted.

He stumbled around just in time to reach out. Kadira grabbed him then lifting him onto the back of the horse. The beast grunted in protest but continued running, the extra weight having no effect on its speed.

"Thank you," Omari gasped. "What kind of horse is this?"

"A damn good one," Kadira said. Her attention was elsewhere. The hill beast was angling toward them. There was no way they could outrun it, if only because of its ground chewing strides. It was then she noticed that the Kashites were gone.

"Damn them to the Cleave," she shouted. "The Kashites have escaped!"

"No they haven't," Omari replied. "Look!"

He pointed toward the beast. The Kashites stood in its path, the acolytes standing on either side of Sebe. The priest held the piece of the Creator's ax over his head.

"It won't work," she whispered.

She watched a few more minutes then the beast shuddered. It uttered a deafening roar as it continued to advance. A moment later it shuddered again. This time it stopped then rose onto it hind legs. It roared again; Kadira thought she heard a hint of pain it its protest.

It shuddered a fourth time. This time it froze, locked on two legs. Sebe and his acolytes mounted their horses. She heard Sebe's voice rise over the din of battle.

"Die!" he shouted.

A part of the beast head cracked then broke free. It tumbled down the body and crashed into the ground. The Kashites galloped away as the beast continued to break apart, its body becoming an avalanche of stone and blood. The morbid flow ceased far from them. When the Kashites reached Kadira and Omari their faces were graced with confident smiles.

"The challenge has passed," Sebe said. "We can proceed to our destination."

Kadira was not so sure.

"What about the . . ."

Sebe gestured over her shoulder. Kadira turned to see that the antelope men were gone. Most of her cohorts were either dead or severely wounded. Only she and Omari seemed capable of continuing on.

"Their share will be split among the living," Sebe said. "Come, we must reach our destination before nightfall."

The Kashites rode toward the rubble that was once a beast. Kadira hesitated.

"What are you waiting on?" Omari said. "Let's go."

"I don't know, Omari," Kadira said.

Omari jumped from her horse and secured another from one of their hapless comrades.

"I've been through too much shit to go home empty handed," he snarled.

He rode after the Kashites. Kadira watched him for a minute before rubbing her horse's neck.

"So what do you think warhorse? Should we follow?"

The horse grunted and followed Omari.

"Look likes this horse is braver than me." Kadira shrugged and let the horse have its way.

Kadira and Omari followed the Kashites into the new forests. She expected Sebe to clear a path for them as he did before but he made no move to do so. Luckily, this forest was not as dense as the other, with plenty of room to maneuver horse and man. She surmised that Sebe has spent considerable power bringing down the hill beast and a closer inspection of his face confirmed her suspicions. He looked as if he had aged decades within a few minutes. How long that would last was uncertain. The pieces of the Creator's Ax contained immense power. It was possible it could rejuvenate Sebe, but Kadira was ignorant of such things. She depended on her skill and what little nyama she could afford. Everything else was in the Creator's hands.

"We're going to be rich beyond our wildest dreams!" Omari whispered. "We started with one hundred, now there is only you and I. I can buy an island. Cleave, I can buy Kiswala!"

"How do you know Sebe will be true to his word?" Kadira asked.

"He has been so far," Omari replied. "If you have doubts then why are you still here?"

"Because I am bound to see this through," Kadira said. "And I don't think I can fight my way through those antelope men alone, despite this wonderful horse."

"Any animal that fight likes that deserves a name," Omari commented.

Kadira patted the horse on its neck and it snorted in response.

"If we survive this I'll name him then give Nguvu a long night of my appreciation."

"You shouldn't talk that way around me," Omari pouted. "It's been a while."

The rest of the day was uneventful. They traveled until night then made camp along a narrow creek. Omari caught a pair of exotic colored fish that tasted as good as they looked and did not make them sick. The Kashites kept to themselves, eating whatever rations they brought then whispering intensely to each other. The acolytes seemed to be in some sort of disagreement with Sebe, leaning toward him with stern faces as they argued in their own tongue. Sebe said little, responding with either a gesture or a word. He finally ended the conversation with a swipe of his hand. The acolytes went to their cots and slept, but Sebe paced between them. He was still pacing when Kadira awoke the next morning. He marched directly to her.

"Today we will reach our destination," he said. "You will have to be very diligent. I had hoped to have more protection at this point, but I did not anticipate such a resistance to our intrusion so soon. I hope you and your friend are as skilled as you say you are."

"You should know by now," Kadira replied.

Sebe frowned. "Then I will pray that you find more skills between here and our journey's end."

They ate a quick meal then set out once again. At midday the forest ended abruptly, replace by a barren expanse. Something rose over the dirt and gravel. She strained her eyes to see.

"It is our destination," Sebe said. "Our journey is almost at an end."

They galloped across the wasteland until they reached the object. It was a temple, a small simple structure consisting of a flat stone on which five thick columns supported a stone conical roof. Kadira could see a pedestal inside. Though the building was sparse, the power it possessed was overwhelming. Kadira felt as if an invisible shield pushed against her as she tried to get closer.

"You two will stay here," Sebe ordered. "Kill anyone who tries to enter."

Kadira and Omari dismounted then took out their bows. Sebe and the acolytes continued to the temple.

"So this is it," Omari said. "This is how we get paid."

"I guess so," Kadira replied. "Looks like this will be the easiest part of the journey."

They had barely positioned themselves when Sebe returned. He held an object in his hand, the bust of a man's head similar to those she had seen in Oyo but with one significant difference. Instead of iron, this bust was made of material from the Creator's Ax.

"It's incredible!" Omari said.

"It's impossible," Kadira replied. It was also foreboding. Such a concentration of the Creator's Ax was killing them as they spoke. That much she knew. It was also a quantity that could make its possessor insanely powerful, and it was in the hands of a Kashite. Suddenly the stacks meant nothing. What use was it to be wealthy in a world that was soon to end? Kadira's shoulders slumped. Nguvu's words were true. This would be her last journey.

Sebe stared into the object, delight in his eyes. The strain of the last confrontation disappeared from his face and he smiled.

"For so long I've sought this, longer than any of you can imagine," he whispered. "The world is now in my hands."

He extended his hand toward his acolytes. They gave him a black cloak and he wrapped the carved head with it. The intense nyama was diminished; Kadira felt the invisible pressure lift. Maybe she would live after all.

"So you have come again," a voice said behind her.

She spun, her sword drawn. Three small women stood before them, each naked with the exception of simple loincloths. The women carried no weapons, only carved staffs.

"Kill them!" Sebe shouted, his voice filled with terror.

Kadira looked at the priest. "These women are not armed."

Sebe glared at her. "They are the most dangerous of all. Kill them!"

Kadira normally followed any order given to her when in a person's employ. It was the reason she harbored memories she'd soon forget. But this command seemed wrong. She looked at Omari for support.

"The Kashites are paying the bill," he said then shrugged his shoulders. He lifted his hand cannon and aimed.

The small woman who spoke moved with amazing speed. She knocked Omari's weapon aside then drove her staff into his chest, the bloody end protruding from his back. She snatched her staff free then attacked Kadira. Kadira desperately blocked his rapid thrusts but it was obvious the woman was faster . . . and stronger. The staff struck her wrist and she dropped her sword; another blow landed across her thighs and she collapsed to her knees. The woman raised her staff; the bloody end aimed at her chest then hesitated. She slammed it on Kadira's shoulder and she collapsed to the ground. She clinched her eyes in pain.

"You will not stop me this time!" Sebe shouted.

Kadira tried to rise but could only roll onto her side. The small women advanced on Sebe and the acolytes, their staffs raised. Sebe threw the cloak from the carved head.

"I have it now," he snarled. "I'm stronger than you!"

He raised the head high and his acolytes fell to their knees. A triangle of light formed between them and Sebe. A similar shape formed between the women and a magical confrontation ensued. A thick beam of light joined the two groups, raising a storm of wind and dust around them. Kadira watched in fearful fascination. Sebe trembled and his acolytes glowed; the women stood still, no signs of any physical movement. Suddenly the acolytes were consumed in a blue white light then disappeared; Sebe fell to his knees, his arms struggling to hold the mystical head.

"You will not take it from me!" he screeched. "It is mine! It is mine!"

The women advanced on Sebe. The Kashite priest began to glow, his features diminishing with each step. Soon he was a only the form of a man in blue white light, the head still suspended over what was left of him. The women gestured toward him with their staffs and the essence of Sebe dispersed slowly into the swirling winds. The carved head fell to the ground.

Kadira rolled onto her back. So the Kashites were dead. She turned her head to see Omari laying still on his back, as handsome in death as he was in life. She looked up and the women stood over her, their faces solemn. She took a moment to remember her family and a slight smile came to her face.

"I'm ready," she said.

The women smiled. "It is not your time, Dogon."

One of the women touched her amber necklace with her staff. The pain dissipated and energy filled her limbs. She sat up rejuvenated.

"Why are you here, Dogon?" the woman who spoke before asked. "We have an agreement."

"I am no Dogon," Kadira replied.

The women exchanged confused glances.

"But you wear the stone," the woman said.

Kadira touched the amber stone given to her by Nubia.

"It was given to me . . . by a Dogon."

The woman grinned. "You are under her protection. That is good."

Kadira finally stood. Physically the women stood no taller than an adolescent child, but spiritually they towered over her.

"What you witnessed was not the end," the woman explained. "The one you know as Sebe is an old spirit, a creature of the Cleave. It craves the power it once knew and constantly seeks it. It will return again."

"You did not destroy it?"

The woman shook her head. "That which the Creator made cannot be destroyed, even that created in His anger."

"Who are you?" she asked.

"We are the Wazelitaka," the woman replied.

The woman's companions left her side. They lifted the head and placed it back into the temple.

"If you know this thing will come for the idol, why don't you hide it?" Kadira asked.

"It must seek it," the woman answered. "It draws it like a moth to light. If it cannot find it, it will cause havoc among the favored. That cannot be allowed."

The woman stepped toward her, her free hand extended. Kadira took it.

"You must go home," he said. "Your family worries for you."

Kadira smiled. "I'm sure they do."

She glanced at Omari and sighed.

"You favor him?" the woman asked.

"I did once. It's sad to see him this way."

"It was his fate," the woman said. "Your path still remains. Go."

Her words were like a command. Kadira gathered her weapons then started for her horse. The animal had remained despite the turmoil that just occurred. She wasn't surprised. She mounted it and patted its neck.

"Let's go home," she whispered.

Kadira mount seemed as anxious to be out of Wadantu as she. It galloped across the barren lands of the temple then sped through the surrounding forest. Even when they emerged onto the ominous savannah where they fought the antelope men and faced the hill beast it did not slow. Unlike before the grassland was empty, but Kadira kept close vigil as her horse streaked across the expanse. Soon they were back to the dense forest. The gash that Sebe, or whatever it was, created was gone, replaced by a trail just wide enough for horse and rider. Kadira shuddered when she thought of the power of the Wazelitaka. They had to be connected to the Creator is some way. She decided not to dwell on it. They spared her life, which was more than she could say for everyone else.

"Keep running, war horse," she whispered. "Don't stop until were out of this strange place."

The horse obeyed her order. It stumbled to a halt only a few strides into Kenja, panting hard. Kadira quickly dismounted then removed her saddle and bridle from the tired beast.

"If you ran off and left me today it would be deserved," she said. Another surprise greeted her as she stripped the horse; two leather bags and a large gourd. The gourd contained fresh water, which she shared with her horse. The leather bags contained relief and joy. One bag was filled with food; berries, edible leaves and strips of dried meat. It was at least enough to last her a few days. She opened the other bag and a giggle escaped her lips. It was filled with gold dust. It was nowhere near eight stacks, but it was enough to make her journey worth it.

"We got paid after all," she said to her horse. The horse ignored her, busying itself with consuming the thick green grass surrounding them.

Kadira set up camp and gave way to the fatigue and pain she'd ignored for days. She planned on setting out for Sati-Baa after a day's rest but stayed at her camp for three days, resting and healing. On the third night a strange sound woke her. It came from the direction of her food bag. She was about to rise when she heard her horse snort. There was a thud and a shout.

"Damn you, you crazy horse!"

The voice she heard was shocking and familiar. Kadira sprang to her feet and ran to the source of the sound.

"Omari!" she shouted.

Omari lay on his back, her war horse standing between him and the food bag. He was filthy and he stank, but he was very much alive. Kadira picked up the food bag and threw it to him.

"You're alive," she said.

"Of course I am!" he spat back. He opened the bag, reached inside and pulled out handful of food then stuffed it in his mouth. A moan escaped his lips.

"Twigs never tasted so good."

Kadira pushed the horse aside then sat beside Omari.

"How did you get here?"

"I walked," he said. "Thanks for leaving me, by the way."

"I didn't leave you. You were . . ."

Omari stopped chewing. "I was what?"

Kadira smiled. "Never mind. What do you remember?"

"I remember trying to shoot one of those women. The next thing I knew I was laying on my back surrounded by them with that damn head on my chest. It felt like an elephant was sitting on me. Then one of the women lifted it off me and told me to go."

"I'm happy to see you," she said.

Omari stopped eating and a sly smile came to his face. "Really? We should celebrate."

Kadira would have laughed if she didn't think it would give Omari the wrong impression.

"I'm not that happy to see you."

Omari shrugged then continued eating.

"Go easy on that," she said. "It's all I have. I'm going back to sleep."

"Alone?"

She shook her head. "Alone. And don't get any ideas. My horse will stomp you to death."

"I'm sure he will. I think that horse is Nguvu."

Kadira finally laughed. "I think you're right."

The morning came with a clear sky. Kadira and Omari broke camp; traveling together in silence. About midday Omari stopped walking and began looking about.

"I think I'll head that way," he said.

Kadira was puzzled. "What are you talking about?"

"I'm not sure, but I think Bashaba is that way."

"Bashaba?"

"It's a Kiswala port."

Kadira finally understood. "So you're not going back to Sati-Baa?"

Omari shook his head. "I think I'll rejoin the Mikijen. They're always looking for men and I'm familiar. Besides, a city like Sati-Baa is no fun without money."

Kadira remembered the other bag. She went to her horse then returned with it and the empty food bag.

"Hold this," she said, handing him the food bag. She poured half of the gold dust into the bag. Omari's eyes teared up.

"I could kiss you!"

Kadira drew back. "You better not."

The sight of money seemed to add a bounce to his stride.

"Then I'm off," he announced. "It was good riding with you again, Kadira. Things didn't turn out as expected, but then it never does."

Kadira nodded. "It never does. Goodbye, Omari."

Omari bowed. "Goodbye sweet lady. Tell that husband of yours he made a fine choice. And kick that damn horse for me."

Omari turned away and marched toward the northeast. Kadira watched him for a while, and then resumed her journey home.

*   *   *

The walls of Sati-Baa never looked so good. Kadira rode toward the mudbrick barrier surrounded by a stream of merchants, farmers and others heading to the city for their daily work. The lax guards barely paid her any attention when she passed through the gates. The patience she possessed throughout her journey home suddenly vanished, replaced by an urgent need to see her man and girl.

"Get us home fast," she whispered to her horse. He snorted a reply and trotted through the throng, gathering curses and shouts along the way. By the time they reached their alley the horse was in full gallop and Kadira's heart pounded against her chest like a celebration drum. The war horse ran up to her home then halted.

"Nguvu! Olea! I'm home!" she shouted.

She jumped off the horse and rushed into the house. It was empty. A bolt of fear struck her until she heard the rhythmic hammering. She sped through the house to Nguvu's shop. Her man's broad back was turned to her as he pounded a strip of red hot steel.

"Nguvu!" she squealed.

He turned and laid eyes on her, smiling as if he knew she would be there. She started toward him but he held up his hand. Nguvu put down his hammer then went to the cradle, lifting Olea into his arms.

"My baby," she whispered.

Then Nguvu surprised her. He set her down on the ground.

"Mama's home," he said.

Olea gave her a look of recognition, clapped and smile. Then she stood, her bowed legs wavering.

"Olea? Are you . . ."?

Olea half stumbled and half walked into her mother's arms. Kadira could not hold back any longer. She cried like a child. Nguvu came to her and hugged them both.

"Welcome home," he said.

She kissed him full and long.

"Are you satisfied now?" he asked.

"Very much so," Kadira replied. "I'm home for good. There is no treasure greater than the one I hold in my arms this moment."

Nguvu nodded. Together they left the shop and entered their home.

SIMPLE MATH

(ORIGINALLY PUBLISHED IN THE KI KHANGA ANTHOLOGY)

Omari Ket stood on the hill overlooking the Kiswala port of Bashaba, fighting to hold back tears. At that moment he was the happiest man in Kenja, if not all of Ki-Khanga. For weeks he'd trudged across the Kenja savanna hounded by Nubia's militias and harassed by the local fauna that viewed him as an easier meal than the thousands of herd animals whose shit his feet had an uncanny ability to find. He wiped away the tear trails with his grimy hands, and then raised them high in celestial praise.

"I don't always believe in you, Creator," he croaked. "But today I do!"

He stumbled down the sandy slope onto the nearest road. A group of farmers with donkeys loaded with grain quickly distanced themselves from him, their pinched faces making their reason obvious. Under any other circumstances Omari would have either beat them up, robbed them, or beat them up and robbed them. But on that day he had neither the energy nor the inclination. All he wanted was a bath.

He made a quick trip to the local brothel. It wasn't hard to find for all Kiswala ports were laid out basically the same no matter where they were located. Two guards flanked the tall wooden doors, their bulk and turbans marking them as Zimbabwans. They snarled at his approach then held their noses.

"On your way," one of them snapped. "Monafiki only services Kiswala and Mikijen."

Omari lifted the tattered sleeve covering his left bicep, revealing the ngisimaugi tattoo.

"What about a Mikijen with gold dust?" He patted the leather back strapped to his waist.

The guards pushed the doors open then stepped aside. Omari walked into the brothel as if he was entering the gates of a palace. The building was empty, as it should have been early in the day. The Kiswala were handling their business and the Mikijen were busy protecting them. He would have the place to himself for at least half a day. No sooner had his foot touched wood did a tall woman emerge from a room opposite him, her shapely body wrapped tight in a yellow kanga. She approached Omari with a suggestive smile and only flinched briefly when close enough to smell him.

"You are quite the handsome man," she said. "Apparently you've spent some time on the road."

Omari's spirits were rising. "Longer than I'd like to remember. I need a bath, and maybe some other things."

He winked and the woman smiled. "All things are possible with the proper motivation."

Omari was not the show off type, at least when it came to his money, but he deserved some pampering after all he'd been through in Kenja. His chest was still sore from his encounter with the short people, and his ego was still bruised from Kadira's rebuffs. He took his bag from his belt and opened it enough for the woman to see. Her eyes went wide.

"I'd like exclusive use of your hospitality for the day," he said. "I think I have enough to make it possible."

"For that bag I will tend to you myself," the woman replied.

"That won't happen," Omari said. "Give me what a pinch of this bag will pay for."

The woman snarled. "You Mikijen are all the same!"

"Thank you," he replied. "Now where's my room?"

"Wait here,' the matron said. 'I'll have a bath prepared for you."

"Thank you," Omari said.

"Don't thank me. It's for our sake. You smell like shit."

Omari shrugged; it was a fair assessment. He plopped down at the nearest table then stripped off his ragged boots. A quick whiff and he put them back on. He'd wait for his bath before taking off anything else.

A woman appeared from a hidden door carrying a simmering bowl. She was pretty despite her unkempt appearance; her kanga barely held her womanly assets. Omari winked at her as she placed his bowl and spoon before him.

"A wonderful meal served by a beautiful woman," he said. "The Creator has blessed me today."

The woman smiled as she turned her head away. She lingered as Omari gulped down a spoonful of stew then moaned.

"Tasty indeed," he lied. "I wonder what else here is just as good?"

"Do not toy with me, stranger," she said. "I'm no village girl."

"Oh, I never play with certain subjects," Omari replied. "And let's not be strangers. I'm Omari."

"Kapera," the woman replied.

"Well, Kapera, you seem to be the only person that doesn't mind that I smell like a rutting camel."

"I tend the livestock. I'm used to it."

Omari frowned. "Maybe after my bath we can discover what other things you do well."

"Don't mess with anything you didn't pay for, Mikijen!"

The matron stormed into the room. "Get out of here, Kapera. You have no business with this man."

Kapera scurried from the room. The matron glared at Omari.

"Your bath is ready. Follow me."

The matron led him to the back of the brothel. It was the worst room in the building, Omari suspected. Inside was a shallow tub filled with dingy water.

"This is it?" Omari said.

"You get what you pay for," the matron replied.

Omari began taking off his clothes. The matron stood before him until he was fully undressed.

"Now you own me," Omari said.

The matron struggled not to smile. "Let me know when you're done."

She walked out the room. Omari waited.

"Creator! He's fabulous!"

Omari grinned. He settled into the lukewarm water and fatigue overwhelmed him. He closed his eyes and was asleep in seconds, drifting slowly into what he hoped was a peaceful slumber. Instead he fell, spinning downward at a speed that made him nauseous and dizzy. He knew he would vomit in moments but mercifully the falling ceased. Light invaded his darkness, illuminating a scene that played out in his life months ago. He was at the temple again in Wadantu standing beside Kadira. Sebe held the strange idol and the persons who called themselves Walezitaka stood before him with their staffs. Omari was raising his bow when he felt a searing pain in his chest.

"By the Creator!" he exclaimed. He bolted up in the washtub and the sword point touching his old wound broke his skin. The brothel door guards hovered over him, the larger one holding his tarnished sword against his chest. The matron peered over his shoulder.

"Don't kill him!" she exclaimed. "The Haiseti will pay well for him. He'd make an excellent pleasure slave."

Omari's eyes narrowed. "Think carefully about what you do. I'm Mikijen. We take care of our own."

The big guard laughed. "You were Mikijen."

"So how will you explain a certain tattoo on my back?" Omari asked.

The guard looked skeptical.

"Don't listen to him!" the matron barked. "The Haiseti won't care and if they do, we'll peel it off. It will reduce his value, but gold is gold."

The matron grinned. "Speaking of gold, search his clothes. I believe we have another bonus waiting."

The other guard went to the pile of odoriferous garments then shifted through it with his sword tip.

"It's not here," he grumbled.

"Here it is." Omari stood in his naked glory. The gold bag rested against his hip, held in place by a thin leather cord.

"Get it!" the matron ordered.

While the life of a Haiseti pleasure slave was not the worst fate for anyone, Omari had no intentions of crossing Kenja again. He twisted to his left, slapping the blade against his chest with the flat of his hand and wincing as it cut his skin. He pounced from the washtub, driving his right fist into the man's throat then catching his sword as the big man went limp. The matron tried to run but Omari swept her feet. She fell hard, her head slamming the floor boards. He turned to face the other guard. The man hesitated, looking at his choking comrade and his dazed boss.

"Looks like you have a decision to make," Omari said.

The guard attacked. Omari parried the clumsy thrust then drove his sword into the man's abdomen. The guard collapsed into the washtub.

Omari looked at the mess around him.

"This was unnecessary," he murmured.

He stripped the big guard of his clothes and donned them. The matron moaned and he hit her on the head with the sword hilt, knocking her unconscious. Omari searched her pockets and found the gold dust he paid earlier in addition to a handful of cowries. He grinned; he'd taken a bath and made a profit. Not bad for a day's work. He decided to go directly to the Mikijen post. He wasn't sure if the matron was dead or not, but he was sure that if she wasn't, she would report him. Once he rejoined, he would be immune to her charges. He stepped over the bodies then sauntered downstairs.

As he left the brothel Kapera appeared. She looked at him puzzled and Omari winked.

"There's a mess for you to clean up," he said. He walked up to her, pulled her to him, kissed her then gave her the cowries.

"I'm rejoining the Mikijen. You should visit," he whispered.

"I will," she replied.

Omari patted her butt then strolled out the door and into the streets of Bashaba, ignoring the curious glances at his makeshift outfit. He'd done worse; he grinned as the memory of Ile-Kanta came to mind. He'd been caught in a compromising position with the head elder's daughter, an embarrassment to the local Mikijen garrison and a blow to the young woman's loloba. He was forced to strip naked in the middle of the village and walk a gauntlet of club wielding village men, but the protests and attention of the village women forced the men to give up the gauntlet idea. They dressed him in women's clothing and gave him a head start to run for his life instead. Luckily for him the village women provided a reasonable obstacle to their jealous men.

As he reached the docks, he felt a pressure in his chest. Omari rubbed it, noticing it was the spot where he received his Wadantu wound.

"I'll have to get a medicine-priest to look at this," he mused.

He massaged the wound as he walked along the mooring. Fishing dhows tainted the sea air with their pungent cargo. A few merchant dhows rested on the calm sea, while further out Mikijen war dhows guarded the harbor entrance. A flood of bittersweet memories invaded his head; Omari began to question why he had returned. But there really was no choice. He was technically broke. True, he could live well for quite some time with the gold dust in his pouch but he had no intentions of doing so. Omari was a planning man; he envisioned a small tavern in a quaint town where he would live out his old age charming the locals with stories of his travels during the day and keeping the old widows company at night.

He finally came to the building flying the Ngisimaugi banner. He walked in and was greeted by a sleeping mercenary, his snores echoing through the small, dingy room. Omari grinned; he walked up to the table then slammed his hand on the table. The mercenary's eyes popped open.

"What in the Cleave?" he shouted.

Omari folded his arms across his chest. "I've come to re-enlist and it looks like I'm just in time."

The man scowled at Omari. "You're former Mikijen?"

Omari turned and revealed his tattoo.

The man stood, walking to a wall of scrolls divided alphabetically. "What's your name?"

"Omari Ket."

The man stopped then turned. "You're Omari Ket?"

Omari grinned. "You've heard of me, I see."

The man nodded. "Yeah, I've heard of you. Decent fighter; ladies' man."

He looked Omari up and down. "You don't look that good to me."

"I'm glad I don't. You're not my type. Too much between your legs."

The man grinned. "Smart mouth. I heard that, too."

The man pulled out Omari's scroll. The Kiswala kept meticulous records. Once a person entered their employ he or she was forever in their archives. He opened the scroll then went directly to the bottom. He went into his table drawer, taking out a quill and an ink vial. With the dip of the quill and a quick scribble Omari was active again.

"You'll come in as you went out, as a soli. You'll be paid accordingly."

"And how soon will that be?" Omari asked.

"Next week."

Omari frowned. "I could use an advance."

"You won't get it. This is Bashaba, not Kiswala."

The man sat, rubbing his chin. "There is an opportunity to make a few extra cowries."

Omari eyes brightened. "How few?"

"Twenty," the man said.

Not a bad amount, Omari thought. "I'm in."

The man smiled. "Give me a minute."

He went into the back room then returned with a lance, a bow, and a quiver of arrows on his hip.

"Haisetti?" Omari guessed.

The man nodded then extended his hand. "I'm Zenawi."

Omari grasped his hand. "Hello Zenawi. Let's get on with it."

He followed Zenawi into the street then waited as he locked up the office.

"This way," Zenawi motioned.

Omari grinned. Now this was more like it.

Omari forced Zenawi to stop at the nearby vendor then feasted on boiled rice and shrimp. He was wiping his face when he heard a familiar voice calling him.

"Mikijen! Mikijen!"

He looked toward the voice and grimaced. It was the young woman from the brothel. She ran toward him, waving her hands as if greeting a long-lost friend.

"How long have you been here exactly?" Zenawi asked.

"One night too long," Omari said under his breath. He forced a smile on his face as he sauntered to meet the woman.

"Well, well, you found me! Why so much joy?"

"I left the brothel!" she said. "I have come to live with you!"

Omari looked at the woman stunned.

"Ah . . . uh . . ."

"Kapera," she said sweetly. "My name is Kapera."

"Jambo, Kapera," Zenawi said. "It is good to have you. Our post has been too long without a woman's warmth."

"Wait a minute!" Omari exclaimed. "What in the Seven Winds are you doing?"

Omari's outburst seemed to wound Kapera. She lowered her head and turned away.

Zenawi cut Omari a mean glance. He went to Kapera then reached into his pocket, taking out the key to the post.

"Here, take this. We will be back in a few days."

Kapera head jerked up, her eyes glowing. "Thank you, bwa!"

She winked at Omari and ran off to the post.

Omari was furious. He grasped Zenawi's shoulders before he could walk away and spun him around.

"What in the Cleave was that? Why did you send her to the post? This is my business!"

Zenawi removed his hands. "The mistress kicked her out. No one quits the brothel. She has no work and would be in the streets otherwise. Whatever business you have with her you can sort out when we return."

Zenawi turned and walked away. Omari considered stabbing him in the back but he needed the money. He shrugged and followed. If he was the cause of the woman's firing, he would give her a few cowries and send her on her way.

They spent the remainder of the day walking along the coast, the ocean a constant companion. Toward nightfall a large structure loomed in the distance, rising over the swaying palms.

"What is this?" Omar said. "I don't remember a Kiswala fort this far south."

"It's not Kiswala," Zenawi replied. "It belongs to Enzi Chande. He was just a local fisherman five years ago before he built a dhow and began trading with the villages to the south. Now he claims to be a bwa."

"I'm sure the Kiswala are not happy with him," Omari replied.

Zenawi nodded. "A Mikijen force from the north came a few weeks ago to deal with him. They did not return."

Omari stopped walking. "What happened to them?"

Zenawi shrugged. "I assumed they dealt with Enzi then sailed home."

"You assume wrong," Omari said. "They were either paid to join Enzi or they were wiped out. Either situation is not good for us."

"Now you assume too much," Zenawi said.

"I'm alive today because of it," Omari replied. "So, I guess your plan is to walk right up to the gate and ask if anyone is home."

Zenawi shuffled about and Omari spat.

"We'll wait until nightfall then have a good look at that fort."

Zenawi frowned. "That is the coward's way. We are Mikijen."

"We walk up to that fort in the open and we'll be crab food. I'm waiting until nightfall. You can do what you wish."

Omari dropped his gear and sat. He took out his dagger and began cleaning his fingernails. Zenawi glared at him then sat beside him. Fatigue settled in as he worked on his nails so he ate what he had left of his meal then slept.

Omari stood beside Kadira. Three elderly women faced them, staffs in their withered hands. He said something to Kadira then attacked the women. One of them stepped forward, stabbing him with her staff. Then he was on his back, looking up at the three women as they lifted a carved head from his aching chest.

"Rise and serve," the women said.

Omari remained on his back, trying to understand what had just happened to him.

"Wake up!"

Omari sat up suddenly, gripping his shirt over his heart. It was dark, the night sky spotted with dense stars. Zenawi knelt before him, his face curious.

"Are you okay?"

Omari ignored Zenawi. He poked and felt about his chest with both hands before opening his shirt. A ragged scar rested over his heart.

"What in the Creator's name is this?" he said aloud.

"Omari, what is going on?"

Omari finally looked at Zenawi then remembered where he was. He closed his shirt.

"Nothing. Just a bad dream."

He stood then proceeded toward the fort.

"Wait!" Zenawi called. "We need a torch."

Omari blew out an exasperated breath. "No, Zenawi, we do not need a torch. If we light a torch they will see us."

Zenawi looked puzzled. "'We don't want to be seen?"

"Not yet," Omari answered. "It will ruin the effect."

Omari put the strange dream and wound behind him. First things first. He moved with care through the dark woods, thankful for a full moon. He stopped at the forest's edge, signaling for Zenawi to do the same. On closer inspection the fort was in a sorry state. The pockmarked walls showed signs of wear, and in certain sections holes punctured the stone.

"This fort is old, probably as old as the Kamit temples," Omari whispered.

"You've been to Kamit?" Zenawi's voice shook with excitement.

"Shut up," Omari barked. There were no guards to be seen, but a soft glow stealing through the wall breaches indicated activity inside. Omari looked about then smiled as he located Enzi's dhows.

"Now you can make your torch," he said.

Zenawi went to work, locating two thick branches then wrapping the ends with palm fronds. Omari inspected them then took them from Zenawi.

"Follow me."

They crept to the dhows. Omari took out his flint then lit the torches. He climbed aboard the first dhow, sword in one hand, torch in the other. Once he located the pitch barrels on deck, he set them on fire. He rushed out of the first dhow then did the same to the second.

"Come on!" he ordered.

He ran to the wood's edge then watched gleefully as the dhow burned. Raised voices came from the fort; moments later a dozen men rushed to the dhows. Omari jumped to his feet, sprinting into the fort through a wall breach. The fort courtyard was empty as he hoped. It didn't take him long to locate Enzi's lair, a large stone room at the rear of the fort. He took a glance behind him; Zenawi was just entering the breach, his face still confused.

"Keep up, damn it!" Omari shouted at him. He ran to the stone room, stopping only to gingerly open the door. Enzi laid sleep in an elaborate bed, his snores filling the opulent room. Omari took out his dagger.

"What are you doing?" Zenawi whispered.

"Eliminating the competition," Omari replied.

"You can't do that! It is not honorable!"

Omari stopped and glared at Zenawi. "You have a lot to learn about being a Mikijen."

Omari went to Enzi's bedside. He raised his dagger and then blinding pain struck his chest.

"What the. . ."

The pain flared again. Omari fell to his knees, dropping the dagger. The blade rattled against the stone floor. Enzi sat upright.

"What is it? What's going on?"

Omari looked into the merchant's eyes, grimacing with pain. Zenawi stood at the door dumbfounded.

"Assassins!" Enzi shouted. "Assassins!"

Omari felt hands slip under his arms. He was lifted to his feet and dragged away from the screaming Enzi.

"No!" he groaned. "I'm not finished!"

"We must flee!" Zenawi countered. "The other will hear him!"

Omari fought past the pain, managing to pull his wrist knife free. He took his best aim then threw it at Enzi. The blade whizzed by the merchant's ear then stuck into the wall behind him. Enzi yelped then flattened against the bed.

"You've been warned, fisherman!" Omari croaked.

Zenawi continued to drag him until they were outside Enzi's room. The pain in his chest subsided; Omari jerked away from Zenawi and stood.

"What is wrong with you?" Zenawi asked.

Omari rubbed his chest. "I don't know."

Zenawi pointed. "There they are!"

Omari and Zenawi both looked across the courtyard. Enzi's guards ran toward them, swords drawn and lances lowered. Omari's pain diminished rapidly as they closed in.

"I think it's time you used some of that Haisetti skill with the bow," he said to Zenawi.

Zenawi hesitated. "Shouldn't we wait to discern their intentions? These men are former Mikijen. They might . . ."

"Take that damn bow and shoot somebody!" Omari yelled.

Zenawi nocked an arrow then let it fly. The projectile sank into the throat of the closest man. Before he could hit the ground Zenawi let two more arrows fly. Two more men fell, another with an arrow to the neck, one with an arrow to the knee. Omari smiled. He was good.

The other guards scattered for cover. Omari scanned the courtyard, spotting the nearest gap in the wall.

"Let's go!"

Omari ran, Zenawi close behind. He was halfway to freedom when a guard jumped in his path, sword drawn. Omari didn't slow his pace. He feinted, raising his sword over his head as if delivering an overhead blow. The guard raised his sword to block then Omari lowered his body, ramming his shoulder into the guard's gut. The guard huffed as he doubled over onto Omari. Omari straightened and threw the guard over his shoulder. The guard slammed into the ground; Zenawi leaped to avoid falling over him.

They were well into the woods before the guards decided to pursue. They stumbled about in the dark, but without torches the guards couldn't spot them. Enzi's men gave up the chase after a time, hurling curses at Omari and Zenawi before returning to the dilapidated fort.

"We'll stay here until dawn," Omari said. "As long as we're on the way back before daylight we should be fine."

"I am not happy with your idea," Zenawi said. "What you attempted to do was an affront to the reputation of the Mikijen."

Omari had to put his hand over his mouth to keep from laughing out loud. "I think you need to take a second look at what you signed up for. We're mercenaries. We do anything we get paid to do. Anything. The Kiswala pay us well for this. I'm assuming that you've came straight from your backwoods home to Bashaba."

Zenawi swallowed. "I did."

Omari shook his head. "Go to sleep. I'll take first watch."

Zenawi found a soft spot in the brush then quickly fell asleep. Omari shook his head again. Times must be hard if the Mikijen recruited men and women like Zenawi. He was a good man, and good men had no place in the Mikijen. He sat, leaning against a palm, and then examined his chest. The pain was completely gone. He rubbed the scar, trying to remember if it was there when he left Kenja. His mind went hazy as he tried to think, so he decided to forget it. He'd find a healer and get an opinion.

He woke Zenawi for his shift then fell immediately asleep. It was a deep dreamless sleep; when Zenawi woke him he was angry.

"What? What?"

Zenawi didn't answer. Omari rubbed his eyes before opening them. Zenawi stood before him flanked by Enzi's guards.

"Is this the one?" one of the guards asked.

Zenawi nodded.

"So you're Omari Ket." The man looked Omari up and down as Omari stood. There was no reason for him to go for his weapons for he was too close and too outnumbered.

"I am. Who are you?"

"Gerial Badogo. We served together in Kiswala."

Omari didn't remember him but thought it prudent to act otherwise.

"Of course. So Gerial, do you plan to kill us?"

Gerial rubbed his chin. "We should. You robbed us of a generous employer."

"That was my plan, but I remember that I didn't kill him."

"You might as well have. The man was so frightened we couldn't get him out of the bed. I tried to convince him that he could have other dhows built and he almost died again. He ran into the night. He could have at least told us where he kept his cowries."

Omari put his hands on his waist. "So, what now?"

Gerial folded his arms across his chest. "We become Mikijen again. You'll speak for us because we didn't kill you and your friend."

"Sounds fair," Omari replied. "There will be no revenge killing? No blood feud?"

Gerial smiled. "The men you killed were our comrades, not our family. If they were family you'd have never awakened."

"Wait!" Zenawi shouted. "They are traitors! We cannot speak for them!"

Gerial glared at Zenawi, his hand finding his sword hilt. Omari raised his left hand, his other hand on his sword hilt.

"He means no harm. Let's not have anyone lose their life over a misunderstanding."

Zenawi was about to speak again but was silenced by Omari's stare. Once Zenawi was silenced Omari turned to Gerial with a bright smile.

"The day gets away from us. Shall we go?"

"Of course."

What began as a two-man task was now a twelve man return. Omari kept smiling while inside he cursed. They would have to split the money with Gerial and his cohorts. This had not turned out the way he hoped. At least Kapera waited on his return. He'd have to thank

Zenawi for that. But first he would see a healer. It was time he learned what was causing him so much pain.

Omari never imagined himself happy to see a backwater like Bashaba, but he never imagined being in the company of such annoying people. Zenawi whined the entire trek back, wondering how he was going to feed all his new Mikijen friends. Enzi's former cohorts were equally annoying, constantly bickering and complaining about various aches and pains and threatening to make him and Zenawi pay for ruining their good work. Omari was about to call them on their threats when the palm tree thicket cleared and the city came into view.

"Zenawi, can you take our new companions to the post?" Omari asked.

"Me? I thought you were coming!"

Omari rubbed his chest, remembering the pain inflicted on him in Enzi's bedroom.

"I'll be along. I'm going to see a healer."

Zenawi hurried to his side.

"I don't know what to do with them!" he whispered. "These are dangerous men!"

"Feed them," Omari replied. "That should hold them until I return. Besides, you'll have help. Kapera is there, remember?"

Zenawi's eye lit. "Yes, Kapera is there!" His face settled into worry again. "Kapera is there!"

Omari rested his hand on Zenawi's shoulder. "I know what you're thinking. Kapera can handle herself. She worked in a brothel."

"I don't know, Omari. This is not a good situation."

Omari shrugged. "We'll handle it the best we can. Once we start assigning duties things will calm down. If it doesn't, I'll pick a few fights and lighten the load."

Zenawi's brows clinched. "You are not a good man, Omari."

"I never claimed to be. Now who's the best healer?"

"Abasi, without a doubt," Zenawi replied. "His stall is behind the cow stables."

Omari's nose crinkled. "The cow stables?"

"He doesn't need to hawk his skills and the smell keeps the casual shopper away. But he is the best by far."

Omari shrugged. "I'll return soon."

He made his way to the marketplace, watching his step as he worked his way behind the cow stalls. Abasi the healer sat before a plain kanga spread over the hard-packed dirt, his healing tools and concoctions displayed on the cloth. He wore a red shirt and pants with charms on his neck and bracelets on his wrists. He appeared too young to be a learned healer, but Omari knew that a healer's looks were deceiving. The healer looked up into Omari's face then frowned.

"Go away," Abasi said.

"Zenawi told me you could help me," Omari replied.

Abasi's frown faded. "Zenawi is a good person . . . for a Mikijen."

Abasi studied him for a moment then signaled him to sit. Omari checked to make sure the ground was dung free before sitting.

"What ails you?" Abasi asked.

"I had a terrible chest pain," Omari replied. "I have no idea what causes it."

"Open your shirt."

Omari opened his shirt, revealing his mysterious wound. Abasi's eyes went wide. He reached out, touching the wound delicately.

"I can't help you," he said.

Omari pushed his hand away. "You haven't even examined me."

"I don't have to. That is not a wound. It is a mark. What affects you is beyond my skills. It's beyond anyone's skills."

Omari jumped to his feet. "This isn't a mark, it's a wound! I was stabbed by . . ."

Abasi titled his head. "By what?"

"By a staff."

"And who wielded this staff?"

"A priestess."

"And why did she stab you?"

"Because we were violating a temple."

"And where was this temple?"

"In Wadantu."

Abasi folded his arms across his chest. "So you were stabbed by a priestess because you violated a temple in a land where no one has ever entered and returned."

Omari nodded.

"Like I said, I cannot help you. She will make herself known when it is time."

"She?"

Abasi looked beyond Omari. He turned to see a young woman holding her wrist.

"Go," Abasi said. "There are people that I can heal that need my help."

"But . . ."

"Go!"

Omari trudged away. What did the healer mean by a mark? He recalled the dream he had nights ago and a shudder gripped his body. He shook his head to clear it of the strange image. This was not mark; it was a wound that was beyond the healer's skill so he made up the story to save face. By the time he reached the post he was already angry. What he saw before him made him boil. Zenawi laid again the wall, trying to stop the bleeding from a chest wound. One of his 'cohorts' was trying pull Kapera out of the post, a rope tied around her wrists. The other men were ransacking the place. Gerial sat behind the desk, a smug look on his face.

"What in the Cleave is this?" Omari growled.

"We're just collecting our payment," Gerial replied.

Omari unsheathed his sword and throwing knife. It was time to pick a fight.

Gerial ducked behind the desk as Omari raised his knife, but he was not the target. Instead the blade found the back of the man holding Kapera. The man collapsed to his knees, reaching in vain for the blade. Kapera screamed then kicked him onto his side, anger clear in her face. She stomped his head until he no longer moved.

Omari was ready when the first man attacked. He sidestepped his charge then severed his spine as he barreled by. The second man swung his blade at Omari's neck but cleaved air as the agile Mikijen ducked the blade. He drove his sword into the man's gut as he rose then kicked him free of his blade. Omari sprinted toward the desk where Gerial cowered, determined to finish him before him before the others reached him. His reason was practical; if any of the others were any type of a skilled sword fighter it would be Gerial. He wanted to rid himself of the most skilled before he wasted his energy on the rest. That way he might just live through this debacle.

Kapera reached Gerial first. Omari watched as the woman snatched the knife from her former captive's back then tackled Gerial behind the desk. Her hand rose and fell, each time the blade covered with more blood. Then she was airborne, shoved away by Gerial. He stood, his chest and arms bleeding. He looked at Omari, then his eyes lost focus and he fell back behind the desk, never to rise again.

Omari smirked as he turned to face the other false Mikijen. Kapera came to his side, gripping the bloody throwing knife in her hand. Gerial's men halted, each looking at the other to determine who would lead them against this formidable swordsman and the crazed woman. The man in the rear fled first; the others soon followed. Kapera relaxed with a gasp, dropping the knife then sitting on the floor before cradling her face in her bloody hands and crying. But Omari was not done. He went to Zenawi's side. The man was still breathing but barely. He picked up Zenawi's sword.

"Tend to him," he said to Kapera. He ran out the door.

Omari was not about to leave enemies alive. Unfortunately for them the interlopers decided to stay together as they fled. They'd underestimated Omari's speed and his intentions. He jumped among them like a leopard on a flock of sheep. In minutes they all lay at his feet in the throes of death. Omari lingered to make sure his work was done before trotting back to the outpost. Kapera sat beside Zenawi, pressing bandages against his chest. He sheathed his sword then knelt beside Zenawi.

"Hang in there, Mikijen," he whispered. "Maybe that healer will work better for you than he did for me."

As he lifted Zenawi he felt pleasant warmth spread from his chest wound throughout his body, easing his fatigue. The feeling puzzled him; this was a sensation that normally came from the ngisimaugi when he was wounded. He shrugged then ran as fast as he could to the healer, Kapera close on his heels.

Omari carried Zenawi through the streets to Abasi's lair. The healer immediately cleared a space before him and cut Zenawi's clothes away to reveal the wound. He reached to his left, grabbing a large gourd then scooped out a handful of a clear cream-like substance. Zenawi yelped when the healer applied the cream to his wound.

"Did you do this?" Abasi asked.

"No!" The question angered Omari. "Why would you think that?"

"How do you feel?" the healer asked.

"I feel. . .rather good, actually," Omari replied.

Abasi nodded. "Open your shirt."

Omari complied. The scar was barely visible, much as it had been when he first arrived.

"What it going on?" he whispered.

"As I said, only She can tell you, and She has not chosen to yet."

Omari wasn't about to get into another argument with the healer. He massaged his chest then changed the subject.

"How is he?"

"He'll live, but he'll need lots of rest."

The healer was interrupted by Kapera's arrival. She scrambled to Zenawi's side, scooting by the healer the cradling Zenawi's head. Omari smirked; he'd seen that look before. Kapera was lost to him. Her feelings were now centered on Zenawi.

"What can I do?" she asked.

"Nothing for now. My paste will cleanse the wound. After tomorrow I'll sew him up. He won't be fit to work for a few weeks."

"I'll take care of him," Kapera said quickly.

"Looks like I'll be running the business for a while," Omari groaned.

For the next two weeks Omari suffered through the daily routine of a Mikijen clerk. He received goods from the local farmers and paid them in Kiswala currency. In the evenings he armed himself and strolled through the streets, fulfilling his other responsibility of enforcer and peacekeeper. His public display with the former Mikijen made the latter roles easy. No one would come near him and everyone bowed to him when he walked by. Omari was utterly and painfully bored. If it wasn't for the fact that Zenawi was recuperating he would pack his things and head north. But he would stay at least until the man was back on his feet.

A week later his prayers were answered. A large Kiswala dhow arrived, flying the Ngisimaugi banner. When the word reached Omari he almost hurt himself running to the harbor. A relieved laugh escaped his lips as a boat filled with Mikijen was lowered into the calm waters. As the boat neared Omari realized he knew the man commanding this dhow.

He cupped his hands around his mouth. "Sonnai Maduo!" he shouted.

"Omari Ket?" Sonnai Maduo shielded his eyes with his ring encrusted hand.

The boat eased onto the beach and the Mikijen waded to shore. Omari greeted each of his brothers with a handshake, but for Sonnai he added a hug and a solid back pat. Sonnai was one of a few Kiswala that served in the Mikijen, for the role of a mercenary was considered beneath the merchants. But Sonnai had the soul of a fighter despite wearing the turban of a merchant.

"I heard you were dead," Sonnai said.

"I was, a couple of times, but the Cleave keeps spitting me back out."

Sonnai chuckled. "Still blasphemous, I see. Anything good to drink in this hole?"

"Of course not, but we'll drink it anyway."

The two walked side by side to the streets.

"So is this a relief visit?" Omari asked.

"No," Sonnai said. "We came to collect you and any other Mikijen in the area. The Kiswala are going to war."

Omari felt a twinge of dread. "Who this time?"

"Axum."

Omari almost giggled. When Kiswala went to war against Axum they spared no expense. There was nothing like war between relatives.

"I have to admit I'm disappointed," Sonnai commented. "I expected more Mikijen here. The census count put you at twenty."

"There were at least thirteen until recently," Omari said.

"What happened to the others?" Sonnai asked.

Omari smirked. "I killed them."

Sonnai stopped in his tracks. "Why did you do that?"

"It's a long story."

Sonnai shrugged. "Then my trip here would be a waste if you weren't here."

Omari was flattered. "Thank you."

"You're the perfect man to command my special warriors."

Omari's rush faded. "Your special warriors?"

It was Sonnai's turn to smirk. "There's a mission within this war that requires special handling, an assassination actually. It pays an astronomical sum and required a unique individual to lead it."

Omari closed his eyes. He knew what was coming.

"Who are these special warriors?"

Sonnai smiled. "Ndoko."

"Shit."

Omari led the new Mikijen to the outpost. They stashed their gear while he checked on Zenawi and Kapera. Zenawi smiled weakly when he entered the room. Kapera studied him with suspicious eyes.

"Who is out there?" she asked.

"Mikijen."

Her hand went to the knife lying beside her.

"Calm down, these are real Mikijen. They've come to gather us for a military operation."

Zenawi tried to sit up. "I must get ready."

"Stay where you are, Zenawi. You're in no shape to go anywhere. You've done a fine job here and with Kapera's help you'll do even better."

Zenawi frowned. "I'm a Mikijen! It's my duty to answer the call!"

Omari rolled his eyes. "It's your duty to get paid as much as possible without getting killed. That's our way. Now relax and get well."

Omari and the others strolled to the tavern, Sonnai catching Omari up on Kiswala business since his departure. They stood before the tavern entrance when Omari remembered his last incident beyond those doors.

"I can't go in there," he said.

Sonnai sighed. "Another long story?"

Omari nodded.

Sonnai patted his shoulder. "Come on. We'll straighten things out."

Heads turned as they made their way to a table.

"No!" a shrill voice screeched.

Omari dropped his head. "Here we go."

"Get out of my place now!" the matron screamed at him. She charged the table followed by two large brutes with studded orinkas in their large hands. Sonnai stood between the woman and the table.

"Is there a problem?" he asked.

The matron jabbed her finger at Omari. "He's the problem! He killed two of my best men and stole the best worker I ever had."

"You're upset, and I understand," Sonnai said calmly. "My friends and I have traveled far and don't wish any trouble. We are hungry and very thirsty. Maybe our patronage will make up for his transgressions."

The matron stood nose to nose with Sonnai.

"Maybe on the day the Cleave becomes Paradise, but not today."

Sonnai gripped the woman's arms then lifted her off her feet as his men stood, their hands on their swords.

"Here's another option. I'll break your arms then we'll kill the rest of your men and burn down this place. I'm sure the next matron will be more pleasant than you."

The brutes slowly turned and shuffled away. Sonnai place the woman down.

"Now please be kind to bring us some food and that swill you call beer."

The matron cut a mean glance at Omari then stalked away rubbing her arms. Moments later servants appeared with large pots of sorghum beer, chaff bowls and drinking reeds. Sonnai took a sip then blew the chaff into a bowl.

"This is bad," he commented.

Omari sipped and agreed. "Tell me about this war."

"Kiswala established trade with Mugadi a few years back. Not long afterwards Kiswali were setting up villages outside the city. The Auxites turned a blind eye to it until some of the settlers started ranting about divine redemption and final homecoming stuff."

"Damn fools," Omari commented.

Sonnai nodded. "Next thing you know an army swooped in from Adisha. They killed every Kiswali and razed their villages. They spared Mugadi with a stern warning."

"So now the Kiswala want revenge."

Sonnai took another sip of the beer then shoved his pot away. "How can you drink this crap?"

Omari shrugged. "You get used to it. Besides, sometimes you just need to get drunk."

Sonnai broke his reed. "Anyway, the plan is to launch an attack on Mugadi. It's actually a diversion. The true objective is to assassinate Adisha's Ras. That's the task of the Ndoko . . . and you."

Omari took a long sip of beer, swallowing the chaff.

"We're talking 30 stacks for each member of the team," Sonnai added, "and an extra ten if you bring back the Ras's head. And you know the stacks are split among the survivors."

Omar cringed. "I know."

"So what do you say?"

"Shit." It was too good of a deal to turn down.

Sonnai laughed. "You're the only person I know who speaks KaNdoko. You can do this."

Omari was torn. The pay would make up for the Kashite disaster and then some. But dealing with the Ndoko?"

Omari drained the beer pot. "Get me another beer. If you get me drunk enough I might say yes."

Sonnai raised his hand. "Another beer pot!"

He smacked his hand on Omari's back. "You won't regret this, brother."

"Yes I will."

Omari didn't remember leaving the tavern. He awoke at the Mikijen post, smelling of fish and vomit. Sunlight stabbed his eyes like knives and he fell back to his cot for another two hours, whether asleep or unconscious he didn't know nor care. His second attempt to wake went much better. He craned his neck to the right and saw a bucket of water resting beside him. His clothes were ruined so he tore them off then tossed them as far away as possible. Whoever brought him the water left a cloth and a ball of fat soap. He cleaned up then changed clothes, ignoring the snickers of his fellow Mikijen as he took his clothes behind the post and burned them. Sonnai waited for him when he returned.

"You won't regret it."

Omari grunted and his head ached.

"I already do. When do we leave?"

"Tomorrow."

Omari struggled to his feet. "I'll be back."

He trudged through town to the healer. Abasi looked at him, shaking his head.

"You drink too much," he said.

"I'm not here for that," Omari replied. "What do you have for pain?"

"I told you I can do nothing . . ."

"I'm not talking about my damn chest!" Omari shouted. "I'm talking about body aches."

The healer rummaged through his concoctions then pulled out a small green pouch. He set it before Omari.

"Do you have any numbing cream?" Omari asked.

The healer tilted his head, then went through his gourds. He gave Omari a wide mouth gourd sealed with a thick cotton cloth.

"Are you in pain?" Abasi asked.

"No, but I will be."

Omari paid the man then returned to the post. The Mikijen had returned to the dhow. Zenawi and Kapera waited for him, their faces drawn.

"So you are leaving," Zenawi said.

"Yes. It's time to move on. There's a war, and war means profit."

Kapera rushed him, throwing her arms around his neck then burying her head in his chest.

"You'll be killed!"

"That's not very optimistic." Omari pushed her back at arm's length.

"I'm very hard to kill."

She looked at him, sorrow clear in her eyes. If Omari didn't know better, he'd think she still had feelings for him.

"You and Zenawi will be fine. Sonnai has a special task that only I can perform."

Zenawi moved Kapera aside then shook Omari's hand.

"It was an honor to serve with you."

Omari did his best not to laugh out loud.

"No, the honor was mine. You have proven your-self a fine Mikijen. We are better because of you."

Zenawi smiled, his eyes glistening.

"Be well, Omari!"

Omari patted Zenawi's shoulder. "Be well, Zenawi!"

He quickly gathered his other things then headed for the dock. It was a good thing Zenawi was hurt. He wouldn't last the journey to Kiswala, let alone a war. He was good where he was. As he neared the docks his mind shifted to other matters. The Ndoko waited for him in Kiswala. Sometimes he wished he's never taken the job on Ors. If not for that he would know nothing of the Ndoko or their strange language. Things always went bad for him personally when he did good for someone else. By the time he reached the docks he was in a sour mood. Sonnai waited with his ever-present smile, which depressed him even more.

"They're on the ship, aren't they?"

Sonnai nodded.

"Let's get his over with then."

Omari handed his items to Sonnai then took off his shirt. He swallowed the entire pouch of painkiller then washed it down with water. He then took the numbing cream and spread it over his torso and face. He waited for a few minutes then pinched himself. He felt nothing.

"I'm ready. Take me to them."

Sonnai led him on board then below deck. They walked to the back of the ship to the hold for animals.

"It's not right for them to be there," Omari commented. "They are not animals."

"It wasn't meant that way," Sonnai answered. "It was the only place left on the dhow. You know they won't share with us."

Omari grunted his disapproval. He grasped the door handle.

"Good luck," Sonnai said.

"Luck had nothing to do with it," Omari answered.

He snatched the door open then stormed inside. The Ndoko sat huddled around a communal eating pot enjoying their evening meal. Omari grunted and the clan leader sprang to his feet. His proportions resemble that of a man, except for the hair that covered his entire body. His face was like that of the Old Men, though the Ndoko were as far from those powerful yet gentle creatures. Omari and the clan leader ran at each other, slamming their chest together. Omari staggered back but regained his feet, surviving the first challenge. They approached each other again. Omari raised his arms, slamming both fists on the clan leader's shoulders. The leader did not budge. The leader the same to Omari and he staggered, but again he did not fall. They circled again, eyes locked. Then the leader's eyes glanced at Omari's chest. He stopped pacing.

"That is a killing wound," he said.

The other Ndoko came to their feet, all of them advancing on Omari.

"Where did you get it?" he asked.

"In Wadantu."

His eyes widened then his body posture relaxed. He gestured toward the food pot.

"Come eat with us, brother," he said. He returned to the pot and ate, the others following.

Omari looked at the faint scar and smiled.

"This gets more interesting every moment," he whispered.

He joined his new clan and shared their meal.

Omari sat among them, eating with his hands as was Ndoko tradition. He kept his eyes down, waiting for clan leader's signal for introductions. It came with a slight shove to his shoulder. Omari looked up and into the clan leader's black eyes.

"Pomu," he said. He looked to his left where his second sat.

"Reth," he said. His brows narrowed as he looked at Omari, letting him know he was not welcomed. Omari returned the gesture, meaning he didn't care. Reth glanced to his left and the others shared their names.

"Agu."

"Bem"

"Senwe"

"Cheelo."

"Fahru."

"Tumo."

"Vembe."

They all looked at him. Omari took a swallow, preparing himself for the worst.

"Ngozi mtu."

The room exploded with shouts. Reth jumped to his feet, swaying from side to side. Omari sprang to his feet as well, repeating the gesture. He studied the other clansmen. Though their eyes were angry, they kept their place. Omari finally looked at Pomu. The elder Ndoko looked at him with a smirk on his face. He stood slowly then put his hand on Reth's shoulder. Reth shrugged it away. Pomu slapped it down his shoulder, pushing Reth to his knees.

"So you are Ngozi mtu?"

Omari stopped swaying then nodded.

He stood before Omari.

"Dumi is dead."

"I know," Omari replied.

"You should have died with him!" Reth spat.

"I know," Omari said. He fought hard to keep the emotion from his voice.

Pomu looked at the others. "He is marked by Her, so he is under Her watch. I have accepted him in our clan and I do not take back my word."

The others shifted about. Omari could tell they were not happy with Pomu's decision but they would abide by it.

"Come," Pomu said. "We'll play."

Omari nodded but on the inside he cringed. He might not survive this after all.

He and the others followed Pomu to the deck. The Mikijen sailors looked stunned for a moment then quickly cleared the deck. Pomu lead Omari to a crude circle painted into the floor planks. He nodded and Omari entered the circle.

Agu was first. He and Omari swayed from side to side in synch as the Ndoko struck the deck in a familiar rhythm. The Game began. Agu was unskilled; Omari swept his feet, Agu crashed onto his back, the momentum sending him tumbling out of the circle. Senwe replaced him quickly, cartwheeling into the circle then falling in time with Omari's movements. Omari played through them all, struggling to raise his 'play' with each turn. Then Reth back flipped into the circle and the Game became deadly. They spun, somersaulted and dodged, landing hard blows with each move. Somehow Omari landed a kick in Reth's chest that sent him sprawling outside the circle. He yelled then rushed back to the circle but Pomu shoved him aside, entering himself. It was then the Game went beyond Omari's skills. Try as he might, he was just too rusty to keep up with the clan leader. A few quick blows and Omari tumbled from the circle.

Pomu appeared over him, his hand extended. Omari grabbed his hand and the Ndoko lifted him to his feet. He heard clapping; the crew was apparently impressed with his skills.

"I see why Dumi chose you," Pomu said. "You will sit beside Reth."

Reth grunted then stomped away. Omari nodded.

"Come, we go back down."

Omari took a step then swayed. His concoctions were wearing off. He crashed into a wall of pain then passed out.

* * *

Omari opened his eyes to Sonnai's face. He immediately tried to sit up but Sonnai pushed him back down.

"You're not going anywhere," he said.

"I have to get back," Omari said.

"No you don't. Those monkey men beat the Cleave out of you. Maybe this was a bad idea."

Omari tried to sit up again. Sonnai attempted to push him down again but Omari shoved his hands away.

"It's part of the process," Omari said. "If you want me to lead them I have to become part of the clan. Playing the Game is part of it."

"You call that a game?"

"It is for them."

Omari swung his legs off the table he'd been placed on. He ached everywhere. Even his hair hurt. The first thing he would do once they reached shore was get more painkillers.

Sonnai folded his arms across his chest.

"You're no good to me dead, you know."

"I'm no good to myself, either," Omari cracked. "I'll be fine."

"I'll have to admit, you held your own. That second to last guy has it out for you, though."

Omari smirked. "Yes he does. I figure his clan must have been on the wrong side of Dumi."

Sonnai's eyes widened. "You knew Dumi?"

Omari nodded. "I was his second."

Sonnai laughed until he saw that Omari was serious.

"That was you? You were The Skin Man?"

Omari frowned. "I always hated that name."

"Toss me in the Cleave! Omari Ket was the Skin Man! I'm surprised they all didn't beat you to death."

Omari stood. His legs were a bit wobbly but he could walk.

"Dumi was a lot of things to a lot of people, but to me he was a friend," Omari said. "At first I fought with him because he let me live when he didn't have to. After a while I found myself believing in him."

"Well, I'm glad he failed." Sonnai rubbed his chin. "Could you imagine the Ndoko as a kingdom?"

"Dumi did. He almost succeeded."

"But then the Skin Man disappeared." Sonnai looked at him as if expecting an explanation. He wouldn't get one. There were some stories Omari would not tell, some he'd rather forget.

He staggered to the cabin door.

"Omari, be careful," Sonnai called out. "You're my friend, too."

Omari turned to Sonnai. "Quit it with the sweet stuff. You need me alive so I can carry out the assassination."

Sonnai chuckled. "That, too."

Omari spent the rest of the voyage submerged with the Ndoko. Every day they played the Game and every day Reth tried his best to kill him. But Omari's old skills gradually resurfaced, making it easier to deal with Reth. He was beginning to give Pomu a challenge as well, but he decided to hold back. The time to confront him had not come yet. He needed to be sure the others were fully dominated before he made that move. Pomu was skilled, but he was no Dumi.

Two weeks after setting sail from Bashaba they arrived in Kiswala. If Omari had any doubts the Kiswala were going to war they were dashed by the huge man-owari fleet assembled in Zanabar Harbor. He stood on deck with his clan, gazing into the city teeming with Mikijen. Omari's mind was on other matters. He looked at Pomu and the Ndoko grunted.

"Go," he said. "I know your needs."

Omari held back a grin until his feet hit solid ground. He placed his hands on his hips, his legs spread wide. Sonnai stood beside him.

"So where do we begin?" Omari said.

"At the bath house," Sonnai answered. "You reek."

Omari sniffed at Sonnai. "And you smell like rainy season flowers."

They laughed and exchanged jabs.

"How many days do we have before we challenge fate?" Omari asked.

"Three."

"Then let's make the best of them!" Omari shouted. They ran into Zanabar like mischievous boys.

Omari was very familiar with the pleasures of the city. No sooner did they enter the city did he stride purposely toward the hostel district with Sonnai and his cohorts in tow.

"This is the wrong direction," Sonnai commented.

"No it's not," Omari replied.

"Yes it is," Sonnai argued. "It's not like this is my first time to Zanabar. I know this city."

"But you don't know it like I do. Just be quiet and follow me. You won't regret it."

They reached the hostel district, rows of stone buildings that served as respite for visiting merchants. The buildings were separated by walls and divided by profession, with each merchant folk claiming their own section. They passed through the hostel district to free lodging, an area set aside for those with no particular origin or occupation. It was a rundown ward, an area where one would not wish to be alone day or night. But it was the district beyond free lodging which was Omari's destination. It was called the Hole, an area where if one fell in, he did not return, hence its nickname. Sonnai and his men stopped following Omari.

"No," Sonnai said. "We're not going in there."

Omari shrugged. "Suit yourself. I have a bath waiting for me."

He walked on alone. Sonnai and his men fidgeted, looking at each other as they silently debated whether to follow him.

"I promise you Omari, if I get killed, I'll never forgive you!" Sonnai shouted.

Sonnai and the others ran and caught up to him.

They could feel eyes upon them, but Omari was familiar with those eyes. Long ago his were among them in a larger, more dangerous city, another beggar preying on the helpless and naïve. His face and his reputation were his passport through the dangerous streets and anyone with him was allowed safe passage. They continued until they reached a battered looking building at the end of an alley, the only redeeming quality a beautifully carved door accented with gold and precious gems.

Omari turned to his friends, his arms spread wide.

"Bwas, welcome to Paradise," he announced.

He approached the doors, which swung wide before he could knock. An elderly man appeared with a smile on his wrinkled face.

"Omari Ket," he said, his voice almost a whisper. "They said you were dead."

"They always say that until I return."

The old man laughed silently. "There are quite a few that will be disappointed you're not."

"Nothing has changed then. Bilal, these are my friends. We require food and baths."

Bilal held out his hand. Omari took the gold pouch he out of Kenja from his belt. He gazed at it longingly, kissed it then tossed it to Bilal.

The old man caught it then tossed it up again, testing the weight. His eyes widened.

"I know this pains you greatly," he said.

"Yes, it does," Omari said. "Please, put it away before I change my mind."

Bilal tucked the bag away then opened the doors.

"Bwas, you may enter. But I warn you, you may never wish to leave."

The interior of Paradise lived up to its name. A wide corridor extended before them, the floor covered with luxurious rugs from Asanteman. Lovely figures of nude men and women decorated the marble walls, each shaped carved into the stone by skilled hands. Two guards stood by the entrance, their stoic faces and broad blades making their purpose clear. Omari and the others followed Bilal down the corridor to a wide rotunda. In the center was a towering statue of Daarila raising his celestial axe, about to deliver the blow that defined Ki-Khanga. Omari wiped a tear from his eye as he gazed upon the magnificent sculpture.

"Are you crying?" Sonnai asked.

"No! Of course not!" Omari replied.

"I wonder about you sometimes," Sonnai said.

On the opposite side of the rotunda were twelve doors.

"Bwas, choose a door and enter. It does not matter which you choose, for in Paradise all is equally satisfying."

Omari walked to the door in the center and entered the room. A porcelain bath resting on squat gilded legs greeted him, herb-scented mist rising from inside. A man and woman stood on either side of the bath. Omari stripped then eased into the warm water, his tension dissipating as each inch of his body submerged under the fragranced liquid. By the time he was completely immersed he was asleep, a relaxed smile on his face. He was awakened by another person entering his bath. He opened his eyes to the woman. Her male companion was gone.

"I didn't pay for this," Omari said with a grin.

The woman smiled. "No one will know if you don't tell."

"My lips are sealed," Omari said.

The others were waiting when Omari emerged from the room. They all looked refreshed, clean and happy. Sonnai sported a wide grin which gradually faded as Omari came closer.

"You didn't!" he said.

Omari smirked. "What can I say? I'm irresistible."

"Damn it to the Cleave! You were to take us to Matalai Shamsi!"

"I will, I will," Omari assured them. "There is no way I can come to Zanabar and not visit the Jewel. Come, we waste time."

A pair of wagons waited for them when they exited the bath house.

"My compliments," Bilal said. "It is not often that our patrons make our staff as happy as we make them."

Bilal and Omari winked at each other. The Mikijen climbed in then were on their way to the Jewel. The city district which held the pleasure house was the complete opposite of the Hole. Tall white washed villas with elegant verandas lined the wide paved streets. Lush fruit gardens divide the villas, the trees pregnant with bananas, oranges and other sweet fruits. Matalai Shamsi rested on the corner of the wide avenue, a tall arch heralding the entrance. Omari was barely out of the wagon when he heard a squeal.

"Omari! Omari!"

A beautiful pair ran to him, a woman with a cloud of hair bouncing over her head and a man with tight red beaded braids. They hugged him like a long-lost brother, which in some ways he was.

"Isabis! Iridis! It is good to see you!"

"Come, come," they said in unison. "Makadisa will be so happy to see you!"

They dragged Omari through the arch and the lush veranda to the gilded doors. The guards opened the doors, winking and smiling at Omari and his companions. The Matalai Shamsi foyer teemed with men and women, the patrons indistinguishable from the servers.

"Everyone look!" Iridisi shouted. "Omari Ket is here!"

All heads turned to the entrance and Omari struck a victorious pose. The foyer erupted in a cheer; somewhere a chorus of drums fell into a vigorous rhythm and everyone broke into dance.

"Now this is a homecoming!" Sonnai shouted.

"Yes it is!" Omari replied.

A vision of beauty emerged from the opposite side of the foyer. The celebrants paused momentarily as she sashayed through, each person acknowledging her with a slight nod before continuing to dance. Omari waited patiently as she made her way to him. She halted before him, her flawless ebony skin and amber eyes glittering with anticipation.

"Welcome home, Omari," she said.

"My beautiful Makadisha," Omari whispered.

"Come, we have much to share." She extended her jeweled hand. Omari took it, his smile radiating his anticipation.

"How many days do we have before departure again?" he asked Sonnai without taking his eyes off Makadisha.

"Three days."

He looked at his friend then grinned. "I'll see you in three days."

* * *

Three days later Omari was awakened by gentle kisses on his eyelids. When he finally opened his eyes Makadisha hovered over him, her dazzling smile brighter than any sunshine he'd ever witnessed. She was the only woman who rivaled Kadira. Although Kadira was not as beautiful as Makadisha, her martial talents and spirit made her just as attractive.

"You must leave me today," she whispered.

"It's probably best," Omari replied. "Otherwise I'd die in bed."

"And what's wrong with that?"

Omari gently pushed Makadisha away and rolled out of her plush bed. He picked up his clothes from the floor where he dropped them three days ago. He dressed slowly, giving Makadisha the last look he knew she wanted. She in turned continue to walk about nude, returning the favor.

"You said you will quit the Mikijen and open a drinking house."

"I will," he replied.

"You said the same years ago," she frowned.

"And if my last commission had gone as it should, that day would have been today." Omari gritted his teeth as he remembered the Wadantu fiasco.

"So, will this new commission help?"

Omari finished dressing then pulled Makadisha to him and kissed her.

"If it does, you'll be the first to know. For now, it's time to serve."

Makadisha threw on a thick silk robe then walked out the room at his side.

"You know I love you," she said.

"And I love you," he replied reflexively.

"No you don't. You love yourself. You love the idea of loving me."

Omari didn't reply. That was what he didn't like about Makadisha. She knew him too well. There was nothing he could get past her. But she wasn't exactly right. If he did finally fall in love, it would surely be her, especially since Kadira was taken and Aisha was a distant memory. But of course, that could change. There were always other possibilities.

"Makadisha, I . . ."

She put her fingers to his lips.

"Don't say anything you don't mean, Omari. Go and be safe. We'll talk more if you return."

"When I return," he said.

She kissed his cheek. "Always the optimist. Goodbye, Omari."

Omari looked back at Makadisha as he met his companions. There was something in her eyes that bothered him. It continued to do so as they returned to the dhow.

"That was amazing!" Sonnai said.

Sonnai's words broke his musing.

"Thank you."

"A man would do well to be your companion," Sonnai continued.

"Most of those who chose to be my companions are dead," he said. "I'm not good luck."

They were about to board the dhow when Sonnai raised his hand.

"Your journey with us is over, Omari. Another dhow will take you to Aux."

Omari's stomach tightened. "You didn't tell me about this."

Sonnai smiled. "Don't' worry. You'll be in better hands. Take care of yourself, my friend. Don't die."

Omari grasped Sonnai's extended hand then pulled him into a hug.

"I don't plan to. May Eda keep you and your sword never breaks."

He heard commotion and looked up. The Ndoko ambled across the deck single file, the other crew members giving them a wide berth. They walked down to the gangplank and directly to Omari, ignoring Sonnai.

"Did you have . . . fun, Ngozi mtu?" Pomu asked.

"Yes," Omari replied.

"Good. We must serve the Goddess now. Come."

Pomu continued past him. Reth tossed him his gear, a scowl on his face.

"Get behind me," he said.

Omari did as he was told. The respite was officially done. In his absence his rank had been decided; he was third, ranked behind Reth. Pomu was a smart leader. Omari's performance in the Game had earned him second status but ranking him such would cause a challenge from Reth that would only be decide by the death of one of them. Pomu needed every one for the task ahead; he couldn't afford to lose anyone yet. Besides, Omari had not been blooded with them. Sure, he was Pomu's second and his reputation was undeniable, but reputation did not supersede experience. Omari didn't protest. If he survived the mission his association with the Ndoko would be done. He'd collect his pay and be on his way.

Curious and fearful stares followed them across the harbor to a large dhow docked a good distance from the other craft. Omari's eyes widened in wonder. There was very little in Duniyaa the traveling mercenary had not seen or experienced, but what lay before him was such a thing. The Tyrak war galley towered over the nearby dhows, a terrible and beautiful craft. He was aware the Kiswali traded with the mysterious guardians of the Cleave, but as far as he knew their ships never ventured away from their martial vigil. His curious eyes swept across every detail, the almost organic design of the dhow, the way it drifted on the waves as if it lived, as if the bones and hide of the indigo joka from which it was constructed pulsed with blood. Sharp bolt tips from the loaded onagers protruded over the deck edge. Tyrak baharia inspected the sails and maintained the decks, oblivious to the file of Ndoko approaching their mooring. They were black skinned, powerfully built men and women, their scalps bare. Intricate ivory tattoos covered their heads instead. Both men and women wore no clothing above the waist, their lower bodies covered by *kangas* which stopped short of their knees, revealing their muscle corded legs. What stood out most were their wide chests and backs. These people were swimmers, a folk who though graceful and sure on land obviously spent much, if not most of their time in the cold waters of their homeland. Maybe the other stories were true as well, Omari thought. He hoped he wouldn't find out.

A female Tyrak broke away from the others and approached them, her only distinguishing feature from the others a small medallion hanging by a leather cord around her neck. She walked directly to Pomu.

"Our cargo has arrived," she said.

She clasped Pomu's bicep in traditional Ndoko greeting to outsiders and he grasped hers as well. Omari wasn't sure, but he thought he saw the Ndoko smile. That would be two miracles in one day.

"It's been a long time, Narsus," he said.

"It has," she replied. "Eda has kept you well, I see."

"As she has you," Pomu replied.

Narsus looked from Pomu to Omari. Omari flashed his smile and Narsus's face became stern. Her eyes narrowed as the look of recognition came to her face. Pomu nodded to her, giving her permission to speak to him.

She advanced on him quickly.

"Omari Ket," she said. "Or should I call you Ngozi mtu?"

"It is Ngozi mtu among my brothers," he replied.

"You are new to Eda's embrace," she said. "We who serve Her are closer than most. Pomu trusts you. Do not let them down as you did Dumi. If you do, you will answer to me."

Omari felt her threat in his bones. He was not a man easily intimidated but the stories he'd heard of the Tyrak nahoda gave him pause.

"I have no intentions of letting anyone down," Omari replied. "Pomu knows this."

Narsus's eyes lingered on his face for a moment then went to his chest. She grabbed his shirt then opened it, revealing the faint scar. Her touch was rough like sand.

"Eda had marked you," she said with a grin. "My mind is at ease now. You will serve her well. You have no choice."

Narsus walked away and the Ndoko followed her onto the warship. The other Tyrak ignored the new passengers, staying focused on their duties. Narsus led them below deck. The innards of the Tyrak dhow were spacious, a requirement because of the Tyraks' bulk. They were taken to a space which was obviously a cargo hold, the only space on a dhow that accommodated the Ndoko communal living style.

"We have made arrangements for your specific needs," Narsus said. "We weren't aware Omari would be with you, but I think we can provide for him as well."

"How long will our journey take?" Pomu asked.

"All the fleets are launching today," Narsus replied. "The Kiswala say they will reclaim Mugadi in two weeks' time but they are always optimistic. We will reach our destination in one week."

"One week?" Omari blurted. "From here to Aux?"

Narsus smiled. "Our dhows are very fast."

Omari and the Ndoko secured their gear then left the room to roam the dhow. Omari went immediately to the deck. The docks were filled with well-wishers waving, ululating and shouting words of encouragement to the fleets. Omari spotted his people as well, the brightly colored and beautiful workers from Matalai Shamsi resembling a flock of birds as they waved scarves at random. Omari whistled and they turned to the Tyrak dhow. A cheer went up among them; Omari was leaving in style. A few folks from the Hole dared to emerge to wish him well briefly then went to work silently robbing the crowd. The Tyrak paid no attention to the celebrants, their efforts focused on getting the dhow under way. If the Kiswali were masters of the sea, the Tyrak were their gods. Omari had never in his life experienced such a fast dhow. He'd heard rumors of Kamite craft so fast they seemed to glide in the air, but people were always saying such things about the Kamites. He'd yet to see any of it proven.

The Tyrak warship raced out of the harbor and into open sea. Narsus had not boasted when she spoke of the ship's speed. Omari was very familiar with dhows as all Mikijen were, and he was impressed. The Tyrak worked the sails with amazing precision, capturing every gust of wind like stingy Kiswali merchants after wealth. He watched the crew for hours, fascinated by their coordination. His time on deck let him witness another skill of theirs; their swimming prowess. A team of Tyrak stripped naked then took up spears, tridents and nets. They dove into the water then disappeared into the clear blue depths faster than Omari thought possible. Minutes later they returned to the surface with the ocean's bounty, easily swimming alongside the ship then climbing back on deck on the cargo nets lowered over the side.

"I take it you like seafood?"

Omari looked to see Narsus standing beside him. Despite her bulk she was able to approach unnoticed. Omari studied her instinctively. It wasn't taking him long to appreciate Tyrak female attributes. A smirk came to Narsus's face.

"You're living up to your reputation," she commented.

Omari flashed a seductive grin. "I'm a man of wide appetites."

"Well, curb your cravings here. I doubt any of my crew would be interested in such a slight man as you."

"We'll see," Omari said with a wink. "And of course I love seafood. I'm Mikijen, aren't I?"

"Your companions prefer land fare. We've made accommodations for them."

Narsus reached into her lap pouch and extracted a scroll.

"Take this to Pomu. It's the map for your mission."

Omari took the map. "I'll deliver it now."

"Please do. You're becoming a distraction. Some of my crew is pairs and the men are becoming angry at your lingering eyes."

"I thought you said I was too slight," Omari replied.

"Tyraks can be curious as well."

Omari chuckled as he headed below deck. As he strolled to their room his mercenary mind began its simple math. With each of them offered 30 stacks for the mission, his payday would rival what he lost in Kenja. He doubted they all would make it back and the Kiswali would honor the payment with those who did. He felt somewhat bad about losing a few of the Ndoko, but war is war. He might as well make the best of the situation. When he opened his drinking house, he would have a drink in their honor.

His chest tightened, a pricking pain rising around his scar. He rubbed it until the pain subsided.

"Got to do something about 'Eda's mark," he said before entering the Ndoko lair.

His clan gathered in a circle as if expecting him. He approached Pomu, map held high.

"A gift from Narsus," he said.

Pomu took the scroll then spread it out. It was a map of Aux, with major roads and cities highlighted.

"We will land here," Pomu said, pointing at an obscure harbor. "We will travel at night. Once we get to Esmeera we'll follow the main road to Qwera. It is their

Ras who led the attack on Bashaba. It is he who is our target."

Pomu looked at Omari. "You will lead us into Qwera."

The others nodded with Pomu. Omari nodded back but was slightly surprised. He knew Aux but not well enough to lead an assassin team into the city. But the clan leader had made the decision and he could not refuse. Pomu rolled up the map then handed it back to Omari.

"We will trust you," he said.

Omari nodded again, absently rubbing the scar as it ached.

* * *

The Tyrak dhow eased close to the Auxite coast on a humid, moonless night. Omari stood on the deck with his clan, straining his eyes to see where the ocean ended and the shore began. His efforts were in vain. It was a dangerous night to attempt a landing, but a perfect night to begin a mission. Omari took inventory, patting his body as he counted his weapons. His hand ended on the etched metal of his hand cannon. He opted to bring the weapon at the last minute. It was cumbersome, loud and inaccurate, but if their task was discovered and their situation desperate it would be a powerful distraction.

The Tyrak lowered their boat over the side then climbed down and entered the warm water. Pomu patted each of them on the shoulder, lingering for a moment before Omari.

"Eda deliver us, either to our home or to her bosom," he said.

Omari and the clan repeated his words. It was a morbid thing to say before going on an assignment, but it was the Ndoko way. They followed the Tyrak over the side, lowering themselves into the waiting boat on thick ropes. There were no oars; the Tyrak decided to tow the boat to avoid the noise of oars against the waters. The guardians of the Cleave prove themselves more than capable. Omari had to grip the side of the boat to keep from toppling backwards when the Tyrak swimmers swam toward the shore. In moments they entered shallow water, the Tyrak standing on their broad feet as they pulled the boat close to shore. Omari eased into the water then waded to the rocky shore. The Tyrak offered them no words as they trotted to the sparse brush; by the time they reached the shore their deliverers had melded into darkness.

"Ngozi mtu," Pomu said. "Lead us."

Omari trotted into the darkness. Though the details were obscure he'd memorized the map. They traveled the entire night then found shelter among a stand of prickly shrubs during the day. It was their pattern for the next week. They covered the miles at a pace that would have worn down the strongest man except the exceptionally long winded Kenjans. Omari would have been included with those incapable if not for his constant playing with his clan members. That was the true purpose of the Game; to build endurance and strength for missions such as this. They avoided cities and settlements except when food and water was needed. Omari's body remembered what his mind had forgotten; by the time the Qweran citadel loomed before them he was primed for action.

The fort materialized over the sparsely forested valley atop a slab of granite extending from the nearby mountain like an open hand. One narrow road undulated from the cluster of villages along the river to the peak. The road was easy to defend; its narrowness prevented mass attack and the fort's position gave its occupants plenty of opportunity to shower death on attacking hordes. Omari chewed on a kola nut as he and the others waited for darkness, ruminating on the citadel's interior details. A servant had been bribed to provide the details and Omari committed them to memory as he had the route to Qwera. The Ndoko sat motionless, holding their infamous serrated edge scimitars in each hand. The sight of them made him reach absently for his left side. Long ago he'd been on the wrong end of one of those blades and almost died. He didn't envy the Auxites they would encounter soon. Pomu watched the sun slowly settle behind the horizon with intense eyes. As soon as the last portion of light disappeared under the horizon, he looked at Omari then nodded.

Omari sprang to his feet then sprinted full speed to the citadel walls; his clan brothers close behind. There was no hesitation, for Qwera was far in the interior of its province and feared no attacks from its enemies and local villagers. When they reached the base of the walls, they took the ropes and grappling hooks from around their waists then threw them up into the ramparts. Omari stepped aside as the Ndoko sped up the ropes. No matter how much he'd trained he couldn't match their natural abilities. He waited until the last Ndoko was on his way up before he climbed. His progress was amazing for a human, but slow compared to his clan. When he reached the top, his brothers feigned sleep. It always amazed him how the Ndoko always chose to display their limited sense of humor in the most dangerous situations.

"It is good you decided to join us," Pomu said to him. "Can we continue now?"

Omari grinned then led the Ndoko down the ramparts to the citadel entrance. According to his internal map the hallway behind the door led to the main corridor which in turn led to the Ras.

"Intruders! To the Ras! Hurry!"

The urgent voices came from behind them. Omari looked at the door to the ramparts then to the gilded portals of the Ras's chamber.

"Go,' Pomu said. "It only takes one Ndoko. We will hold here."

The rampart door crashed open and Auxite soldiers spilled in like water from a failed dam. The Ndoko twisted, somersaulted and leapt into the mass, striking with sharp blades and hard fists. Omari sprinted to the Ras's chamber. He smashed his shoulder against the door but it did not budge.

"Damn it to the Cleave!" he hissed.

He swung his hand cannon from his back the loaded the weapon with a double charge. He braced it against his chest, not knowing exactly what would happen. He discovered the answer moment later. The charge exploded; Omari sailed through the air then landed hard at the heels of his fighting comrades. He stumbled to his feet then ran back to the Ras's chamber. The doors were open, a splintered hole where his shot struck. Five bodyguards sprawled on the marble. Three were definitely dead, the others too wounded to stop him. The five remaining guards stood before the smirking Ras, blades drawn and spears lowered.

"Sonnai sends his greetings," the Ras said.

"Can't trust a mercenary," Omari whispered as he attacked. He threw his hand cannon at the guards as he sprinted, slowing them down just enough to gain more speed. As the warriors converged, Omari jumped. He cleared them then tucked his body and flipped twice before landing on his feet before the startled Ras. His sword was in and out of the man's throat before he recovered.

The guards had failed but they were determined to avenge their Ras. Their fury made them clumsy; Omari deftly worked through them with sword and dagger, staying close to take away the spearmen advantage. He kicked the last man off his sword then looked into the hallway. The Ndoko still held the soldiers back, though not without a price. Two lay dead on the stone.

Omari looked about the room and found the window. He began unraveling the rope around his waist as he sauntered to the opening. This was even better than he imagined. He could escape alone, leaving the Ndoko to die the noble death. As the only survivor with confirmation that the Ras was dead, he's be the wealthiest merchant in Sati-Baa. Forget a drinking house; he'd purchase a mooring, a warehouse and a couple of dhows.

The pain struck suddenly. He clutched at his chest as he fell to his knees, overwhelmed by the excruciating sensation. Omari tried to stand but the pain increased. It surged through him, taking away his sight, his feeling and his voice. The Ras's chamber faded into an empty darkness.

"You would leave my children?" a voice asked.

A female form emerged from the dark. Amber eyes opened before him, followed by a solemn smile. There was no doubt that this was the most beautiful woman Omari had ever seen. But then she was not a woman.

"Eda?" he managed to say.

Her smile removed his pain and filled him with joy.

"You belong to me, Omari Ket," she said. ***"You became mine in Wadantu."***

"How?" Omari rose from where he lay to his knees.

"When I gave life back to you."

He remembered everything. Three old women stood between him, Sebe and Kadira. He drew his sword to kill them and Kadira tried to stop him. Then one of the women stabbed him with her staff. The next thing he remembered he laid at their feet, the woman holding the idol they sought.

"So, I was dead."

"Yes," Eda answered.

"You gave me my life back," Omari said. "Why?"

"Kadira asked me."

"Kadira belongs to you, too?"

"Yes, although she is not aware of it."

Omari stood. He didn't like belonging to anyone or anything, not even a beautiful goddess.

"Would you prefer I rescind my gift?" she asked.

"No, no!" Omari said. He was trapped. There was no way out of this one.

He sighed. "So what must I do?"

"Save my children, then wait for me to come to you again."

Omari dropped his head. "So be it."

Light flooded the room. Omari stood by the dead Ras, his sword and dagger in his hands. He sheathed them then collected the Ras's golden cap, medallion and one ear to prove the deed was done. He jammed the items in a pouch then secured it to his waist, his anger rising with each second. He didn't ask to be saved in Wadantu. He didn't ask for this mission. He didn't ask to be bound to a god. He picked up his hand cannon, reloaded it with a handful of shot then stomped his way to the melee at the end of the hall. By the time he was in the hand cannon's effective range he was furious.

He lit the hand cannon fuse.

"Get out of the way!" he shouted in baNdoko. The Ndoko somersaulted away from the Auxites, coming to rest behind him just in time. Omari braced himself as the fuse disappeared. The corridor echoed with the blast; he saw scores of Auxites fall before smoke obscured his view.

Omari turned then stomped away.

"Follow me," he said.

They hurried to the throne room window. Omari uncoiled the rope around his waist, secured it to a column then lowered it to the ground below. He stepped aside and the Ndoko climbed down. They carried their dead brothers on their shoulders as they descended; Bem, Fahru and Reth. Omari's gaze lingered a moment on Reth's glazed eyes. At least the bothersome Ndoko would trouble him no longer.

Omari was the last to descend. They set off on a run that continued without rest for three days, each one taking his turn to carry their fallen comrade. The Ndoko was silently surprised that Omari kept the pace and did not ask for rest. The truth was that Omari's stamina was fueled by his anger. His fatigue did not emerge until they were on the Tyrak dhow and well on their way to Kiswala. He slept the entire journey, too tired to be angry. When Pomu woke him, they were moored in Zanabar harbor. He rubbed his eyes clear to a comforting sight.

His Ndoko brothers sat in a semi-circle, each with the promised stacks before them. Omari's stack sat before him as well. Then a surprising thing occurred. His brothers, one by one, added their stack to Omari's.

"What is this?" Omari said.

"You saved our lives," Pomu answered. "Besides, we have no use for this."

Omari struggled between absolute joy and down-right suspicion.

"If you didn't want to be paid then why take the mission?" he asked.

Pomu smiled. "This mission was your test, Ngozi mtu. Eda needed to know if She could trust you."

"So you risked your lives to prove that her yoke on me was secure?" Omari's bitterness flavored his words.

Pomu shook his head. "We are Eda's children. We serve as she asks, for we know she will let no harm come to us. Now you are her child as well. You will find what you consider a yoke is truly a blessing."

"How can I consider this a blessing when I cannot live my life my way?" he retorted.

"None of us know true freedom," Pomu said. "We all are subject to the whims of others."

Omari was done talking to Pomu. He was wasting his words on a zealot. He looked at the stacks before him and a smile came to his face.

"I thank you, brothers."

They stood in unison. Omari went to each of them, pressing his chest against theirs. Their ritual was interrupted by Narsus.

"Good, you said your goodbyes. Omari Ket, get off my ship."

There was playfulness in her voice that let Omari know her words were made in jest.

"And what of my brothers?" he asked.

"They will stay on board. Eda wishes us to spend some time together. I believe you have a drinking house to build."

"That and a bit more," Omari replied.

Omari nodded his goodbyes to the Tyrak crew as he made his way to the gangplank, Narsus by his side. He was about to disembark when another grim thought came to him.

"There's some business I need to take care of," he said.

"Sonnai?" Narsus asked.

Omari nodded.

"Don't worry about him. He and his men were killed during the initial assault on Mugadi. There are no secrets among the Kiswala."

"Saves me the trouble," Omari said.

A clear sky ruled over the harbor city, the air warm and slightly sweet. Omari soon saw the reason why. Makadisha waited resplendent as ever, flanked by the twins Isabis and Iridisi. He could tell by her smile she was genuinely happy to see him. The twins met him halfway down the plank, showering him with hugs and kisses. Their brother had returned. They backed away when he reached Makadisha. She gave him a subdued peck on his lips.

"You didn't die," she said.

"No I didn't."

She peeked behind him to the bags of stacks being carried by a Tyrak. It placed the bags by their feet.

"It seems you have enough for your drinking house," she commented.

"And some," Omari replied.

"So you will stay for a time?" The tone in her voice was expectant.

Omari rubbed his chest wound. A feeling of contentment rushed through him.

"Until Eda calls," he replied reluctantly.

"That's all I can ask," Makadisha said. Their second kiss was more personal.

Omari lifted his bag over his shoulders then took Makadisha's hand. Together they strolled from the docks and into the wonders of Zanabar.

ABOUT THE AUTHOR

Milton Davis is a Black Speculative fiction writer and owner of MVmedia, LLC, a small publishing company specializing in Science Fiction, Fantasy and Sword and Soul. MVmedia's mission is to provide speculative fiction books that represent people of African and African Diaspora descent in a positive manner. Milton is the author of seventeen novels; his most recent is the Sword and Soul adventure *Son of Mfumu*. He is the editor and co-editor of ten anthologies; *The City, Blacktastic! The Blacktasticon 2018 Anthology, Terminus: Tales of the Black Fantastic, Dark Universe* and *Dark Universe: The Bright Empire* with Gene Peterson; *Griots: A Sword and Soul Anthology and Griot: Sisters of the Spear*, with Charles R. Saunders; *The Ki Khanga Anthology*, the *Steamfunk! Anthology*, and the *Dieselfunk anthology* with Balogun Ojetade. MVmedia has also published *Once Upon A Time in Afrika* by Balogun Ojetade and *Abegoni: First Calling* and *Nyumbani Tales* by Sword and Soul creator and icon Charles R. Saunders. Milton's work had been featured in *Black Power: The Superhero Anthology and Rococoa* published by Roaring Lions Productions; Skelos *2: The Journal of Weird Fiction and Dark Fantasy Volume 2, Steampunk Writers*

Around the World published by Luna Press; *Heroika: Dragoneaters* published by First Perseid Press, and *Bass Reeves Frontier Marshal Volume Two*. Milton's story 'The Swarm' was nominated for the 2018 British Science Fiction Association Award for Short Fiction.

Enjoy more exciting stories of the world of Ki Khanga in The Ki Khanga Anthology. Available now from MVmedia.

https://www.mvmediaatl.com/product-page/ki-khanga-the-anthology

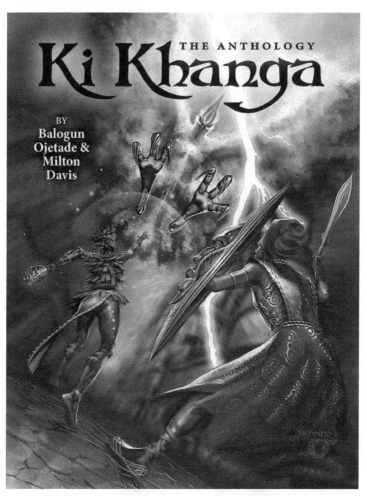

Ki Khanga: The Sword and Soul Role Playing Game allows you to create fantastic adventures in this amazing world. Get your book and begin the journey today! https://www.mvmediaatl.com/product-page/ki-khanga-sword-and-soul-role-playing-game-basic-rules

Be sure to check out these Ki Khanga titles available wherever books are sold!